'Who ar

A cool, ang ks,
and stirred a

He bowed. 'I am Sir Guy Jarvis, mistress, riding on the Duke of Gloucester's business. I would be obliged if you would identify yourself.'

He caught a sharp intake of breath as if his words had dealt her some shock, then, with her immediate reply, understood the reason.

'I am Mistress Margaret Rushton.'

Dear Reader

Happy New Year! We open 1995 with your favourites—Joanna Makepeace is back with CROWN HOSTAGE, where Margaret and Guy are caught up in the power play over the young Edward V, and Stephanie Laurens gives us another delightful Regency with THE REASONS FOR MARRIAGE.

Our American offerings are TRUST by Muriel Jensen, with two people who had hoped for fresh beginnings, and GIFTS OF LOVE by Theresa Michaels, when Erin badly needs a refuge. Forget the January snows and indulge!

The Editor

Joanna Makepeace taught as head of English in a comprehensive, before leaving full-time work to write. She lives in Leicester with her mother and Jack Russell terrier called Dickon, and has written over thirty books under different pseudonyms. She loves the old romantic historical films, which she finds more exciting and relaxing than the newer ones.

Recent titles by the same author:

CORINNA'S CAUSE
RELUCTANT REBEL
BATTLEFIELD OF HEARTS

CROWN HOSTAGE

Joanna Makepeace

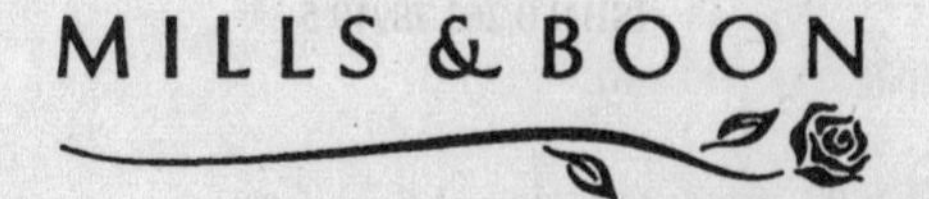

MILLS & BOON LIMITED
ETON HOUSE, 18–24 PARADISE ROAD
RICHMOND, SURREY, TW9 1SR

All the characters in this book have no existence outside the imagination of the Author, and have no relation whatsoever to anyone bearing the same name or names. They are not even distantly inspired by any individual known or unknown to the Author, and all the incidents are pure invention.

First published in Great Britain 1994
by Mills & Boon Limited

This edition 1995

ISBN 0 263 78919 5

Set in 10 on 12 pt Linotron Times
04-9501-83855

Typeset in Great Britain by Centracet, Cambridge
Printed in Great Britain by
BPC Paperbacks Ltd

CHAPTER ONE

MARGARET hurried into the great hall to a scene of frenzied activity. Serving men were erecting the trestle-tables while the maids waited with snowy drapery, drinking-mazers and wine jugs. A red-faced groom was rounding up the quarrelsome hounds to lock up in the stables until the expected exalted guests had departed. Margaret paused near the dividing screens, her eyes anxiously scanning the preparations. She had not realised she had been quite so long on her morning ride to the village. The fresh spring air had brought a rosy glow to her cheeks and the exercise had exhilarated her.

Sir John Rushton, coming hastily from the buttery, beckoned her urgently to him.

'Margaret, is your gown laid ready, girl? You are late. We must not keep his lordship waiting. I thought you would have been more excited by the thought of receiving your betrothed here at last.'

His eyes appraised her, noting the tendrils of dark hair which escaped from her hood, the rise and fall of her breasts beneath the drab woollen gown, the brightness of her dark eyes. Yes, she was agitated by the thought of today's ceremony, as he had expected. That was no bad thing. It emphasised the animation of her oval face with its determined, firm chin and well-shaped, though slightly over-large nose. She was not beautiful, his Margaret, but comely, tall for a woman, in pattens, as she stood now, as tall as he and, at eighteen, all mature woman. It was a pity she was not yellow-haired, he thought regretfully. The Queen, the Marquess of Dorset's mother, was famous for her gilt-pale hair and such colouring was admired at Court. He had waited for so long for this moment and now, on this twenty-eighth day of April in the year of our Lord 1483, in the reign of King Edward, he was about to betroth his daughter to Bennet Hartwell, a gentleman in the Marquess's train. Sir John's breast swelled with pride at the thought and he reached out and touched Margaret's hand in an unaccustomed gesture of affection.

'Hurry, child. I will come up and see you when you are dressed and ready.'

She nodded and hurried up the winding stair to her own chamber behind the solar.

Her maid, Jonnet Cross, was waiting anxiously as she entered and had already laid out her betrothal gown ready on her bed. Before the fire blazing cheerfully in the hearth the wooden tub was steaming, while two other maids from the kitchen were carrying up further heavy ewers of hot and cold water in readiness for her needs.

'Mistress,' Jonnet twittered nervously, 'I thought as 'ow you might 'ave forgotten. . .'

'Hardly,' Margaret replied tartly as she signalled for the girls to put down their jugs and return to their work in the kitchen, where the cook would be needing their help in the last-minute hectic arrangements.

Jonnet helped her undress and into the tub where she stood, her dark hair pinned high on her head, while her maid rubbed her body with scented soft soap, and she let the remnants of tiredness from her ride drain away in the herb-strewn water. Her hair was washed and rinsed in rosemary water and she stepped out, was shrouded in towels and rubbed dry.

Her old nurse would have rubbed her hard till she was almost sore, she thought with a sudden pang, but old Alice had died last Martinmas and missed this great occasion. Jonnet was new to her service, willing enough but inexperienced and clumsy, often tongue-tied in her new mistress's presence. Margaret missed the sharp reminders and rejoinders old Alice would have made, and moved with a slight sigh to the bed where her splendid gown and soft linen undershifts were laid ready.

The gown was splendid, the rich materials brought specially to their Northamptonshire manor by a London merchant and sewn by two seamstresses normally employed by the Mother Abbess of the nunnery in Peterborough. Her father had spared no expense for this day, the culmination of all his ambitious plans for her marriage. She stood docilely while Jonnet dressed her, patient today at the girl's stolid cautiousness. There must be no mishaps, no tearing of veil or catching of costly brocaded cloth. Sir John's eagle eyes would miss nothing and there would be recriminations, and punishment too, if the final effect failed to please him.

Margaret had wanted to wear green, a colour she found pleasing to her creamy complexion, but her father had blanched at the idea.

'God's wounds, no, not for a betrothal. Don't you know, girl, green is unlucky, a pagan colour? There must be no suggestion of that.'

Margaret knew there had been gossip concerning the Queen's secret marriage to King Edward, that marriage which had caused such dissension between the King's Grace and his powerful cousin, the great Earl of

Warwick, the quarrel which had almost lost him his throne. That had been celebrated on May Day, believed to be uncanny, and the Queen's mother, Jaquetta, Duchess of Bedford, was said to be a known witch who had laid a spell upon the King for the purpose of advancing her family's interests. She must not insult the noble Marquess by any notion of heretical practice on this, her betrothal day.

So she had chosen crimson brocade trimmed with sable over an undergown of white samite. As Jonnet arranged her fashionable butterfly hennin and filmy veil, Margaret viewed herself in the polished iron mirror fixed to the wall which had been her mother's. Recently her father had made her a gift of a smaller one of fine Venetian glass which stood upon her dressing-chest, but in this old one she could see more of the full effect and she sighed with satisfaction at the sight of herself. Yes, she did look magnificent. Her father would have no fault to find, nor, she thought, would her betrothed or the noble Marquess.

When her father knocked Margaret dismissed Jonnet. He murmured to the girl at the door, possibly his approval of her handiwork, and came on into the room, drawing Margaret towards the light from the oriel window.

'Yes, indeed. You chose the colour well. It complements your dark hair and brings a faint blush of colour to your cheeks.'

'You think the Marquess will approve, and my betrothed?'

'Certainly, certainly, why should they not?' He waved away her doubts. 'He gets a fair dowry with you; he can have no reason to complain.'

'You have seen this man, Bennet Hartwell, only once, you say. Tell me again what he is like.'

Sir John shrugged. 'He is presentable. You need have no fear that I would wed you to some old lecher or to some puling weakling. He is not over-tall, but well-built without portliness. His hair is brown. I have no idea what colour his eyes might have been—brown, I suppose, or grey. Dorset tells me he is twenty-two years old, a good age to embark on matrimony——'

She interrupted him. 'I mean what kind of man is he—quiet and reserved or choleric, well-mannered or aggressive? How did he take this notion of marriage to some country maid from the wilds of Northamptonshire? Would he not have preferred one of the ladies at Court in the Queen's train?'

Sir John stared back at his daughter belligerently from beneath bushy brows. He was a big man, broad-shouldered, large-boned, a man who issued orders on the manor demesne in a harsh, dominating voice which brooked no argument. Like Margaret he was dark, with small black snapping eyes which missed not the slightest breach of duty or misdemeanour. He was universally respected by most and feared by many. Though Margaret loved him dearly, she would not have thought to defy him nor even question his decision. Her eyes fell beneath his glare and she moved very slightly from him, as if avoiding the possibility of a blow for her forwardness.

'God's teeth, lass, how should I know what the man thinks? He is anxious to please the Marquess, his patron, and hopes for knighthood soon at the King's hand. He is sufficiently wealthy to keep you in some style and has promised to present you at Court. You will like that, will you not?'

Margaret nodded a trifle nervously. She did, indeed, long for a more exciting life than her present one as chatelaine of her father's manor near Cold Ashby. Her mother had died three years earlier in childbed in a final, unsuccessful attempt to give Sir John an heir, and Margaret had waited anxiously for him to marry again, for he was still in his forties and physically attractive to women. She knew, only too well, that life would not be so pleasant under the control of a stepmother and was willing enough to marry and take charge of her own household, but she had still not seen her betrothed. Though this state of affairs was in no way unusual, she would have been grateful for more reliable information about the man who was shortly to order her life.

Her father moved purposefully to the door.

'Are you coming below stairs to wait for the Marquess's arrival?'

She shook her head, sinking down on the window-seat with care so as not to crease her gown unduly.

'No, I would prefer to spend this last hour quietly in my chamber.'

'Shall I send up the girl?'

'No, I will be best alone.'

His black eyes surveyed her thoughtfully then he gave a little grunt, inclined his head and left her in peace.

The noises from below in the courtyard—clinking of stone on anvil, mewling of hawks from the mews, clatter of pattens on cobbled stone as the maids went about their duties from kitchen to dairy and buttery—gradually quietened. Most of the preparations were concluded to the cook's satisfaction and it wanted only the arrival of the betrothal party now to begin hectic activity once more.

Margaret gazed across at the hearth fire and thought of another time when she had sat uneasily waiting for her father to summon her down to the hall.

How long ago was it? Five years, winter, in 1478. That must have been soon after the death of the King's brother, Clarence, in the Tower. Why, yes, that was it. The King's other brother, Richard of Gloucester, would have been travelling north after his failure to persuade the King to pardon Clarence. He had stayed at Fotheringhay and, naturally, Guy Jarvis, in service to Sir Dominick Allard, a knight in the Duke's household, had taken the opportunity to visit his betrothed and suggest arrangements for the formal ceremony.

She remembered vividly that memorable meeting. A messenger had arrived at the manor with news of the impending visit. Her father had been sitting in the great chair in the hall and his face had darkened with choler as he'd pushed aside the letter.

'Here's an unfortunate reminder from the past,' he'd muttered thickly as Margaret's mother, Jane, had lifted mild hazel eyes to view her lord as he strode irritatedly back and forth, raising dust and pungent herb scents from the scattered rushes.

'What is it, John? Must you leave on some errand for the King?'

'No.' He had stopped in his pacing and stood, thumbs hooked in his belt, glaring down at Margaret who had been seated by her mother's chair untangling silks for her embroidery. 'No, I thought it all forgotten, it has been so long, but now it rises to haunt me.'

'Father?' Margaret, feeling she was the cause of her irascible sire's displeasure, had shifted awkwardly on her low stool.

'You heard me talk of that fellow, Jarvis, whose prompt action I had cause to thank at Edgecote?'

'Indeed,' Lady Rushton had smiled, 'I had cause to thank him too, for you would not have returned to me after that encounter if he had not cut down the mounted knight who was riding down at you with axe poised to strike. You have told the tale so many times I would be forgetful indeed if it did not stick in my memory, but I thought Sir Ralf dead, some months before Barnet. Surely this letter cannot concern him.'

'Aye he is, and this note does. It's from his whelp, Guy. He writes to say he is at Fotheringhay and wishes to call and see our Margaret here.'

A flush had dyed Lady Rushton's pale cheeks. 'Margaret's young betrothed. But it is years since we heard from him. . .'

'Not so young. Now that I recall he must be nigh on twenty-one years of age.'

'Then he comes to see Margaret and plan for the wedding?'

Margaret had known from babyhood that she had been betrothed from the cradle. After that near brush with death at Edgecote near Banbury, her father and Sir Ralf Jarvis had struck up a friendship and agreed to betroth their children. Though she had understood that it would be her destiny eventually to marry Sir Ralf's son, Guy, it had always been a vague thought in Margaret's mind, one so far off that she could forget it for months, even years at a time. Later her nurse had told her brusquely that Sir Ralf's fortunes had declined and he and her father had seen one another rarely and, finally, communication between them had ceased. But betrothals were serious commitments, needing a dispensation from papal authority to break, and Margaret had realised that, though her father might now have second thoughts concerning the wisdom of that binding of his one child, he had no course but to accept the consequences of his vow. Her heart had pounded fiercely. At last she was to see Guy Jarvis.

Her father's voice had grated across her racing thoughts.

'I'll not be bound by it, Jane. The man is little better than a pauper. He has some piddling manor in Gloucestershire with scarce enough good land to make it profitable and to cap all the man is bound in service to Gloucester who spends all his time at his castle of Middleham in Yorkshire. Margaret would be buried there in the Dales with no prospect of presentation at Court and, besides, it's the Queen's kin who count these days. I had already tentatively talked with her eldest son, Thomas of Dorset, concerning the possibility of a match between Margaret and one of his friends. There will be no problem about obtaining a dispensation. Dorset's uncle, Lionel, Bishop of Salisbury, has agreed to arrange that for us. I had thought to write to the young man explaining my reason for breaking the betrothal. It is a plaguey bad business that he is now so near, and wishes to call in person.' He'd shrugged. 'It will be embarrassing but that cannot be helped. Margaret, take yourself off to your chamber and put on one of your good gowns. It may be necessary for me to call you to repudiate the match. If possible I shall avoid that. Best if you never set eyes on the fellow at all.'

Margaret had gone obediently, but she had, after all, been forced to confront Guy Jarvis, there in the hall, where soon she was to welcome her new betrothed.

And he had summoned her. Margaret would never

forget standing at the head of the stair, her nurse behind her, staring down at the two men facing her father. The older one, brown-haired and stocky, she'd known to be Sir Dominick Allard, known as Wolf Allard, partly for the wolf's head device he bore and partly for his fierce courage in the battles of the recent wars. Her eyes had gone instinctively to the other, the man her father had said it would have been better if she never set eyes on. He was looking upwards, one hand resting on his sword-hilt, slightly ahead of Sir Dominick who had placed a restraining hand on his shoulder. So there had been hard words between them, she'd realised. Her father's announcement of alternative plans for her future had not been well-received.

She had felt pierced by the icy glitter of those bright blue eyes. Her hand had slipped on the stair's rope support and she had stumbled so that her nurse had pulled her sharply back to a safe position on the top stair. He was tall and slender, taller than the knight in whose service he had been since boyhood, and fair. Tumbled golden curls had hung to his shoulders, and at first sight she'd thought how very young he appeared for his twenty-one summers, but coming closer, as she'd begun to descend the stair, she could see that he was incredibly handsome. His brow was high and smooth, his nose well-shaped, the nostrils flaring slightly, the mouth beautifully chiselled. Even then, at thirteen, she had thought the ladies of his acquaintance must have longed for a kiss from those curling lips. He had been so very different from what she had expected that it had prevented her from being as embarrassed in his presence as she had feared.

She had thought to confront a fighting warrior and instead met the angry eyes of an elegantly dressed young courtier. Her own lips had curled in response. She'd had no wish to be matched with this boyishly attractive youth. She'd wanted a man like her father, strong-willed, dominating, a man to be obeyed and, possibly, feared.

His voice, though, had not been that of a youth, nor his words.

'I understand, sir, that you do not consider me a good enough match for your daughter,' he began. 'It would seem that my father's opinion of you was faulty. He spoke of a brave comrade, one who valued courage and honour more than position and influence. Either he was mistaken as to your character from the first, or you have trimmed your sails to the fresh wind which blows at Court. Am I to believe that your daughter has been brought to consider silks and jewels and the honeyed tongues of Court flatterers more to her taste than marriage with a plain man who is pledged to protect her from any ills which might come in these unsettled times?'

The ice-blue stare was directed full at her and Margaret turned anxiously to her sire for guidance.

Her father's tone remained bland, unruffled. 'Master Jarvis, times are no longer so bad that old values hold good. Then we were all forced to make circumstances fit necessities. Now the King has his own again and my opinions have changed. All men desire the best for their daughters. . .'

'Especially if what they consider best advances their own ambitions.' The reply was couched as a sneer and Margaret found herself trembling with sudden anger. How dared this young puppy speak so to her father?

She said coldly, 'Know that my father speaks for me,

sir. I too wish for a match which will ensure my comfort. I've no desire to bury myself in the wilds of the north.'

She knew she sounded childishly petulant and greedy, as if all she wished for her future were a succession of pretty baubles and sweetmeats, which was far from the truth. Even at thirteen she knew what she wanted—domination over her own household, a powerful man at her side, one she could respect and admire, possibly the cut and thrust of Court intrigue to add spice to her life. What she would find unbearable would be a dull, quiet existence, far from the bases of power. She had had too much of that. Her mother was a submissive mouse of a woman who was bullied from pillar to post by her strong-willed husband and, though Margaret knew she was content, it would not have suited her daughter. Margaret liked to sit near her father's side while the news of the day was discussed and, very occasionally, was allowed to offer an opinion, received with amusement and bluff disdain by her doting sire, it was true, but she knew that, for all that, he was proud of her expressions of forthright good sense.

Guy Jarvis said harshly, 'So, the child is spoilt and opinionated. I might have expected that, having listened to her faithless sire. Perhaps, as you say, sir, I am well rid of a bad bargain.'

Margaret tossed her head in fury and bright tears sprang to her eyes but her mother lifted one hand to silence her. Margaret was surprised by the determined set of her mother's gentle mouth and realised she was extremely angry. So rarely did Lady Rushton show her feelings that it came as a severe shock to her daughter. Her mother's disapproval, she was sure, was directed not at their visitor but towards her father, and presumably herself, for what she considered her daughter's unchastised rudeness to a guest beneath their roof. Margaret opened her mouth to justify herself but her mother's face darkened with unaccustomed, angry colour and she signalled to nurse to draw Margaret away, back to her chamber.

Catching her father's eye and his silent signal to do her mother's bidding, she made to move towards the stair-foot again. Swiftly her young suitor forestalled her.

'Am I to believe that it is truly your wish to seek a dispensation and break the formal betrothal between us, mistress?'

He had put one slim brown hand on her arm, preventing her from stepping up on to the first stair. He was blocking out her view of her father's face so that she was unable to read his expression. She swallowed hard. This decision to break a solemn vow, which she had been led to believe from childhood was her duty, was hard. She knew she had only to nod her head, for her father would expect no less from her but instant obedience to his wish, but she was impelled to do more. The arrogance of this handsome stranger instilled sudden and instant antipathy for him in her mind. How could she think of leaving her comfortable home, where her loving parents granted her every wish, for life in the cold north, where she knew no one and would possibly be expected to wait upon the Duchess of Gloucester, in whose service this man was?

Deliberately she stared down at the detaining hand. 'I think you blot your oath of chivalry, sir, by laying hands upon me. I have no desire for your touch, or your hand in marriage. My father is right. You are no true match for me.' She gave another toss of her head in what she hoped was a proud gesture of defiance and swept by him as he hastily removed his hand.

Now, as she recalled the incident, Margaret made a *moue* of disgust for her own foolish behaviour. How humiliated Guy Jarvis must have been by those proceedings. Of course he must have said something which had prompted her father to send for her and personally back his own decision, but she should certainly have kept silent. Later her mother had made no reference to the occurrence but Margaret knew she had displeased her, for Lady Rushton's retiring and gentle nature would have withdrawn from any word or act which she thought might harm another. Ruefully she thought that her performance today must be much more circumspect.

Another suitor had been chosen for her shortly after the Bishop of Salisbury had obtained a papal dispensation to dissolve her betrothal, but she had never met the man. During that summer he had taken a fever and died very suddenly. Margaret had wondered, fleetingly, if she had angered God by her own refusal to keep the vow made for her so long ago, but surely that sin could not have doomed her innocent suitor and she had tried to dismiss the notion, though at the back of her mind there had lingered a sense of regret she had been unable to explain, even to herself.

No other suitable gentleman had presented himself, till Master Bennet Hartwell had distinguished himself in the Marquess of Dorset's service and her father had been delighted to accept an offer for Margaret's hand from him. She was eighteen now, and ripe for the marriage bed. This marriage would prove beneficial to both parties. Margaret's considerable dowry would enrich Master Hartwell's coffers and this favour would please the Marquess of Dorset well.

Her betrothed would arrive very soon now and Margaret was eager for her first sight of him. She judged he must be roughly the same age as Guy Jarvis. Her dark eyes flashed at the memory of that young man's fury. She had never again dared to mention the man's name to her father and was unaware if he had married. The Duke of Gloucester would surely be instrumental in finding a suitable bride for a loyal member of his household. It was rare that the King's remaining brother travelled south, spending much time settling disputes on the Scottish border. Only recently, however, he had journeyed to London to receive the grateful plaudits of Parliament for his great achievement of winning the border town of Berwick for the English crown. Probably the handsome Guy Jarvis had fought in that engagement. Margaret gave a little secret smile at the thought. Somehow she could not imagine that handsome, golden-haired young gentleman living rough in camp or wielding a broadsword or axe.

She rose to her feet as sounds of arrival from below told her their guests were even now riding into the courtyard. She gave one final glance in the mirror at her finery and prepared to descend the stair for this fateful meeting with her bridegroom-to-be.

Sir John signalled to her to stand by his side and she could tell by a slight tic moving in his neck that he too was nervous about this meeting.

The hall door was jerked open and Sir John's steward stumbled abruptly into the chamber. Margaret was startled. She could see, even from here, that the man was troubled and something unexpected had occurred to put him out of humour. Suddenly a second figure stepped into the hall and, with one brawny arm, pushed the steward aside before he could open his mouth to announce the new arrival.

The newcomer advanced the length of the hall to face Margaret's father. He was bespattered with mud and wore leathern jack, plain woollen hose and long riding boots. This, clearly, was no gentleman of the Marquess's coterie. He gave a brief soldier's bow and cast a hurried glance in Margaret's direction.

'I'm the Marquess of Dorset's sergeant-at-arms,' he announced without preamble. 'His lordship regrets he is unable to attend you as he promised but circumstances have forced him to ride at once for London.' Again his eyes, under level white brows, swept over Margaret and back to Sir John. 'Can we talk privately, sir? My master sends me on a vital and urgent errand.'

Sir John's arm steadied his daughter, who had clutched at him in alarm. She could feel he was trembling and decidedly disturbed by this sudden departure from the expected arrangements.

'My daughter is in my confidence. As you doubtless know, this was to be her betrothal day. Do you bring word from Master Hartwell? Has he too ridden to London?'

The man's eyelids flickered, whether from anger or irritation Margaret could not tell, but he shifted his weight from one booted foot to the other and nodded.

'Aye, sir, Mistress Rushton has the right to learn immediately what is the reason for what must be a postponement of her betrothal. Master Hartwell, too, is prevented from coming here since he is busy on the Marquess's business. Know then, Sir John, that His Grace King Edward died on April the ninth. Naturally the Marquess feels the Queen his mother has more pressing need of his presence.'

Sir John fell back apace at the man's astonishing tidings. Margaret gave a little inarticulate cry. Surely not! This could not be. His Grace was scarcely more than forty, and, though grown over-heavy and disinclined to ride recently, and suffering several minor ailments, had apparently been in excellent health when last they'd heard.

'Dead?' Sir John's mouth gaped open and he released Margaret and placed her in a chair while he moved hurriedly to the table, splashed malmsey wine into two goblets and offered one to his guest, who swallowed it gratefully. 'I don't understand, cannot believe. . . Suppose you tell me how this—monstrous thing could have happened? Was there an accident?'

'No, sir. I am informed His Grace took suddenly ill a week before his death. Soon after Easter he went with a party of friends and courtiers on a fishing expedition to the eastern marshes. We heard he must have suffered a seizure, possibly brought on by over-exertion—we cannot tell. It would seem unlikely on such a planned trip but you know His Grace is inclined to over-indulge. . .' He checked himself and coughed discreetly. 'At all events he collapsed and was carried in a litter back to Westminster. He never recovered and died on Wednesday April the ninth. As you know the young King's Grace is at Ludlow and must be brought hastily to London for his coronation—alas, too late for his father's funeral. The King was laid to rest with all pomp in St George's chapel at Windsor on the eighteenth. The Marquess realises that it is essential for the young King to make no delay.'

Sir John and Margaret had crossed themselves reverently as the news of the King's untimely death was told. The messenger hastily followed suit.

'We all know, none better, how dangerous this state of affairs could be to this realm—a lad scarce thirteen on the throne after all the wars of the last decades. King Henry Sixth, of blessed memory, was but a boy when his noble father died, and we are all aware what happened then. Those uncles and men of power about the child vied constantly for position. God forfend it should happen again. The Marquess begs every man who offers him friendship to show his support for the Queen in her hours of grief and desperation.'

Sir John said instantly, 'How can I be of service to his lordship?'

The sergeant sank on to a low bench near the trestle-table set so ornately for the now abandoned feast.

'Lord Rivers, the King's uncle, is with the boy and has received word to start off at once for London. The Marquess is anxious that supporters should meet the royal party on the way. He suggests that you, Sir John, with a party of retainers, should take yourself to Northampton to meet the young King when he arrives shortly.'

Margaret put in hurriedly without thinking, 'But what of the King's last surviving brother, the Duke of Gloucester? Should he not be consulted about the arrangements?'

She coloured hotly as she found the intent gaze of both men boring into her.

There was a pause. The sergeant said thoughtfully, 'It is thought that the Chamberlain, Lord William Hastings, has sent north advising the Duke what is planned.'

Margaret's thoughts raced to a frightening conclusion. Surely Gloucester, as a royal Plantagenet duke, should be the legal guardian of the young King and all his brother's children. Why was the Marquess so intent on involving her father in his scheme to rush the King to London before his royal uncle? Was it feared that Gloucester would seize power and oust the Queen's kin from positions of influence and wealth they had long held? That was likely. Margaret knew there was no love lost between the Woodville clan and the Duke of Gloucester, who had made it plain, on more than one occasion, that he thought his brother listened too readily to the Queen's numerous relations, all of whom had made powerful marriage alliances, some of them scandalously unsuitable, but for the ambitions of the recipients of land and dowries. So, with the sudden death of the King, all those days of glory could be doomed and her father's ambitions with them, as well as her own bridegroom's hopes of preferment.

The Duke of Gloucester would be riding south soon and would Guy Jarvis be in his retinue? Strange that her thoughts earlier had flown to her former betrothed and had now instantly gone to him again. It was more than likely that Jarvis would accompany his Duke. She stifled a desire to giggle hysterically. It seemed that her father's offhand treatment of his old friend's son might not be so practical and profitable as he had hoped. Should Gloucester come to power, Guy Jarvis might have proved a more useful ally than Master Bennet Hartwell.

The men were talking of their plans and she gave her attention to what was being decided.

'Lord Rivers will by now have been in communication with Gloucester.' The sergeant cleared his throat awkwardly. 'I feel you should know, Sir John, that the late King, by a codicil to his will, left the guardianship of his children and the care of the realm in the hands of his brother.'

Margaret's father's eyes caught and held those of the visitor and he inclined his chin in a little decisive gesture.

'Well, it seems that indeed the Queen will need allies. I will make arrangements to ride for Northampton at once to make myself available to Lord Rivers, should he need me.'

The sergeant shook his head like a dog shaking himself after swimming, then said, 'Aye, I'll be off for London to report to the Marquess, if you could provide me with a fresh mount, Sir John. Master Hartwell will be in Northampton. There you two can confer about how to proceed with the betrothal ceremony.' The man had risen and was in the act of pulling on his mailed gloves. 'I'm sure all will be well very soon, mistress, and this unfortunate postponement soon mended.'

Margaret inclined her head graciously and waited while her father conducted his guest to the hall door and shouted for his steward to give him instructions. When he returned and prepared to mount the stairs, she called to him softly.

'You ride, then, immediately for Northampton?'

'Aye, daughter, you see how matters stand.'

She said evenly, 'You have considered carefully what you are doing?'

He paused and stared at her, his eyes bulging at her impertinence in questioning his decision.

'Certainly I have.'

'Then can I not ride with you? I too would like to see the young King. It will be a memorable occasion before his arrival in London and the coronation.' She hesitated. 'Also, it would give me an opportunity to meet my betrothed at last.'

He hesitated, frowning. 'I don't know if this is wise.'

'You fear trouble with Gloucester?'

'No, no,' he blustered. 'How can that be so, quarrels with his brother's kin and His Grace scarce cold in his grave? Why should there be?'

'Then there can be no harm in my accompanying you. Besides,' she added, 'my presence will make it clear that you expected no trouble and escorted me to see the new King. Natural enough, don't you think, especially as my betrothed will be in the town?'

'Aye.' His tone carried a considering note now. 'You could be right. You have a head on your shoulders, daughter, and it can do no harm to have you prominent in the new King's service, proving us loyal to his half-brother, the Marquess.'

'Then that is settled.' She rose to accompany him up the stair. 'I will call for Jonnet to pack necessities and attend me on the journey.'

At the stair-foot she stood for a moment. Her father had given way easily. Could it be that he really *did* think this was simply a formality, this show of force for the Queen's relatives, this haste to procure the person of their young sovereign? If he was wrong things could go very badly for him, and for Master Hartwell. She could not have borne to remain here constantly on thorns to know the outcome of this affair.

CHAPTER TWO

Sir Dominick Allard rose from his seat near the fire in The Angel's taproom to welcome his friend and former squire as Sir Guy Jarvis strode in, stripping off his mailed gloves and rubbing his hands against the cold, for it was still chilly on this late April day in Northampton.

'Come and take some spiced ale, man. You need it on this raw night. Brr. . .' Sir Dominick grinned. 'I had heard tell it was much milder here in the south. I can't say that I've noticed it during this ride.'

Sir Guy gratefully sank down on the bench beside him and nodded his thanks as the young inn wench handed him the warmed tankard.

'Is all well at the Duke's lodgings?'

'Aye, well enough. He's comfortably settled and was waiting supper when I left. Sir Richard Ratcliffe was in attendance and sent me off to see about my own quarters.' Guy sipped thoughtfully at his ale. 'His Grace was quiet, as he's been throughout the ride, but I think he's well satisfied with the arrangements you've made for him.'

Sir Dominick nodded and stared deep into his own tankard. 'He has never been hard to please, praise God.'

Sir Guy stirred moodily and stretched out his booted legs to the blaze. 'You have known him longer than I. His quiet reserve can be expected. The King's death has been a grave shock to him but. . .'

'But?'

Sir Guy grinned nervelessly. 'It's my opinion that, though he has passed no comment on recent events, His Grace is in a royal rage.'

'Ah! You know him better than you think. He is indeed, and who's to blame him?'

'What will he do, Dominick? The King has already been hurried off to Stony Stratford, more than ten miles nearer to London, though it was understood that the Duke and Earl Rivers would together escort His young Grace into his capital. Do you fear the move sinister?'

'Coupled with Lord Hastings's grave warnings, I do indeed, and the significance of the move will certainly not have escaped Richard.' Sir Dominick sighed. He had been in the Duke of Gloucester's service since before the battles of Barnet and Tewkesbury. At both those events Sir Guy had been his squire and now, knighted these two years past, for loyal service and courage in the border skirmishes, remained still his friend and ally in the Duke's household.

Both men had been in attendance at Middleham when the news of his brother's death had reached Gloucester, and had ridden with him to York where masses for the King's soul had been celebrated. Sir Dominick's wife, Aleyne, had remained in Middleham Castle with the Lady Anne, Duchess of Gloucester, until it was thought fitting for the ladies of the Duke's household to join him in the capital. Sir Dominick's children—his heir, young Richard, and his small baby, Anne—were with their nurse at his manor near Jervaulx. Moodily he considered that this catastrophe within the realm bade fair to destroy his family's peace. It was as well young Guy here was still unwed, though privately he considered it advisable that his friend put behind him that unfortunate affair at Cold Ashby and give serious attention to the task of finding himself a wealthy wife. His dark eyes surveyed his companion from under bushy brows.

'Our arrival here in Northamptonshire brought to mind that business with Rushton. I'm wondering if he's allied himself with Dorset. He was known to be his man.'

Sir Guy gave a small grunt, whether of anger or interest Sir Dominick was not to discover.

Sir Dominick continued, 'The fellow Rushton hoped to wed to his daughter died, you know.'

'Yes, I heard.' Guy's retort was uncompromising.

'Aleyne heard from Lady Scrope that there was talk she was to marry Bennet Hartwell, one of Dorset's gentlemen. Apparently it was planned for the King to knight him at the Smithfield tournament set for Whitsuntide.'

Sir Guy drained his tankard and slammed it down on the scrubbed table before him. 'Well, this certainly dooms the man's hopes.'

'It may well doom *all* our hopes,' Sir Dominick said gloomily.

'But our Duke is named Lord Protector of the realm by the King's will. Who can dispute that?'

'The Queen will dispute it, Dorset will dispute it, all the Woodvilles will rally round her and most of the southern nobles will back her and jockey for position. Remember Richard is not so well-known and respected here as he is in the north.'

'Then Richard must take matters into his own hands and take possession of his nephew.' Guy's reply was explosive.

Dominick grinned at him amiably. 'Here's heat,' he murmured mildly.

Guy had been a handsome, even an effeminate-looking youth, which had belied his capabilities. Even at twenty he had appeared younger than his age. All that had changed now. He was still devastatingly handsome, so much so that Dominick had to smile constantly as he glimpsed the admiring gazes directed at Guy by the Duchess's ladies. His former squire was tall, almost as tall as his late sovereign, who had been past six feet in height, and whipcord-thin, with the grace and restlessness of one of the lions in the King's Tower menagerie. The finely chiselled features had not lost their perfection but for one slight scar which winged his right eyebrow, the wound made by a stray arrow which had caught Guy when that young man had scorned to wear his helmet one morning when thwarting an attack by thieving Scottish reivers. But every line of his stern features and the firm set of the mouth bespoke the true warrior. If this young sprig Hartwell were to win his spurs for some skill with tournament weapons, he would never match the worth of Guy Jarvis's service in Gloucester's eyes. Fairly he had won his knighthood and it was a pity he had little wealth to allow him to enjoy the privilege. Gloucester had several times attempted to make a match for his loyal young captain but, as yet, Guy had excused himself from acceptance. Dominick sighed again. He had witnessed the harm that stupid young child had done that fatal day five years ago. Always proud, despite his slender means, Guy had been withdrawn and uneasy with gentlewomen ever since.

The noise of horses' hooves in the street outside brought Guy to his feet and he went instantly to the window. Since the horn gave him little view of the road, he pushed the casement wide and peered outside.

'This is probably the Duke of Buckingham arriving,' Dominick called. 'His harbingers informed Richard that he would be joining him here. Good, it appears he is in time for supper. There is accommodation for him at Richard's lodging?'

'Yes, I had instructions to see to it.' Guy leaned further forward and gave a sharp whistle.

'This isn't Buckingham. It's Rivers.'

'What?' Dominick joined him at the window. 'You're right. The insolence of the fellow! He ignores protocol, carries the King on without permission from the Lord Protector, and here he is, daring to face Gloucester.'

'He'll have some excuse, like as not.' Guy closed the window and turned, yawning. 'One thing is sure—I shan't get to bed as soon as I'd hoped. Let us order supper now, Dominick, and enjoy it while we can. One or both of us will be summoned to attend the Duke before the night is out.'

Dominick nodded and went to the door to summon a serving wench. Before he could do so he saw Guy's squire, Owen Lewis, coming hurriedly across the courtyard from the stables.

'A message for your master?'

The youth nodded. 'And for you, sir. A messenger came in only a moment ago. He asks that both you and Sir Guy attend the Duke of Gloucester as soon as possible at his lodgings. Supper will be provided.'

'Ah.' Dominick stood back for the boy to enter the tap-room.

'As you feared, Guy. Owen comes to summon us to the Duke.'

Guy made a wry movement of the lips. 'Such a life it

is, when one waits on princes. I wouldn't have minded had I taken supper first.'

'Sir.' Owen looked uncommonly earnest. 'The messenger wishes me to inform you that the Duke needs an armed escort to be ready at first light. Shall I go and see to that immediately?'

'Aye, lad.' Guy turned back to Dominick, his brows raised.

'It seems that the Duke has in mind what you were suggesting. He will see to it that the boy is in our hands when we enter the capital.'

'With Rivers present here?'

'At least that should give Richard an opportunity to hear what Rivers has to say. We are told to be present for supper, by the way.'

Again Guy made a grimace. 'In that case I had best change my doublet.'

Dominick nodded and stood in thought, while his friend mounted the inn stair.

Margaret pushed her plate of cold meats away with an impatient hand. Jonnet looked up nervously. Her mistress had been irritable since their arrival in Northampton and the departure of Sir John in Earl Rivers' train, leaving his daughter to cool her heels in this somewhat dubiously appointed inn. The town was crowded with men-at-arms wearing various liveries, and little accommodation had been available. Harbingers for both the Dukes of Gloucester and Buckingham and Earl Rivers had bespoken what respectable lodgings were available well in advance, and Margaret and her father had been lucky to find this place with a private room, otherwise they might all have had to share the common room opposite. Even Jonnet would have scorned that, sharing her bedplace with farmers' wives and, possibly, women of less respectable callings.

Margaret sighed and once again moved to the window, but there was nothing to see. The inn was situated off the main thoroughfare and, though she could hear the noise from the centre of the town, it told her little. She had hoped to catch a sight of the young King, but Earl Rivers had ridden straight through the town and on to Stony Stratford and her father had left her with a small escort and taken the rest of his men on towards London to swell the Earl's force of almost two thousand men. More annoying even than that, her betrothed had been with the Earl, and Margaret had not so much as caught a glimpse of him either. She tapped her foot in frustration and turned back to Jonnet.

'It seems there will be no news tonight. You say the men are bedded down in the stables?'

'Yes, mistress, and the horses well cared for.'

'Well, that is that. Since there is nothing to do but sleep, we'd best get to bed. Call the serving wench, Jonnet, to fetch the dishes, and go down to the kitchen for water. I'll wash and prepare for bed. You did see that the sheets were aired and are clean?'

'Yes, mistress, patched but perfectly clean. I made the wench change them while I stood over her and I insisted she pass the warming-pan over them to ensure they were aired.'

'Well done.' Margaret forced a smile. She knew she had been surly with the girl since her father's desertion, and young Jonnet had stood up to the unaccustomed hardships of the journey quite well. 'I'm sorry, Jonnet. I'm being unfair to subject you to my mood of disappointment. Father will either ride back first thing tomorrow or send for us to join him. Till then we must just make the best of the situation. You must be tired yourself. Let us try to get what rest we can in spite of that racket from the soldiers.'

Jonnet curtsied and hurried out. Margaret undid her gilded belt then reached up to remove her hennin. She had dressed finely in a dress of blue velvet trimmed with marten fur in the hope of a meeting with Master Hartwell or possible presentation to the Earl. She dared not believe that she might kiss the young King's hand—but none of that was to be. The messenger who had arrived so hurriedly had been anxious to have her father leave at once and there had scarce been time to ask after the health of the young King's Grace.

Margaret frowned uncertainly. Her forebodings appeared to be coming true. The Earl was determined to keep control of his nephew at all costs. There had been so many men-at-arms in his train that Margaret thought the escort from Ludlow could have been taken by the populace to be an army on the march. There had even been carts carrying armour. Surely this would not please the Protector.

Now he had entered the town and one of her men had informed her that he guessed the Duke had with him about two hundred men or more. The Earl's force certainly outnumbered his and Gloucester would not challenge him—he was too experienced a soldier—but Earl Rivers and the Marquess of Dorset must first convince the Council of the rightness of their cause before they could establish themselves in the seats of power behind the throne. Margaret shivered slightly as she thought that, if they should fail, all who supported them might well be considered traitors.

The serving wench scurried in, made a clumsy half-curtsy and carried out the tray. Jonnet arrived with a ewer of hot water and came to Margaret's side to help unhook her gown. It would be hard to sleep with the constant noise of men chattering, the rattle of iron wheels of carts and baggage waggons on the road and the shouted commands of sergeants-at-arms, but at least the two of them could stretch out and rest. The truckle-bed had been pulled out for Jonnet. Nothing could be gained by sitting anxiously through the hours of darkness until Margaret received word from her father.

She was about to get into bed when there came a hard knocking on the door. Jonnet gave a frightened little cry and Margaret silenced her maid with an upraised hand.

'Who is it?' she called imperiously.

'The innkeeper, Jake Stockes, Mistress Rushton.'

'Go away, man. I am about to retire.'

'I'm right sorry to disturb you, mistress, but there's a gentleman below requesting to see you. He says his errand is urgent.'

'A gentleman?' Margaret's question was sharp. 'You mean one of my father's men?'

'No, mistress, a gentleman certainly, by his dress and manners, a young gentleman. He says he is sure you will receive him despite the lateness of the hour. He is Master Hartwell.'

Margaret's heart skipped a beat and she raised a hand to her breast. Jonnet stared at her incredulously.

'Mistress,' she whispered hoarsely, 'your father'll not want you to see your betrothed until he is present.'

'Well, he isn't here, is he?' Margaret snapped.

Really! Was everything about this business set to try her temper? She had wanted to see this man days ago, when she was properly attired for the occasion. Indeed, she had dressed with care just this evening in hope of a meeting with him. Now, when she was alone with her maid and her father some miles distant, undressed, her hair unpinned, the wretched man had arrived and was demanding to see her.

'Tell him to wait below until my maid comes for him,' she called to the waiting innkeeper.

The man's feet could be heard descending the stair and Margaret turned on the wide-eyed Jonnet.

'Hurry, get my furred bed-gown from the saddle-bag and bring me my small mirror and a comb. Let me at least make myself presentable.'

'Mistress, I'm sure Sir John would not approve. . .'

'Things are not normal, you foolish wench. Cannot you hear the commotion in the streets? For all we know Master Hartwell comes from my father. At all events you are here with me so there can be no impropriety. Hurry now; we mustn't keep him waiting any longer than necessary.'

Within moments Jonnet had returned, ushering in their visitor. Margaret sank into a curtsy, so, for a moment, was unable to get a good first view of her betrothed. He bowed and, when he straightened, she found herself staring intently into his eyes.

He was of medium height, sturdily built but with no suggestion of plumpness, brown-haired and eyed, with a broad, open countenance she found reassuring. He was clad, of course, in unrelieved mourning, since he had been one of the gentlemen of the King's escort, but the fine black wool of his cloak and doublet was powdered with dust from the road and she understood that he had not stopped to change his garments before presenting himself so he was, clearly, in a great hurry.

She knew him to be twenty-two years old but he appeared younger. He hesitated for a moment, as if a trifle bashful, a tendency she found endearing, and then came hurriedly forward to kiss the tips of her fingers.

'Mistress Margaret, I am indeed sorry that we have been forced to meet for the first time under such unfavourable conditions.'

She glanced regretfully down at her velvet bed-gown and put a hand up to her hair. Had she realised the truth, she would have known what a wonderful picture she made for him, tall and stately, her dark locks flowing almost to her waist.

He made a quick awkward gesture and stood back a trifle.

'Forgive me. I am too forward.'

'Indeed n-no, sir,' she stammered. 'I am sorry that—' She broke off and gestured him to seat himself on a wooden stool near the table. 'Please, sit down. You appear to have been riding and. . .'

'I fear I stink of the stables. I rode with my Lord Earl from Stony Stratford.'

'There is nothing wrong? The King is not ill?'

'No, certainly not. The King is in good hands and has his chamberlain, Sir Thomas Vaughan, and his former tutor with him.

'I don't understand.' Margaret sank on to the bed and Jonnet, plucking nervously at the skirt of her gown, moved a little closer to her mistress. 'Why has the Earl returned to Northampton? I understood from the message which came to my father that it was thought sensible to move on closer to London.'

'Yes, indeed.' Master Hartwell adjusted his sword-belt as he wriggled into a more comfortable position on the stool. Margaret's eyes flickered to the weapon and she was made aware that he had come to her armed, though he was not wearing mail. 'The Earl thought it wise to inform Duke Richard of his reason for taking the King on—er—er—without his permission. The villages round here are small and unable to accommodate our combined forces—er—escorts. It seemed appropriate to leave the best accommodation in the town to the Duke. He called at the Duke's lodging and—and was invited to take supper with the Protector.'

Margaret had the uncomfortable feeling that this had not been a wise move. Surely it would have been more strategic to keep distance between the two uncles, since both had much to gain by the control of the youthful King. She gazed back steadily at this young man who was a total stranger to her and whom she had been so eager to meet. Now she was more anxious to receive his news than to sum up his personality.

Again he shifted awkwardly and she was aware that he was as nervous in her company as she felt in his.

He swallowed. 'The Earl instructed us to remain on the outskirts while he pushed on with Sir Richard Grey and two members of his guard.'

Sir Richard Grey was the Marquess of Dorset's younger brother, the Queen's son by her former marriage to Lord Grey of Groby.

'I waited for a while then moved into the centre of the town. There is considerable chaos, as you can imagine, with so many men-at-arms moving about, jostling one another for accommodation and looking for ale and—and women,' he finished in a faintly embarrassed tone. 'At the Duke's lodging I was aware that his cousin, the Duke of Buckingham, had arrived to join him and——' he paused deliberately and looked full at Margaret for the first time in their talk '—and that Gloucester's men and Buckingham's had drawn into a tight circle round the inn. They were allowing no one in—or out.'

Margaret blinked rapidly. 'You mean. . .'

'I mean that it is possible—no, likely—that the Earl and Sir Richard Grey have been placed under house arrest and will not be allowed to proceed to Stony Stratford as they planned.'

'But the King has a strong escort.'

'Yes,' he said grimly, 'but Gloucester's is now strengthened by Buckingham's force and, without the Earl to give a lead—' he shrugged '—I think Sir Thomas Vaughan will be forced to give up the person of the King into Gloucester's charge.'

Margaret sat silent for a moment. 'You are saying that all those supporters of the Earl could be in an invidious position. They—could be accused of treason, since the Protector has been appointed by the Council and the late King's will.'

'Such a construction could be put on their conduct.'

'My father is in Stony Stratford, I believe.'

'I saw him there.' Hartwell rose. 'Mistress Margaret, the moment I saw how matters stood I came straight here, thinking it my duty to escort you immediately back to your manor. Once I am assured of your safety I must ride hotfoot for the capital to inform the Marquess and the Queen how matters stand.' He looked quickly at Jonnet. 'I will go below. Instruct your maid to help you dress and pack and we will leave at once. It will be full dark soon but I imagine your men know the area well and will be able to guide us. At present there should be no bar to your leaving Northampton but I cannot know how the situation will change by the morning.' He glanced significantly at the window from which they could hear snatches of raucous song. 'It will not be pleasant to be trapped here and, unfortunately, I must ride south as soon as possible.'

Margaret nodded. 'Thank you, sir, for your timely warning. I will dress at once. Will you be good enough to summon my two men for the stable?'

He stood up and moved to the door.

'I have no time to express my true admiration of your good sense and courage, mistress. I shall be waiting in the tap-room and will pay your score.'

'No, no, sir,' she said firmly. 'You must ride at once for London. That is your first duty. Mine is to my father. I shall go to Stony Stratford.'

He stopped dead in his tracks.

'Mistress Margaret, that is unthinkable. Two men only to escort you with roistering soldiery at every street-corner and in the villages along the way? Your father would insist——'

'My father is not here to insist. You say yourself he could be arrested. I have to find him and warn him. The King will be safe. No one would dare to harm him, but if my father is involved in this faction——' she drew a hard breath '—he could lose his head, as you could, sir, if you do not immediately take yourself out of the vicinity of Northampton.'

His brown eyes widened and he made to expostulate, but she brushed aside any argument he might put forward.

'Go, sir. Tell my men to be ready. As you say, we know the byways well. I can be in Stony Stratford before morning and give the alarm. I am grateful you delayed to come to me and—and I pray we shall meet again and become further acquainted when times are better suited.'

He gave a little regretful smile then bowed deeply and went from the chamber. Margaret waited only until the door was closed behind him and Jonnet had securely latched it against intrusion before she began to tear off her bed-gown and reach for her clothing.

Sir Guy Jarvis's squire, Owen Lewis, presented himself to his master in the tap-room of the Duke of Gloucester's lodgings, his face grave.

'Earl Rivers' servants are beginning to question the guard, sir. They demand to know why they are no longer free to go into the town. I feel it cannot be long before one of them informs the Earl of the situation.'

Sir Guy nodded. 'I'll come myself. Did you check that the road to Stony Stratford was adequately patrolled, as I ordered?'

'Yes, sir. Will Scroggins is in charge. You can depend on him utterly.'

Sir Guy smiled somewhat grimly. Scroggins had been a sergeant in Dominick Allard's company during the time Guy had served Allard as squire. He knew Scroggins well. The fellow was an arrant scoundrel but had settled down over the last years since his marriage to Kate, Lady Allard's maid and companion. Scroggins was a captain of a troop now and experienced enough to hold the Stony Stratford road against all-comers until either Guy, Dominick or the Duke himself gave him leave to withdraw his men.

He felt a savage satisfaction at the way events had turned. The Duke of Buckingham had arrived in Northampton scarcely an hour after Earl Rivers had ridden in. The two Dukes and the Earl had supped together. Dominick and Guy, served their supper in the taproom, in company with Sir Richard Ratcliffe,

Gloucester's friend since his early days as squire to great Warwick, at Middleham, had caught the sounds of genial conversation and laughter from the private chamber above stairs. The Earl's explanation that the town and villages near by had been too crowded to accommodate their combined force, and that for this reason he had carried on his nephew the King to Stony Stratford, had, seemingly, been accepted, though Guy had ground his teeth in fury at the Earl's duplicity. He knew Rivers' plan well enough. The Earl had most likely given orders for the royal party to leave early next day and press on to London. Gloucester would be left to trail ignominiously in his wake. Doubtless Dorset and the Queen had put their heads together, determined to foil Gloucester's chance of taking his rightful place as the boy's legal guardian. Then, abruptly, Gloucester had left the upstairs chamber and descended to talk with his gentlemen below. Instructions had been given to escort Rivers to his lodging at a nearby inn and see to it that he remained there, guarded by a troop of Guy's men-at-arms. To make doubly sure, Scroggins would deter any attempt to join the King's escort in Stony Stratford.

At Rivers' lodging Guy was faced by an angry and defiant steward.

'It is necessary that I and other servants ride on to Stony Stratford to see to it that all is in hand for the young King's comfort,' he said icily. 'It is a direct order from my master, the Earl.'

Guy smiled reassuringly. 'I'm sure that errand cannot be urgent at such an hour. The King is amply provided for. I understand his chamberlain and tutor are with him.'

The man blustered, his eyes uneasily sliding from the

blue ones of this man who was appearing more and more to resemble their gaoler.

'The Earl should be informed. . .'

'Certainly inform the Earl of the Protector's wishes. He desires him and Sir Richard Grey and all members of his accompanying party to remain within their lodgings until the Duke is himself ready to join his nephew at Stony Stratford. You will appreciate, I'm sure, how anxious the Duke is to offer his condolences in person to His Grace the King and as soon as possible.'

There was a steely note in Jarvis's voice and the man bowed stiffly and withdrew to confer with his masters.

It was merely an hour later that the Dukes of Gloucester and Buckingham emerged from their lodgings, professing themselves ready to ride for Stony Stratford. Guy had never seen Harry of Buckingham before this and thought the man resembled George, the late Duke of Clarence, Richard of Gloucester's older brother, who had died in the Tower, on King Edward's warrant. Like Clarence, Buckingham was taller and heavier than Gloucester, younger by perhaps one or two years. He was floridly handsome, with the fair hair of the other Plantagenet princes, while Gloucester was slighter and darker. Buckingham rested his arm familiarly round the Protector's shoulder, a gesture which Guy found irritatingly bold. Buckingham, he knew, was not enamoured of the Woodville clan, though he was wedded to Katherine Woodville, the Queen's sister, more than likely against his will since the marriage had taken place when he had been scarcely more than a boy. There was a gleam of triumph in the prominent blue eyes which showed openly his pleasure in the discomfiture of the Queen's brother and son.

Gloucester signalled to Guy and Dominick Allard,

who was following the Duke's party in company with Sir Richard Ratcliffe.

'Very well, gentlemen, we ride. Dominick, I leave you in charge here. Earl Rivers and Sir Richard Grey are to remain in Northampton under house arrest. I will decide what further action to take when we return here with the King's Grace.'

Dominick bowed and turned to Guy as if he expected his friend to accompany him, but the Duke lifted one hand imperiously.

'I shall need Guy with me in Stony Stratford, Dominick. There will be further arrests and I understand others in the Earl's service are abroad in the vicinity. I shall require someone I trust to be in charge of patrolling the district when I proceed south with the King.'

Buckingham, Guy thought, had either not proved himself in that capacity or he had established himself more nearly in the Duke's confidence and would be needed at his side when they entered the capital. He was not sure why he felt a moment's disquiet at the notion, but there was no time for doubts, only for prompt action, and he turned instantly to give orders to Owen Lewis to see that his troop was mounted and ready.

Stony Stratford was but a short ride and it was full early when Gloucester's company, strengthened by Buckingham's retinue, arrived in the little market town just as the young King's chamberlain was settling him comfortably on his mount preparatory to setting off on the final stage of his journey to London.

The boy looked anxiously at the two Dukes in their mourning velvets, then past them as if in search of the familiar features of his uncle Rivers, and his half-brother, Dick Grey.

Gloucester reined in immediately, dismounted and strode over to where the boy's mount was curvetting nervously. Momentarily, young Edward was too much occupied in reining him in to give his full attention to the size of this armed company. Guy, with Owen in attendance, watched the proceedings with grave attention. He was near enough to catch the gist of what was said. Buckingham had joined his cousin Gloucester, and waited until Gloucester had dropped to one knee in the dust of the road to kiss the young King's hand once he had regained control and was able to proffer it to his uncle.

'Your Grace, at last I am able to offer my condolences and pledge of loyalty. I wish we could have met again after these months of separation in happier circumstances.'

Guy was unable to catch the boy's reply but obviously Gloucester was presenting Buckingham to the King, for he rose and motioned for the younger Duke to make his obeisances. Gracefully Buckingham too knelt to salute his youthful sovereign.

Like his handsome Neville father and his beautiful mother, young Edward was fair, tall and slender. He bore himself with dignity but without arrogance and it was plain that he was bewildered by the sudden arrival of his father's brother. Guy's brows rose in surprise. Had the boy not been informed that he would enter the capital with the Lord Protector? Possibly not. Had Rivers wished to keep the initiative, he would have doubtless kept the youth in the dark concerning his intentions.

Obviously so, for Guy heard the high, youthful voice raised in bewildered objection.

'Return to Northampton? I don't understand. My chamberlain, Sir Thomas Vaughan, has prepared everything for our immediate departure for London. I see no need for delay and where is my uncle Rivers, and Dick, my brother? Surely we should wait for them. . .'

Gloucester's voice was calm and as clipped and businesslike as Guy recalled it before going into action on the Scottish border.

'Your uncle and brother are in Northampton, Sir. Earl Rivers, I'm sure, must have informed you that your late father, of blessed memory, left you and your brother and sister in my charge. There are several matters to be decided before we proceed further, matters which cannot be discussed while we remain in the open street. If Your Grace will oblige me by riding by my side we can return to my lodging, where, I assure you, you will find everything provided for your refreshment and comfort before departing for the capital.'

He signalled silently to Sir Richard Ratcliffe who, with an armed escort, moved immediately to detain Vaughan and others of the King's party. The elderly chamberlain protested volubly and the King turned towards him agitatedly, but Richard had once again mounted and ridden up close to his nephew while Buckingham ousted the man on the King's other side. Gloucester's cool grey eyes held the King's blue ones for a moment, then the boy dropped his gaze and allowed himself to be escorted between the two royal Dukes back on to the Northampton road.

Ratcliffe motioned to Guy as he made to take up his position at the rear of the company.

'Guy, I need you to see to it that any other malcontents are apprehended. I shall return my prisoners to Northampton and wait for further orders. I think it would be sensible for you to do the same. Rivers and Dorset had several followers. Many of them must have realised the situation and just taken off, but it would be unfortunate were His Grace to be challenged by any other noble once he has resumed his journey with the King. Would you remain here and question the senior servants? Any you think dangerous should be arrested and sent to Northampton, the rest should be allowed to disperse.'

Guy nodded. He left his mount in charge of a groom and, with Owen, went into the King's lodging to discharge the duty Ratcliffe had laid on him. It did not prove difficult. This sudden alteration in plans had completely shaken the young King's retainers who had come with him from Ludlow. One or two professed their disquiet at being separated from the King but most remained timidly silent. Guy assured them suavely that they were at liberty to return to Ludlow if they so desired or if they preferred to remain in Northamptonshire to await the Protector's orders that would be acceptable. He made it clear that they would be unwise to attempt to communicate with the King unless given leave by His Grace of Gloucester, or to have any further dealings with the King's Woodville relations. There was no one whom he felt it necessary to arrest and, at length, prepared to leave the inn and ride for Northampton to join Gloucester.

Owen Lewis's dark young face appeared a trife clouded with doubt and Guy glanced at him grimly. His squire came from the Welsh Marches and knew how the young men of the Ludlow escort must be feeling, uncertain how best now to proceed. But Lewis knew better than to question the actions of his masters and, since Guy made no comment, mounted silently and rode at his master's side at the head of the small company.

Halfway between Northampton and Stony Stratford Guy was met by Scroggins and his patrol. The grizzled veteran of Barnet and Tewkesbury looked somewhat disgruntled and appeared to have in tow a group of prisoners. Guy's lips twisted in a slight grin. Will Scroggins had been out all night and was not a man who missed his creature comforts without complaint.

'Well, Scroggins, I see you appear to have detained someone of note. What have you to report?'

Scroggins pushed up his metal salet to scratch his head.

'I don't know as 'ow I 'ave anybody important, Sir Guy, but I did apprehend this 'ere lady and 'er servant with a couple of men-at-arms.' He indicated the prisoner with a jabbing finger. 'Very 'aughty, she be, sir. Says as 'er father is one of the Marquess of Dorset's gentlemen with the King and she be riding to join 'im. Since I was told not to let anybody join the Earl Rivers' company I took her under guard. And a lot of trouble she's been, sir, what with all 'er complaining—worse than my Kate. I'll be obliged if you'll interview the lady and decide what's to be done with 'er. Couldn't we let 'er go?' He turned again and gave his prisoner a disparaging glance not unmixed with some suspicion of grudging respect. 'I can't see as 'ow she can 'arm the Duke's cause, sir, and she says 'er 'ome is near 'ere.'

Guy dismounted and strode towards the disconsolate group guarded by four of Scroggins' troop. A frightened girl, her wimple awry, shrank back at his approach and Guy surmised she was the lady's attendant.

A cool, angry voice stopped him in his tracks.

'Who are you, sir? Someone in authority, I hope, who can assure this person that I have right and reason to go on my way without hindrance. Please instruct him to release me and my servants so that we can proceed on to Stony Stratford. I presume, since he has consulted you, that he is under your command.'

Something in that cool, authoritative voice stirred a chord in his memory. Guy glanced up at the mounted figure, shrouded in a dark velvet cloak, who was glaring angrily down at him. Her hood had been pulled up to shade her face but he could see that she was young and proud, and believed that the eyes which flashed fire at him were dark.

He bowed. 'I am Sir Guy Jarvis, mistress, riding on the Duke of Gloucester's business. Since he is now Lord Protector of England, I have his instructions to see to it that no unauthorised persons are travelling upon this road. I'm sure you are aware that His Grace the King will soon be setting out for London. We must see that the way is both safe and clear for his passage. I would be obliged if you would identify yourself.'

He caught a sharp intake of breath as if his words had dealt her some shock, then, with her immediate reply, understood the reason.

'I am Mistress Margaret Rushton. My father, Sir John, came to Northampton to join Earl Rivers' escort of the King on the Marquess of Dorset's orders. He instructed me to join him in Stony Stratford but I was detained on the road, as you see. May I proceed now?'

Margaret Rushton! Yes, Dominick had said something earlier of Rushton's association with Dorset. So Rushton had joined Rivers and was willingly involved in the coup to oust Richard from power, an act which could now be construed as treasonable. Was she aware of it? Yes, Guy believed that she was, and was probably on her way to warn him that the Protector's company had now been strenghtened by the addition of Buckingham's men.

He smiled a trifle grimly. Where was Rushton now? He himself had taken charge of the waggons laden with armour and weapons which had accompanied Rivers' escort. There was no doubt that the Woodville faction meant to challenge Gloucester's authority. Oh, yes, Rushton was involved in the Woodville plot, up to his ears. It seemed that his ambitious plans to wed his daughter to a gentleman of Dorset's choosing had gone sadly wrong for his hopes of preferment. Gloucester would wish to have Rushton in his hands, and where Margaret Rushton was her father would surely try to join her.

She was waiting impatiently for his reply and added, 'It seems we are doomed to meet in unfortunate circumstances, Sir Guy. On the last occasion neither of us was pleased by the other's reaction to planned changes.'

Her voice was still cool in tone, even, as if she had no intention of betraying any unease at this sudden embarrassing encounter. She put back her hood now and he was able to see her face more clearly. She had become a very comely woman. He judged she must be now turned eighteen, if his memory served him correctly. Perhaps some would not term her beautiful. Her features were too strongly marked for femininity: those arching dark brows, not shaved in the fashion at Court that he personally found displeasing, for it tended to leave the lady who did it expressionless, without character, that firm mouth which informed him that there had been no change in her determination to express her own opinions forcibly as she had done when scarcely more than a child, and that jutting chin. All spoke of a strength of character and a waywardness which Scroggins had found so unnerving. Her seat on her mount pronounced her a practised horsewoman and betrayed no sign of weakness, though he knew she must be feeling decidely weary and probably apprehensive.

'I regret, Mistress Rushton, that my orders force me to take you and your escort in charge. We will return to Northampton, if you please.' His embarrassment at this unexpected meeting caused him to speak more coldly than he had intended.

'And if I do *not* please?' The arrogant tone he remembered was still noticeable in her voice.

'Then I shall be forced to compel you.'

'My father will, by now, have returned to the manor and be anxious about me.' This statement was less confident and revealed a measure of growing concern.

He shrugged. 'That is possible. If that is the case I am sure Sir John will present himself before the Protector to explain his reason for joining Earl Rivers' escort without being requested to do so by His Grace of Gloucester.'

Recognising the steely quality of the implied threat, she swallowed uncomfortably.

'The Marquess of Dorset sent, asking——'

'The Marquess of Dorset is not Protector of the realm, mistress.'

Her shoulders drooped only slightly but her imperious dark eyes stared into his hard blue ones as if seeking reassurance. She sighed.

'Since you insist, I must accompany you, sir. I have no wish to anger His Grace of Gloucester by defying his orders.'

His lips twitched as he bowed coldly in acknowledgement of her surrender.

'That would not be wise, Mistress Rushton.'

Her maid gave a little despairing sob and Margaret Rushton turned on the unfortunate girl with the ferocity of a tigress.

'Be silent, you foolish wench. These gentlemen intend us no harm. The moment we return to Northampton and our errand is explained we shall be allowed to return to Cold Ashby. Come, sir, let us proceed. The sooner all this is sorted out, the sooner we shall be relieved of the discomfort of each other's presence.'

Guy signalled to Scroggins. 'Right, we return to Northampton and report to Sir Richard Ratcliffe. You will want to be relieved of duty and get some food into your men before we take the road south again.'

He walked back to his own mount, taking only one quick glance at his prisoner, who sat immovable in the saddle, waiting for his next move. He met Owen Lewis's puzzled expression with an irritated gesture of his hand.

'Oh, come, let's get on,' he snarled testily. 'I'm as anxious as Scroggins is to take some refreshment and have the responsibility for this tiresome woman off my hands.'

CHAPTER THREE

MARGARET had ridden without conscious thought the few short miles back to Northampton. It was only when they entered the bustling town, crowded and noisy with soldiery, that she realised how terribly exhausted she was. When they drew rein before the largest and most prosperous inn in the town, she leaned back in the saddle wondering just how she was going to summon the strength to dismount without falling and making a spectacle of herself before her captor.

Sir Guy materialised at her side and, without waiting for permission, lifted her down. She gritted her teeth and forced herself to stand proudly, head thrown back in defiance.

'Well, sir, what have you in store for your prisoner, a dark dungeon somewhere?'

'I think first we should find you some accommodation where you can wash and make yourself presentable,' he said coldly.

She flushed with embarrassment. She had been up all night, in the saddle most of it, and must appear bedraggled and unkempt and, most likely, stank of horseflesh. She said, with frigid politeness, 'That would be kind.'

A soldier had lifted Jonnet down and the girl was artlessly rubbing her bottom, without the least show of feminine modesty. Really, the girl was impossible!

'Jonnet,' Margaret called sharply, and the maid raised her head, startled, then saw her mistress's disapproving countenance and the broad grin of the young soldier who had helped her. She trotted obediently to Margaret's side, her face showing a mixture of puzzled apprehension and resignation.

Guy Jarvis led his two female prisoners into the inn and sent Owen Lewis to procure some private place for them. The innkeeper was not best pleased. He had been honoured by the presence of the two royal Dukes within his establishment but they and their attendants had put considerable stress upon his staff, unaccustomed to such exalted company, and his supplies, so he had been relieved to see His Grace of Gloucester ride out but dampened to see him and the Duke of Buckingham return soon after with the young King. He blustered that he could in no way find a private room for the ladies but, meeting Guy's cold blue gaze, wilted and waddled up the stair to his own private chamber which he grudgingly placed at the new guests' disposal.

Guy looked round haughtily and gave a brief nod of acceptance.

'We shall be here only a matter of hours,' he told the sweating man. His glare of dismissal took the fellow down the stairs again at a run, an unaccustomed haste for one of his bulk. In more pleasant circumstances Margaret would have found the brief exchange amusing, but she was too wearied and heartsick to register any emotion and thankfully sat down upon the bed. Jonnet waited apprehensively for her to explode into angry speech but she too found this tall, fair young man alarming and was relieved when he said coolly, 'I shall send up a maid with some water and towels, also some food, for I imagine you have not broken fast since last night. Meanwhile you will remain within the chamber. An armed guard will be present outside. I shall inform

His Grace of Gloucester that you were taken on the road and he will doubtless issue orders as to what is to be done.'

'He will send me home?' Her words almost fell over each other in her eagerness.

'It would seem likely. Probably you will be issued with an escort and ordered to remain on your own manor until your father returns or word of him is sent to you.'

He gave a quick bow and took his departure. Margaret sank back against the pillows of the bed and rubbed her tired and smarting eyes. She was still wearing her hood and shoes but Jonnet did not dare approach to help her remove them. An inn wench arrived with amazing haste which spoke again of Sir Guy Jarvis's method of persuasion, and Margaret sat up thankfully and washed off the dust and grime of the evening ride. Jonnet shook the dust from both their cloaks and did her best to tidy her mistress's hair.

Margaret was consumed with concern for her father. Sir Guy had not informed her of anything which had taken place in Northampton or Stony Stratford but it seemed evident that the Protector was completely in charge of the situation and she realised that Sir John Rushton was either in the hands of Gloucester's men-at-arms or at large in the district, possibly in danger of being apprehended at any moment. She was anxious now to get back to the manor as soon as possible. If her father were to seek refuge there it was essential that she be present to do her best for him. Her thoughts also flew to the fate of Bennet Hartwell. Had he managed to avoid the Protector's men and reach London to carry his tale to the Queen's kin?

Her reverie was cut short by the return of Sir Guy.

She answered his knock coldly and he stood on the threshold regarding her steadily. Before his cool appraisal she lowered her head to hide angry tears.

'Well, sir?' she demanded huskily.

'The Duke of Gloucester had commanded your presence.'

'Now?' She was startled by the summons. It had not occurred to her that she might be called to explain her presence on the road at such a strange hour.

'Certainly, at once. One does not keep His Grace waiting,' he chided her.

She was thankful that he had had the consideration to give her the opportunity to put to rights her appearance but possibly he had expected this to happen.

She was surprised by the youthful appearance of the Protector, though she reminded herself inwardly that he could not be much older than thirty. He had been scarcely eighteen years old when he had taken such an eventful part in the Yorkist victory at Tewkesbury. He looked tired now, his mouth held in tightly as if to control signs of stress or pain, and his gold jewelled chain was the only relief to his dress of sombre black velvet mourning. She had expected him to look bigger, more robust, and saw that he was slightly built, dark, with a pale, narrow countenance, but the grey eyes were wide-set and luminous. This was not the face of a cruel man, nor, did she think, a particularly calculating one. He had seized power and was in no mood to countenance disloyalty—she saw that in the set of his mouth—and she had heard he was a fearless warrior but, as she curtsied low, she felt no fear that he would treat her badly.

'Mistress Rushton.' He acknowledged her curtsy with a nod and gestured her to approach his chair. 'Sir Guy tells me you had come to Northampton with your father, Sir John, but that he left you here to join Earl Rivers.'

A bluff-faced, brown-haired man stood behind his chair. There were five of them in all in the chamber. Margaret wondered where the Duke of Buckingham was with the young King, for she had been made fully aware of the King's return with his uncle, from the conversation between the men on the road.

'Yes, Your Grace,' she said, and hoped the effort she had made to keep her voice steady had taken effect. 'My father was called away urgently but later I set out to join him in Stony Stratford, but was detained on the road.'

'By my orders.'

She felt her legs tremble and waited for his further comment.

'Know, mistress, that I have placed Earl Rivers under arrest together with his nephew, Sir Richard Grey and Sir Thomas Vaughan, the King's chamberlain.'

Her eyes must have registered shock for he smiled a trifle grimly. 'There was considerable evidence to prove that Earl Rivers and his party were seeking to overset my authority. By the late King's will I am Protector of the realm, guardian of King Edward's children, and those who try to thwart me will suffer for it. I cannot allow the peace of the realm to dissolve into a state of lawlessness because of the uncontrolled ambitions of those who should know better. I have seen too much of that in my youth.'

The words betrayed no anger, but were clear and rather clipped, decisive, in the fashion of a man who was unused to having his commands questioned. 'Your father would have done better to remain on his manor until he received news that I had need of him.'

Margaret swallowed and forced back her rising sense of panic.

'There were waggons of weapons and armour in the Earl's train,' The Duke explained with gentle irony. 'I came south with a small escort to meet my nephew and offer him my loyalty and express my great grief at his loss, to be met with a vastly superior force. Had it not been for the assistance rendered by my cousin Buckingham, I might not have reached London.'

Feeling herself bound to answer in her father's defence, Margaret murmured faintly, 'I am sure my father meant no disloyalty, Your Grace. Like you, he merely wished to support the King and offer his condolences.'

The Duke's lips twitched slightly. 'I'm sure when he presents himself before me he will offer his own explanation of his conduct.'

Margaret moistened dry lips. Behind her she felt Sir Guy stir only slightly. Jonnet, by the door, shifted uncomfortably. She had no understanding of the cause of the friction within the room but felt the chill quality of the atmosphere and, like Margaret, wished passionately that they were all back safely on the manor.

Gloucester was leaning back in the chair, absently playing with a cabochon-set ruby ring on his left hand.

'Naturally, mistress, you are anxious to return home.'

She had to make two attempts to find her voice. 'If you would be so kind as to release me, Your Grace.'

One eyebrow arched upwards and again the mobile mouth curved in a smile. 'Oh, I have no intention of releasing you, Mistress Rushton, though I will send you home. Sir Guy, I wish you to accompany Mistress

Rushton to her manor and remain there with your company until I send orders to the contrary. Mistress Rushton will feel safer with a guard while the district is in some disarray. There will be masterless men abroad and it is our duty to see the lady is kept safe.'

Stung to sudden anger, Margaret's dark eyes flashed dangerously. 'You intend to hold me as hostage, my lord?'

The grey eyes twinkled with some amusement. 'I do not intend to have you held above the walls in a threat to hang you before your father's eyes if he continues to defy me, as King Stephen was said to do to the youthful William the Marshall, but yes, I think that your presence in my hands will ensure that your father thinks carefully before he decides on any further act of disobedience,' he said drily.

Margaret drew a hard breath. She dared not utter any further complaint and contented herself with another deep curtsy, which she hoped he might find in some way a gesture of silent insolence.

The action was not lost on him, she was sure, for he bowed his head in an equally ironic acknowledgement.

'You are dismissed, Mistress Rushton. I trust we shall meet again in more pleasant circumstances. My wife, the Duchess, would be charmed to receive you, I know, should you travel to London in due time.'

She moved gracefully backwards, Sir Guy skilfully leading her by one strategic hand on her elbow. At the door she heard him speak respectfully to the Duke.

'Would you grant me a private word, sir?'

'Of course, Guy. See the lady safely disposed under guard and come straight back to me. I cannot delay. You know we must set out soon for the capital.'

Guy returned Margaret to the room placed at their

disposal by the landlord and curtly suggested that she prepare herself for riding within the hour. She forbore to say one word to him. He saw to it that a reliable guard was placed outside her door and hurried back for his audience with the Duke.

Richard looked up at him over the rim of his wine cup.

'Well, Guy, what is so urgent?'

Sir Richard Ratcliffe had withdrawn and the two were alone.

'Sir,' Guy began hesitantly, 'I. . .'

'Heavens, man, when have I ever given you cause to fear making requests? What is it?'

'You will perhaps recall, sir, that I was once betrothed to Mistress Rushton.'

'Certainly. The whole affair was a disgraceful breach of trust on Rushton's part.'

'Yes, sir. I understand from what Dominick said that her father now plans to betroth her to Bennet Hartwell, one of the Marquess of Dorset's gentlemen. Aleyne heard it from Lady Scrope, I believe.'

Richard's lips curved in a broad smile. 'Lady Scrope appears to have a remarkable ear for current gossip and Anne informs me she is seldom wrong. Well, if that is the case, it is more essential than ever that we keep a sharp eye on the lady's movements.'

'I agree, Your Grace, but. . .'

'But?' The imperious tone was there again.

'Would it not be better, sir, if someone else were given the task of guarding the lady? I would feel somewhat embarrassed by—by the circumstances and would be grateful if you would relieve me of this duty.'

There was a short silence. The Duke placed his wine cup down on the table very deliberately.

'Understand, Guy, that I need someone on that manor I can trust. Dominick comes with me to London. I shall have need of his services and when Anne arrives to join me later Aleyne will be in attendance—it will be appropriate if Dominick is there to welcome his lady. Dick Ratcliffe I have sent north with the prisoners. I tell you now in confidence that I shall have no mercy on these three ringleaders. This isn't the time for clemency. If I don't exercise my authority now the country will suffer for it, unrest and insurrection breeding like rabbits. Frank Lovell, of course, will also be needed in London. If Rushton arrives I want you there to take him into custody.' He looked intently back at Guy who was fiddling with his dagger-hilt, frowning uncertainly. 'Come, Guy, it isn't like you to be put out of countenance by the presence of some green girl. Rather I would think it would give you the opportunity to repay Rushton for the humiliation you suffered at his hands.'

Guy let out his breath and nodded slowly.

The Duke continued. 'Not that I wish you to treat the girl badly. I know you would not do that, but you are unlikely to be seduced by the light in her bright eyes either.' The tone was dry. 'If I'm not mistaken she's quite a termagant and will need a firm hand. The only other man I could send would be Scroggins.'

Guy made a brief murmur of remonstrance.

The Duke grinned. 'Quite. The man's loyal enough but he still has the instincts of the mercenary and the lady requires gentler treatment, to say nothing of possible depredations to the manor he might allow his men to make.'

Guy straightened his shoulders, then bowed. 'I'm

sorry I troubled Your Grace. Naturally I am unreservedly at your service.'

'Good man, I knew I could rely on you. You should not need to be gaoler for long. I shall require you by my side in London before the month is out. If Rushton is not in the net then, I shall send instructions to you to bring Mistress Margaret south.'

At the door Guy paused. 'If Rushton resists arrest, sir?'

'Then you will take steps to compel his compliance but, if you can, send him alive to London. I need to know just how deeply he was involved in this threatened coup and who his associates are.'

'Hartwell?'

'We have no grounds on which to arrest him, or,' he said regretfully, 'reason to interrogate him, as yet. The lady might know something more. See what you can discover.'

'I doubt she will be in the mood to offer confidences, sir.'

The Duke shrugged slightly. 'No, I grant you, but occasionally one discovers more from ill-chosen words when one's prisoner is in a towering rage.'

Guy's lips twisted in a gesture of reluctant resignation then he nodded, bowed again and withdrew.

Hastening back towards the chamber where he had left Margaret Rushton, Guy encountered Dominick.

'Ah, I wanted to see you before I left for London. I understand you have been commanded to escort the lady to her manor and stay there.'

Guy nodded gloomily.

'Have you recently been with the Duke?'

'I asked to be relieved of the duty but he impressed on me how important it was that I should stay.'

Dominick inclined his head. 'I could leave Scroggins with you. You'll need a good man. Under you, he'll behave.' He smiled. 'He knows reports will go back to Kate.'

Guy was forced to laugh. Kate Scroggins, Will's lame wife who was also Lady Allard's maid and confidante, had complete control over her mate. Since Will Scroggins had answered to no one from the moment he could walk unaided until Kate appeared in his life, it was a source of amusement to his masters and the men under him that he was now so much under the thumb of his sharp-tongued wife. Scroggins was dependable, when under supervision, and Guy knew his services at the manor would be invaluable.

'Thank you, I'd be glad of that. I shall be pleased when I'm summoned to London. I can only hope that Sir John is, by then, in our hands.'

The two gripped hands, Dominick staring intently into his young friend's troubled blue eyes. He was, perhaps, the one person in the world who knew how badly that repudiation had hurt Guy Jarvis. Even Lady Jarvis, Guy's gentle mother who continued to live widowed in Gloucester, had not thoroughly understood the harm to her son's pride that that foolish chit of a girl Guy now held prisoner had dealt him.

'I haven't seen her,' Dominick said a trifle gruffly. 'Not since that afternoon. Has she grown comely?'

Guy averted his eyes. 'One could almost say beautiful,' he said coolly, 'if one admired a determined chin and eyes which flash fire whenever she's crossed, to say nothing of a haughty disposition. Even her maid seems terrified of her tempers. I tell you, Dominick, this will be no easy task. Had not Gloucester enjoined on me the necessity of keeping the wench under my eye at all times, I'd keep well out of her way. Hartwell is welcome to her. Once she is installed on his manor there will be no question as to who rules the roost.'

'And if she were installed in your household?'

Guy shrugged then turned back deliberately. 'But there is no possibility of that. If there were, she might find things very different.'

He murmured a hasty farewell and mounted to the chamber. A frightened Jonnet opened the door to his knock and he pressed inside despite her agitated effort, doubtless at her mistress's command, to keep him waiting on the threshold. Coldly he regarded Mistress Margaret, who stood near the window, head thrown back, spine stiffened to rigidity, in the pose he was beginning to find habitual with her.

'We are ready to ride now, mistress. I trust you are prepared.'

'Since it seems I must.' She moved only slightly nearer. 'I have left a saddle-bag containing my baggage at the White Swan. Can it be collected?'

'Certainly; we'll call there before leaving the town.'

He waited for her to precede him to the door but she said abruptly, 'What of my two men-at-arms? Are they to be kept here under arrest?'

'I see no reason why they should not ride home with us. If there is thought need to question them they will be at hand.'

She gave a slightly relieved sigh. He was surprised. He had not expected her to be concerned about the fate of underlings.

Outside the White Swan, Guy instructed Margaret to remain in the saddle and sent the maid with one of his men to retrieve their belongings. Margaret remained stiffly tall on her mount, in total control even when the animal sidled nervously at the delay. She ignored Guy totally. Soon the maid and man returned and the saddle-bags were packed on one of the sumpter mules which the escort kept with them for the conveyance of supplies. Guy was about to give the order to ride when one of the inn girls rushed out, agitatedly waving some garment he thought must be a veil. Irritably he reined in his horse again until the girl approached Mistress Margaret.

'You left this behind, mistresss,' the girl gabbled urgently, pushing the length of rather coarse veiling into Margaret's hands.

'You're mistaken, girl,' she said somewhat tartly. 'This is no stuff of mine. It must have been left by some other guest.'

The girl continued to grip Margaret's saddle and leaned towards her, her eyes imploring.

'Please look, mistress, I'm sure it must be yours. We've had no other lady present.'

Wonderingly Margaret peered at the inferior cloth and the girl spoke quickly.

'I had to speak to you, mistress. The guest who arrived late last evening, he came back. He seemed in a rare taking and asked if I knew where you were. When I said I did not, that you hadn't come back, he said I was to try and get a message to you that he couldn't reach his destination.' The girl pronounced the word carefully as if its meaning eluded her. 'He'll be in the district, he said, close to you, and will get word to you right soon. That you was to look out for news of him and keep up your heart about—those you love.'

Margaret looked nervously to where Sir Guy Jarvis was impatiently chatting to the captain who had formerly detained her on the road. She had been further angered that the man was to form one of her guard. She had found him less then respectful in his attitude. Now she was relieved that neither of the men was observing her closely.

'Thank you,' she said fervently, taking the veiling and reaching within her hanging purse for a noble, which she pressed into the girl's hands. 'You have done me good service and relieved my heart. Now go before someone insists on knowing what you said to me.'

The girl was off and into the inn before Sir Guy looked up.

'Merely something I forgot to pack, sir,' Margaret explained, thrusting the veil before her on the saddle. 'It was torn accidentally and the girl took it off for repair. It had slipped my mind.'

'Very well, then, now can we get on?'

She nodded agreement and fell in by his side as he was clearly expecting her to do.

For the next few miles her mind was busy with the import of Bennet Hartwell's message. Obviously he had found it too dangerous to proceed on to London as he had planned but was in touch with her father. So far both were unharmed and free. She uttered a silent prayer of gratitude to the Virgin.

Their arrival caused quite a stir at the manor. The grooms looked askance at the murrey and blue liveries of the men-at-arms and Margaret's father's bailiff, Wilf Charlesworth, looked positively alarmed as he came running to the door to greet them, his eyes sliding uneasily from the figure of the tall mounted knight to his mistress's face.

Sir Guy forestalled one of the grooms and lifted Margaret from her horse, then, without waiting for her to explain or introduce him, gave crisp orders to the bailiff.

'I shall be staying here for some days. See to it that my men are found suitable accommodation and the horses and sumpter mule adequately cared for. You can present yourself to me each morning in the hall for your orders. For now your mistress is wearied. Arrange for maids to attend her in her chamber and for a speedy supper.'

'Yes, sir.' The man looked anxiously towards Margaret. He was a thin, spindly little man in late middle age who lived in constant fear of her father's disapproval, but he was honest and reliable and Margaret often felt sorry for the scant respect he got from Sir John. The man deserved more appreciation for his loyalty and would have served the family even better if he could have gone about his business with a quiet mind and not in a continual panic about Sir John's wrath.

'Has my father returned, Wilf?' she enquired in a kindly tone, for Sir Guy's benefit, knowing only too well that Sir John's presence at the manor was most unlikely.

'No, mistress. There 'as been no message from the master since he left for Northampton. We thought as 'ow you might all 'ave gone to London—'

'No, no,' she interrupted what might have been a spate of unfortunate surmises. 'Sir John left me in Northampton to return to the manor and went on to join Earl Rivers in Stony Stratford.' She looked defiantly at Sir Guy. 'However, there have been several changes in plan and I thought he might have ridden home, but no matter.' She moved briskly towards the main door. 'I'm sure we shall have good news of him soon. I shall want supper in an hour. Perhaps Sir Guy would prefer to be served in his chamber? I see he has his squire with him and he will make sure that the rooms provided are satisfactory.'

Sir Guy said smoothly, 'I would not dream of putting your servants to so much trouble. I shall eat in hall with you, mistress, tonight and—always.' There was a slight pause before the final word, as if he was delivering a definite statement of intent, and Margaret gritted her teeth in annoyance. It was going to be bad enough putting up with the man's presence on her land but now she would be forced to treat him, outwardly at least, as an honoured guest. He was waiting now, his hand outstretched, as if to conduct her inside and, angrily, she placed her own upon his arm and went meekly though reluctantly. Jonnet, who had ridden pillion behind one of the men-at-arms, was chattering volubly and Margaret's voice floated coldly back to her.

'Jonnet, I need you in my chamber, at once.'

At the stair-foot Margaret turned to face her gaoler. 'I hope my servants will be able to make you comfortable, sir. I'm sure you are no more anxious to be here than I am to have you as guest. For that reason I thought it best we should eat apart, seeing each other as little as possible. Perhaps it would be best if *I* were to eat in my chamber from now on.'

'No,' he said evenly. 'You will eat in hall with me. That way you will be able to ensure that things are progressing normally on the manor and that my men are not overstepping their authority, and——' again he paused and smiled '—I shall be able to keep my eye on you, at least for most of the time.'

Her face darkened with angry colour. 'Then I am indeed your prisoner?'

'As you put it yourself, to the Duke's face, with amazing discourtesy, you are hostage for your father's good behaviour. Within the manor you will act as chatelaine as you have always done.'

'But not outside it?'

'You will not leave the manor unless I accompany you.'

She stepped back a pace, for the first time fully aware of her position.

'But I must be allowed to go to Cold Ashby. I do, regularly, to visit the sick and—'

'I'm afraid, for the next few days at least, they will have to make shift without you.'

'But to church—to mass?'

'I will make arrangements for a priest to come here to hear confessions and celebrate the mass.'

A slight breath escaped her lips. She was virtually to be held under house arrest. How would it be possible to receive news from Bennet Hartwell? Would her servants be able to move freely? Somehow she must find one of the grooms she could trust to watch out for any stranger in the village. . . Her thoughts ran on until she found Sir Guy looking at her intently, his fair head held only slightly on one side.

She said coldly, 'I will go up and wash. I suggest, sir, that you do likewise, if you are to eat at my table.'

It was a calculated insult and misplaced, since he did not appear in the least dishevelled from the night's activities or the final ride here, and, she felt, she most probably looked anything but her best. Without waiting to see if her arrow had gone home she swept up the stairs with Jonnet trailing behind her.

Once within her chamber she regretted her waspishness. She was becoming a positive shrew lately. Jonnet's alarmed, wide-stretched eyes told her that as the maid came apprehensively to help her change. She must try to be more kind towards Jonnet. She told herself often that her impatience was unjustified. As for this knight, he was merely obeying the orders of his Duke. She could not hold him responsible for her imprisonment. The circumstances of their last meeting did not give her cause to treat him with such scant respect. The outcome had been brought about by her father and Guy Jarvis had been in no way at fault. At the time she had merely been obeying orders, as he was now, yet she felt extreme embarrassment at his presence. She was shy with him, even more so than she had been last evening with Bennet Hartwell. Why? The man meant nothing to her. Soon this unpleasantness would be over and he would leave Rushton. But what would bring about that state of affairs—the arrest of her father, or the overturning of the Duke of Gloucester's plans in London? She bit her lip thoughtfully. The latter did not appear to be likely. From what she had seen of him, Gloucester looked more than competent to deal with his rivals, and the combined escorts of his and Buckingham's made a formidable force.

She decided to dress in one of her finest gowns, gold brocade over a cream undergown which complemented the creaminess of her complexion. Since she was forced to play unwilling hostess, she would put on a good show and impress the plain knight from Yorkshire.

She realised her mistake when she joined him at the high table in hall, for he too had changed but wore sombre mourning for the dead King as his master, Gloucester, had done. She stood uncertainly, biting her lip and regretting her crass lack of sensitivity. He moved to take her hand and lead her to her place at table. Wilf had impressed on the servants the need for speed and efficient service and they did not put her to shame. If she had expected any awkwardness from this man who rarely went to Court she was mistaken. His table manners were excellent but in no way showy. He helped her to meat after delicately rinsing his fingers in the proffered bowl of rose-water and she noticed that, though he ate heartily, it was without undue haste, nor did he drink heavily.

The silence between them seemed oppressive until he requested politely, 'I did not hear how your mother came to die, Mistress Margaret. I remember her from our only meeting as a very lovely, courteous and gentle lady.'

Tears pricked at her eyelids as she recalled her mother's tragic passing. 'She died in childbed, sir. The child, as your must realise, did not survive.'

'I'm sorry. You must miss her sorely.'

'She ran the manor beautifully and, as you observed, she was very gentle and deeply loved by all who served her.'

He did not reply and she wondered, uneasily, if he was comparing her shrewish behaviour with her mother's show of courtesy.

He turned his head as his captain, Scroggins, entered the hall and took his seat at the lower table. For a moment Margaret was able to observe him while he appeared to be watching the conduct of his men. She had avoided staring too obviously, over the last hours, and now she was curious to see clearly what changes time had wrought in his appearance.

He was tall, taller than her father, and she was forced to look up at him, a situation she did not face too often. She remembered him as tall and slender, almost boyish.

He was still slim-built but she was in no two minds about the muscular development of that tall frame, deep-chested and slim-hipped, his hose fitting those long legs to perfection. He was, if anything, she thought, not for the first time, *too* handsome. His hair had been cut short now, probably for simplicity of style while serving on border patrols in the north, but curled on to his broad, high forehead and into the nape of his neck. His fairness had not deepened to brown and was still the glorious colour of ripe corn. The features had hardened, the nose more acquiline, the cheekbones high and well-accentuated. The lips only had remained womanly, long, well-shaped, sensuous, she thought, though she had no experience of men so described. The scar which winged his brow in no way detracted from the manly beauty of his proud face. She would have liked to know how he came by it. She flushed awkwardly, to be caught watching him so closely, as she now saw that those devastatingly blue eyes were boring into her, as if he would read her thoughts.

'Something disturbs you, mistress?'

'No, no, sir.' She looked away towards the group of Yorkist men-at-arms. 'No, the men seem admirably behaved.'

'They had better be. They have had their orders.'

'You are a hard commander?'

'I hope I am a fair commander, as, I am sure, you hope to be thought a considerate mistress.'

She drew a hard breath and followed his gaze to where Jonnet sat in animated talk with the man behind whom she had ridden pillion.

'Jonnet is new in my service,' Margaret said defensively. 'Sometimes she forgets herself and needs to be reminded sharply.'

'As do my men,' he observed drily, 'on occasion. Make no mistake, Mistress Margaret, they have been informed of their duties and what is expected of them. Each man knows I do not excuse any lack of attention when on guard.'

She knew he was reminding her that she should make no covert move to leave the manor and her lips compressed in anger.

Abruptly she asked, 'What is to become of Earl Rivers and the King's half-brother?'

'I was told Sir Richard Ratcliffe will escort them north.'

'Where the Duke of Gloucester's will is law.'

'Where the Lord Protector's authority is respected, yes, madam.' His tone was curt but she was in no mood to be silenced.

'The young King will miss his uncle and brother, be frightened.'

'He has no cause to be. Richard of Gloucester is his uncle and as near in blood.'

'Yet his mother's brother, his maternal uncle, is to be imprisoned.'

'Had he not chosen to ally himself with the Protector's enemies, he would be free at this moment and eventually riding south with his nephew at Gloucester's side.'

'You believe Earl Rivers to be Gloucester's enemy?'

Guy smiled grimly. 'All men desire power, Mistress Margaret, and advancement. Your father taught me that lesson all those years ago. Now who holds the person of the King holds the balance of that power. Why do you think Rivers was so anxious to hasten the boy on to London without Gloucester's agreement? If Gloucester were to step meekly aside in this contest for influence, how long do you think he would remain free on his own lands in Yorkshire? He is the late King's brother, a man to be feared. Do you think his rivals behind the young King's throne would let him live to oppose them? You know your history, I'm sure. What happened to the late Harry VI's uncles?'

She gave a shiver of fear. Suddenly the warmth of the hall had turned chill again. Gloucester, she knew, had a wife at Middleham and a young son about the age of the King's younger brother, Prince Richard. Now she understood Gloucester's need not only to hold power as his brother, the late King, had wished, but to protect his own. How terribly the unexpected death of the King had affected the peace of the realm, beside the fates of each and every member of that royal Plantagenet family, not to say interrupted her own planned betrothal and forthcoming marriage.

Before she could bite back the obviously curious words, she heard herself saying, 'And what of your wife, Sir Guy? Does she remain in Yorkshire in attendance upon the Duchess of Gloucester?'

He replied stiffly, 'I have no wife, mistress. Past experience has taught me to regard the loyalty of women with extreme caution.'

Her eyes fell under his chilling scrutiny.

He continued, 'I believe I heard that the suitor originally chosen for you by your father died. That was unfortunate—for all of you.'

Her fingers were trembling on the lip of her wine cup. 'Yes,' she breathed. 'Recently my father planned another alliance, to Master Bennet Hartwell. We should have celebrated our betrothal but the ceremony was postponed when we heard the sad tidings of the King's death.'

'You appear to be unfortunate in your chosen husbands, mistress.'

Was he sneering openly at her discomfiture? She saw no sign of it on that coldly impassive countenance.

So he was not married. Perversely she felt an acute sense of satisfaction. Neither of them had prospered after her father's calculating decision. She could not help thinking that he must have been offered opportunities. He was in service to one of the most powerful princes in Europe. Had his excuse been made to cover the fact that those ladies offered such an alliance had found him too cold for their tastes? Certainly they could not have found him unattractive in appearance and she judged him fearless in battle, probably ruthlessly efficient.

She asked diffidently, 'Does your mother still live?'

'Yes. She remains much of the time in Gloucestershire, on my manor, and sometimes in Bristol where she stays often with my aunt who is also a widow.'

'She must see little of you, now you are so occupied in the Duke of Gloucester's service.'

'My mother is pleased for me and I visit her as often as I can. When my father died things went hard for her and she was relieved that another colleague of his in service under the Yorkist princes, Sir Dominick Allard, consented to take me as his squire. I followed him into exile during the brief return of King Harry VI to the throne and served him in the decisive battles of Barnet and Tewkesbury. He honours me with his friendship and, since he is one of Gloucester's gentlemen, it was natural that I should take service with the Duke during his campaigns on the Scottish border.'

'Then you were knighted by him?'

'By Gloucester, yes, after the taking of Berwick.'

She shook her head as he proffered the bowl of fruit at the close of the meal, but watched with interest as he delicately peeled an apple. They had come to the last of the stored fruit and it was wrinkled. She wondered, vaguely, if she would be here when they began to gather the early strawberries.

She glanced down to the lower table where the men had begun to drink more heavily and were growing more noisy. She turned back to Sir Guy.

'If you will excuse me, sir, I will retire now.'

He rose immediately to escort her. Jonnet scrambled up from her bench and scampered up the stair before her to prepare her chamber.

Margaret paused at the stair-foot and could not resist a last calculated thrust.

'Are you to mount guard over my very chamber door, Sir Guy?'

'I should find it hard to report to the Duke if I failed to secure your safe-keeping,' he said evenly, without a trace of self-consciousness. 'I shall see to it that my men keep constant watch in the hall, outside, and within the corridors.'

She turned from him and began to mount the steps. He followed her to the door of her chamber.

Jonnet stood in the doorway curiously fingering the veil handed to her by the inn wench in Northampton.

'Mistress,' she said guilelessly, 'I found this among your baggage. I cannot believe it to be yours. It is such poor stuff.' Her eyes went to it longingly despite her disparagement of its worth.

Margaret said hurriedly, 'I think the wench at the inn must have been mistaken and it got packed in my saddle-bag in our haste of departure. Throw it away, Jonnet, or keep it yourself if you wish.'

Sir Guy was staring at the garment and Margaret's heart missed a beat. Those gimlet eyes missed nothing. She hoped her tone had conveyed her complete uninterest in the veiling.

He reached over and took the thing gently from Jonnet's fingers.

'Strange that it should have been packed as yours. As you say, the material is of poor quality. I do not think any other lady was lodged at that inn, or so Scroggins reported to me.'

'Perhaps it belonged to the girl herself.'

'And she made you a present of it? Unlikely,' he commented. Handing it back to Jonnet, he said mildly, 'The girl must have had a pressing need to speak with you alone, Mistress Margaret.'

She flushed darkly. 'Why should you say that?'

'Surely that could be her only reason for offering you something she no doubt prized. I hope you paid her well for the message.' He waved the maid back inside the room and, gripping Margaret's arms with his two hands, turned her to face him directly. It was dark now on the landing, but the torch, set in a sconce on the wall, played upon his high cheekbones and aquiline nose, giving him a faintly sinister look. She trembled in his grasp.

'I want no repetition of such conduct, mistress. The Duke has ordered me to treat you well but he will not be pleased if you flout his commands.'

She said gratingly, 'The Duke of Gloucester is not my father. He has no authority over me and you certainly have none. Release me at once.'

'Gloucester is Protector of the realm, as I keep

reminding you. He stands in place of your sovereign lord. You will obey him and me as his captain.'

He released her and she put both hands up to the places on her arms where he had gripped her. She was dry-mouthed and her knees threatened to let her down. She put out one hand to steady herself on the rope railing to the stair.

'I have no choice but to obey you, sir, but, I warn you, my true allegiance is to my father and I will contrive to warn him of this ambush even if I hang for it.'

Her dark eyes were flashing fire at him and he gave her a thin smile and bowed.

'I doubt it will come to that, mistress, but be equally warned that I shall do anything I must to prevent you.'

They continued to glare at one another until he bowed again and, turning, went back down the stairs.

She was still trembling as she entered her room. Jonnet stood open-mouthed, staring at her. Though she was not sure about the reason for it she was aware that her mistress was in a furious temper. Surprisingly Margaret said nothing but began to undo her girdle. Jonnet sighed with relief. She had had the uncomfortable feeling that she had done something dreadful by showing Mistress Margaret the piece of veiling.

Once in bed, Jonnet snoring peacefully on the truckle by her side, Margaret stared up at the ceiling, despondent. The man was insufferable. Fate had made them enemies, it seemed, from the beginning, but need he have handled her so roughly? Bruises were already beginning to form on her upper arms. She had to face the fact that he would prove a formidable gaoler. She was forbidden to leave the manor, even to attend mass. How was she to know if Bennet's messenger was in the vicinity? Despite everything, she had failed to think of any way of communicating with him. If she were forbidden to ride there would be no reason to go to the stables where she might have bribed one of the grooms. Jonnet was such an innocent that it might be possible to send her into the village without suspicion being aroused, but could she trust the girl to carry an important message back, and when would she know the right time to send her maid? Sir Guy would surely realise that Jonnet would be the one person she might try and would flatly refuse his permission. Margaret sighed. He had so easily seen through the inn girl's ruse and he would be one step ahead of her in all her attempts to outwit him.

She turned on her side and tried to woo sleep. If she thought of Bennet Hartwell's comely face she would calm herself, but, try as she might, she could not picture the man. It was the piercing blue gaze of Guy Jarvis's eyes which harassed her down the dark corridors of her dreams when she managed to sleep at last.

CHAPTER FOUR

MARGARET sat sewing in the little pleasance her mother had loved so much. Her grandfather had created it for his wife but Margaret's father had neglected the scented flowers which grew there until his wife had come to Rushton and made the enclosed garden live again. It was late May now, warm in the spring sunshine and redolent with the fragrance of the lilac blossom and remaining gillyflowers. Jonnet sat a short distance away, the veil she was hemming neglected in her lap, her gaze abstracted. Margaret smiled a little wistfully. Jonnet's thoughts were on William Grimshaw, the man-at-arms behind whom she'd ridden pillion back to the manor. Jonnet was happy and showed a new-found confidence. Margaret's face clouded as she feared that that happiness might soon fade when Sir Guy's company was summoned back to Gloucester's service in London or the north.

She had tried to warn Jonnet that Grimshaw would go and leave her, and that, despite his promises, he might well be married with a family of babes back in Yorkshire. On Jonnet's behalf she had attempted to question Sir Guy. He had looked puzzled at first at her worries about her maid and curiosity about one of his company, then had shrugged off her doubts.

'I don't know the fellow that well. If he says he's willing and able to marry your serving wench then he most likely will do so. He belongs to Ratcliffe's company and Scroggins knows no more about the man than he's told us himself. Has your maid given way to him? If so, she's a fool, but aren't they all at some time or other?'

Margaret had been indignant. His plain speaking had outraged her. Surely he must hold some sense of responsibility for what his men did here, but in this case, it seemed, he did not. His men were disciplined. They did not steal the pigs and chickens nor make themselves obnoxious to the manor serving wenches. In hall they were tolerantly well-behaved, though she would have liked them to be more temperate with the ale they swilled, but so far no damage had been perpetrated on her property and no man had dared to insult her by so much as an insolent glance. Sir Guy expressed himself bluntly. He'd have no lass raped nor threatened but if Mistress Margaret's maid had been stupid or trusting enough to believe the fellow's artful wooing, then she must suffer the consequences. If there was no compulsion, Jonnet was free to choose. Margaret had felt reluctant to spoil Jonnet's happiness by outspoken warnings of dire disasters if the girl were too free with her favours.

At least Jonnet could see the object of her affections frequently. Margaret had no such advantage. Over these weeks she had received no word from either her father or Bennet Hartwell and was beginning to think there was no hope of freedom for her at all.

News had filtered in from Northampton, brought by the carrier with supplies and a strolling pedlar whom she'd insisted on seeing despite Sir Guy's sour objections. She had bought one or two trinkets and had learned from the man that the young King had entered London on May the fourth, flanked by his uncle of Gloucester and cousin of Buckingham. The populace had welcomed him joyfully and the mayor and principal citizens had come in procession to offer their young sovereign the keys of the city. The Council had met and bestowed the chancellorship on John Russell, Bishop of Lincoln. Rotherham, Archbishop of York, the last chancellor, had too openly showed his hand when he had conveyed the Great Seal of England to the Dowager Queen in the sanctuary of Westminster where she had fled so hurriedly with her second son and daughters.

Margaret had gone back on her promise to herself not to discuss the intrigues at Court with Sir Guy. Her sense of outrage at the Queen's undoubted fear of the Protector had made her lash out at her gaoler when they had sat together at supper.

'The poor lady is clearly fearful for herself and her family. How dreadful it must be for her to be mewed up so uncomfortably when she is used to so much state.'

'Hardly uncomfortably,' he'd returned, unruffled. 'She fled with so much baggage that the sanctuary walls have had to be breached to allow through such a wealth of possessions. God knows why she feels she must go there. Gloucester has not threatened her or her children. The young King is living in state at the Bishop of London's palace and, more than likely, misses his brother and sisters sorely. Likely the lady suffers from an uneasy conscience. Sir Edward Woodville sailed from London with the greater part of the royal treasury and Dorset has taken himself off to France, it's thought.'

'Is it any wonder when his uncle and brother are prisoners of Gloucester in Yorkshire?' she'd retorted with more heat.

'Their passage from Ludlow with such a force of

arms, to say nothing of the quantity of armour and weapons, is plain proof of treason, which I have explained before. If Dorset was not involved in that treason he has damned himself now by this precipitate flight, which brings me to the question of your father's whereabouts, mistress. If he has a clear conscience there is no reason for him to absent himself from his own manor, wouldn't you agree?'

Tears had pricked at her lashes, but they were angry tears, then at any rate; later she had wept openly within her chamber as her fears for her father's uncertain position had grown to alarming proportions.

Apart from one or two angry exchanges between them, Guy Jarvis had treated her civilly enough. She had little to complain of but the curtailment of her liberty. Thinking to spare her pain of embarrassment, he kept from her sight much of the time except for his insistence that they eat together at supper in full view of the household.

'In this way your servants can assure themselves that you are in no danger and that my orders come with your authority also. There will be less friction on the manor under this arrangement.'

With this she was forced to agree. There would be no sense in her people challenging the newcomers and getting harmed for their pains.

She looked up enquiringly from her embroidery as she heard sounds of someone galloping into the stable yard. Jonnet, startled, jumped to her feet and went, at Margaret's nod, to the archway which led from the pleasance into the main courtyard.

She called softly, 'It's a man in Yorkist colours, mistress, probably a courier with letters for Sir Guy Jarvis.'

Margaret stifled an exclamation of disappointment. Against all reason she had hoped, desperately, that it might be her father or someone sent from him. She knew, in her heart, that this was unlikely yet she had tried to think optimistically all through these past days. Surely John Rushton was not entirely compromised by his ride to join Earl Rivers. If he were to provide a satisfactory explanation to put before the Council, Gloucester could have no reason to charge him with any crime against the state. Yet, if Rivers himself was still held prisoner, what hope could Rushton have of clearing himself of complicity in the Woodville plot to seize power? Dorset was not near to stand by him, so he was forced, by the very nature of his predicament, to leave his daughter in hostile hands on her own manor.

She nodded to Jonnet to sit down again and determinedly returned to her own embroidery. If there was news, good or bad, she would soon be informed. Better, at this stage, to show no eager curiosity concerning this messenger.

Sir Guy arrived in search of her very soon after. He made no apologies for disturbing her and stood in his usual pose straight before her, one hand thrust into his ornamental sword-belt.

'I have direct orders from the Duke of Gloucester,' he announced without preamble. 'We are to leave for London at first light tomorrow.'

Despite her pose of disinterest, Margaret moved awkwardly on her seat and pricked her finger, dyeing the fine cloth of her embroidery with an ugly stain of blood.

'That is quite impossible, Sir Guy,' she said when she

had regained her composure. 'It would take far longer than that notice to be ready for such a journey.'

Her head was bent over her work and she was unable to read his expression. There was a brief silence.

'We leave as I have stated, mistress, at first light.'

She looked up at him then, her eyes widening, partly in disbelief at his discourtesy in immediately dismissing her objection, and in sure anger at his impertinence.

'I can fully understand the Duke of Gloucester's commanding your obedience,' she said evenly, 'but there can be no need for me to journey to London. I'm sure he will find me another gaoler to take your place.'

'I would not dream of countermanding his orders, mistress, nor even questioning them. He commands me to take you to London and to London you will go, tomorrow, if I have to tie you into the saddle.'

She gave a sharp exclamation then, and averted her head. Her lips were trembling. If she looked at him she would weep, from pure temper.

'Jonnet,' she said, her tone kept deliberately level, 'will you please go up to my chamber and begin to pack sufficient clothing to last me for the short time I must be absent from this house?'

Jonnet dipped her a curtsy, and another somewhat nervous one in Sir Guy's direction.

'Yes, mistress, and—and am I to accompany you?'

'That you must ask Sir Guy. It seems he makes all the decisions without concerning himself in the slightest about my needs or comfort.'

Sir Guy said, 'Certainly you must accompany your mistress. Pack everything you will both need for a protracted stay. Mistress——' he bowed formally to Margaret '—pray excuse me. As you will realise, I have important preparations to make and in some haste.'

She inclined her head coldly and he left them. Within moments she heard him issuing orders to Scroggins and the stable lads concerning their departure.

She was seething but, worse, very frightened. Why was she being summoned? Had her father been arrested? Was he being held in London, in the grim Tower perhaps? But surely Sir Guy would have informed her. He was not in the habit of sparing her pain. Even if her father was still free, how could he get in touch with her once she was securely held in some London household loyal to Gloucester? Had Bennet Hartwell made attempts to contact her unsuccessfully? She knew she was being unreasonable to tax him and her father with neglect. It was too difficult and dangerous to reach her but, despite her understanding of their situation, she still felt anger at being left to her fate.

At supper Sir Guy made one or two attempts to mollify and reassure her.

'You must not be alarmed, Mistress Margaret. The Duke of Gloucester means you no harm.'

'You would know that for certain,' she said savagely. 'You consider it no harm to keep me here a prisoner then force me to journey far from my home in these dangerous times?'

'It is probably because he considers it safer for you to be in the capital that he recalls me. I know him to be ever gentle and courteous to the ladies of his household. Even when the Countess of Warwick was held in disgrace at Court following her husband's rebellion and subsequent death in battle at Barnet, he welcomed her to Middleham that she might be with her younger daughter, Lady Anne. The Countess has lived there happily, as if the castle still remained her own home. I can bear witness to that.'

'Yet the Queen remains in sanctuary.'

'Entirely of her own volition. There could be nothing to prevent her returning to live at Westminster Palace.'

'With the man she fears is her enemy?'

'The Duke is not, nor is he in residence at the Palace. When he first entered London he stayed at Baynards Castle, his mother's home, and has now settled into his own town house at Crosby Place. His courier confirms that the Duchess of Gloucester has now left Yorkshire and will soon join him there. If so, it is likely that Lady Allard will be with her. I served Mistress Aleyne when my master was first married and I know she will be willing to extend a hand of friendship.'

Margaret sniffed her disapproval. Why should she wish to become friendly with a woman so plainly in Gloucester's favour? Likely it would be a simple method of spying on her, even during those moments when she was not open to Sir Guy's scrutiny. She sighed. She had longed to escape the confinement of the manor. Now, it seemed, she would be allowed even less privacy.

Jonnet managed most of the packing before they retired but Margaret found it hard to sleep. Her one gnawing fear was that she was putting herself totally beyond her father's help by being forced to this journey.

Hope was to come from a completely unexpected source. She woke and breakfasted early, eating very little under Sir Guy's watchful and impatient eye, then, reluctantly, made her way to the courtyard where her palfrey was being led up to the mounting-block. She could see that Sir Guy's troop had already saddled up, packed their belongings upon the sumpter mule and were waiting now only for his command to mount. Sir Guy insisted upon lifting her into her saddle and she averted her head coldly as she thought of his threat to tie her in her saddle if she refused to accompany him. Jonnet, she saw, was mounted behind Will Grimshaw and, even from this distance, Margaret could tell from her maid's expression that she was quite willing to go anywhere he was sent.

Sir Guy mounted and rode to the head of the company, issued his order to leave, and the troop began to move towards the gateway, four men preceding Margaret with Scroggins riding close in attendance and the remaining members of the company moving in behind.

Margaret was relieved that, for the present, she was excused the necessity of conversing with her gaoler and rode in sullen silence. It was a pleasant summery day, too early to be excessively hot as yet, and a small shower they had had two days ago had refreshed the earth and settled the dust of the road. A few miles out, Sir Guy summoned Scroggins to his side, presumably to seek his advice as to where they should stop for a midday rest, and another fresh-faced young soldier took his place near her. She was not pleased when he suddenly drew in close and bent over her, ostensibly to check that her girth was tight and secure. Angrily she assured him that everything was correct and she needed no assistance, but he rode so close that she could almost smell his breath, fumed with the not unpleasant scent of his morning ale.

His head was lowered to his task so she could not gauge his expression when he startled her by saying softly, very near to her ear, 'Please do not look alarmed, mistress; I have been trying to have a private word with you for days.'

She checked her gasp of astonishment and forced herself to remain rigid, showing him only the disdainful look she bestowed on all Sir Guy's men-at-arms.

He went on quietly, 'Be assured your father knows of your plight and has not abandoned you. You must trust me to find some opportune moment during the journey to get you away to him. Be on your guard and ready.'

Her eyes met his dark ones, and she inclined her chin only very slightly. He moved his horse away with a respectful salute and, before she could draw breath or evaluate the import of his words, Sir Guy had dropped back to her side.

'Is something wrong?' he demanded tartly. 'Everything should have been checked and re-checked. I'll have the hide off the fellow who neglected his duty and gave us cause for delay.'

She managed to say almost sweetly, 'Your man thought my girth was working loose, sir, but he was mistaken.'

He shot her an intent look from beneath his level fair brows and nodded his satisfaction. She was relieved that he made no attempt at further talk, riding silently, his brows drawn together in a frown of concentration, his eyes on the road ahead and the cover of hedgerows on either side, as if he feared some ambush might be set for them.

Her thoughts raced together as she dared not look back towards the soldier who had offered her, at last, some hope of rescue. Sweet Virgin, he must manage to get her free before they reached the capital. Once there, she was convinced she would be so thoroughly guarded that any such attempt would prove utterly impossible.

They stayed the first night at an inn in Stamford.

Margaret marvelled at how busy the place was on the Great North road but was relieved that Sir Guy had managed to find a private chamber. She watched anxiously while her baggage was unpacked and carried up to her chamber by the man who had spoken with her earlier. Though he gave her a smilingly obsequious glance in the presence of his commander, he gave no indication that there might be any chance of escape for her at this stage of the journey.

'Since this appears to be the only quiet place in the inn, I will sup with you in your chamber tonight with Owen in attendance,' Sir Guy announced.

He left, not waiting for any objection. Margaret had grown to like the reserved young man from the Welsh border country who served Sir Guy as squire, but she had no wish to eat with any of the company, especially while her mind was teeming with the possibilities of evading Sir Guy's surveillance soon.

The meal was somewhat poor and indifferently served, the serving wenches who attended them running hectically from one room of the inn to another. Margaret could not help wishing that this had been the designated place, since there was so much frantic activity that there might have been some time lapse before her absence was discovered.

She said, as casually as possible, 'The young man who tried to help with my girth this morning—what is his name?'

'Smallberry, I believe,' Sir Guy said, without interest. 'He is not one of Scroggins' men, nor, I think, of

Ratcliffe's company. He may have come from Sheriff Hutton. I do not think I've seen him around Middleham.'

Thinking to put him off guard, Margaret questioned him more fully about the people she would meet in London.

'You speak well of Lady Allard. What of the Duchess? Is she very haughty and proud?'

He laughed out loud. 'The Lady Anne? No, indeed. She is the most gentle lady I know.'

'And a very wealthy heiress. How does she find enforced marriage to Duke Richard? I imagine he neglects her, now she has given him an heir.'

He stopped, his wine cup halfway to his lips. 'Duke Richard was deeply in love with Lady Anne from his boyhood. He fought against all opposition to the match; for a time Lady Anne's very life was threatened and she was forced into lowly service in a cook shop. Her brother-in-law, Clarence, had no wish to share the Warwick fortune and tried every trick he knew to thwart Richard from his purpose. The King consented to the match only after the Duke agreed to accept only the Yorkshire castles of Middleham and Sheriff Hutton as the marriage portion. He was then his brother's favourite and the mightiest prince in Europe. He could have married some foreign royal princess. Lady Anne was a widow, the disgraced daughter of an avowed traitor, but he wanted no one else. He loved her the moment they were wed in the chapel at Westminster, when she placed his heir in his arms, and every moment since. I'll not have such scurrilous talk about the master and mistress I revere so greatly. He will be missing her sorely and praying for the moment she arrives in London.'

Margaret was chastened. So many times she had listened, somewhat wearily, to Sir Guy's praise of the Protector, but such open admiration for what he saw as a true and abiding love caused her to reassess her judgement concerning Gloucester. Well, it was possible that such a man, cunning and ambitious as he undoubtedly was, might still be deeply attached to his wife. She found herself watching Sir Guy covertly while he ate, as she sometimes did. He often seemed so cold and distant that she thought he must never have known love, yet he recognised its true worth when he saw it between others. Could it be that he had loved some lady truly and been again repudiated? She had never dared to question him or his squire about his amorous adventures.

She swallowed hard and gave her attention to her wine cup.

Sir Guy pushed his chair aside roughly and rose hurriedly at the close of the meal. 'I suggest you retire immediately and try to get what sleep you can. We must get on at first light tomorrow. It will be noisy here but you are well guarded.' He gave his usual half-bow and, with his squire, left the chamber. She had discovered from Will Scroggins that the two of them were to bed down in the stables with the rest of the company. The men, then, were to sleep in shifts, making sure that the women were closely watched during the night. Margaret would have been reassured in normal circumstances. She knew only too well that populous inns were haunts for footpads and highway robbers and that all travellers needed protection, the reason why many banded together whenever it was necessary to embark on any lengthy journey.

Before retiring she abruptly went to the door and opened it. Jonnet, surprised, started towards her.

'Is there anything you want, mistress?'

Margaret stared down, discomfited, at the sight of Owen Lewis stretched uncomfortably before her door. He scrambled to his feet immediately.

'Mistress, I am at your service. I can call one of the maids. . .'

'No, no,' she amended hastily, 'it is nothing. The room seemed so close I wondered if I might catch an extra breath of air.'

'Would you like me to open the window?'

'Yes, it appears to have stuck.' She was not at all sure that that would prove to be the case but needed some excuse for examining the possibility of leaving her room should the occasion offer itself. It did not seem likely. Sir Guy was taking no chances. Smallberry would not find rescuing her a simple task.

The window, fortunately, did resist his effort to open it, though he was openly surprised that she should wish to do so, to admit possibly harmful night air, but he obeyed her wish, bowed and returned to his watch near her door. She had the uncomfortable feeling that he would be relieved by Sir Guy some hours later.

Jonnet stared at the open window, outraged, and Margaret sighed. She had not taken Jonnet into her confidence. She must do so soon, despite the fear that the girl would blurt out her mistress's plans to her admirer. Biting her lip in outright frustration, she went to her bed and waved Jonnet to the truckle beside her. Obviously Smallberry had no chance tonight, yet he had assured her that he would make an opportunity despite the difficulties. She could only pray that he would prove capable of such a devious and dangerous undertaking.

If Owen Lewis had reported to his master that she had attempted to leave her chamber during the night, Sir Guy made no comment on the fact the next day. He hastened her impatiently through breakfast and into the saddle again and she was not sure whether she should be relieved or angered by his reluctance to talk to her or even acquaint her with his plans for the rest of the journey.

The following night they spent in a small Benedictine priory guest house which was certainly more quiet and restful, but secluded, protected by high walls, and Margaret realised that again there was no possibility here of leaving the company.

She did, however, take the opportunity, while they were alone in her small, cell-like chamber, to explain to Jonnet what the man Smallberry proposed. She had expected fearful protests but Jonnet merely regarded her open-mouthed and nodded her agreement when her mistress demanded her solemn oath not to acquaint anyone with their secret.

'Of course I wouldn't, mistress,' she averred stoutly. 'Did you think I'd be so disloyal?'

'I know you are very attracted to Master Grimshaw.'

'Ah, well.' Jonnet had the grace to blush darkly. 'That be so, but he knows well enough that I'm your maid and close to you in all things. What comes, if anything, of our—our liking for each other will come in its own time. He's got 'is duty and I've got mine and there it is. Course you want to join Sir John if'n you can and I'm willing to help. You do want me to come with you?'

Margaret had not considered that, nor was sure if Smallberry would wish to include her maid in his plans, but knew she would be lost now without Jonnet and, besides, the girl should not be left alone to face Sir Guy's undoubted fury when he discovered what had happened.

'Yes, certainly, if it is possible,' she said quickly. 'But we must be prepared every moment to be ready to leave if he calls us.'

Jonnet's expression revealed how dangerous such a move would be and again Margaret felt a stab of guilt at embroiling the girl in her plot to outwit their captor. But she thrust it aside. Such consideration did not matter now. Every day her father remained in England to be near his daughter left him in greater danger. It was not only her wish to join him but her duty.

When they arrived at the White Swan in St Albans, Sir Guy informed Margaret that next day they would be in the capital and at Crosby Place. Her heart pounded as she stared round the inn bedchamber. This, then, was their last chance. Smallberry must make his move here, yet he had given her no sign, nor so much as approached her. If she was to be as closely guarded as she had been at Stamford, how could their escape be managed? When they were alone together she instructed Jonnet to pack one small saddle-bag with necessities then waited, dry-mouthed, for Sir Guy to arrive to take supper with them privately as he had done throughout the journey.

He arrived as Jonnet completed her preparations and hastily pushed the packed bag under the bed with the truckle.

Sir Guy seemed abstracted and Margaret said coolly,

'I imagine you will be glad when this journey is over tomorrow and your responsibility done.'

He looked up at her very directly. 'I am a soldier, Mistress Margaret. I confess I find my enforced role as gaoler not to my taste. It may be that the Duke will release me from service here in London and I shall be able to return north. Keeping the peace on the border is what I know and am best at.'

'Then you will not find life at Court pleasant?' She was toying with her food, her attention strained, striving to make easy conversation. 'Surely there will be ladies at Court you will find engaging, and dancing and feasting for your pleasure.'

'I doubt that,' he said shortly. 'I've said before I am in no mood for the marriage market and it is unlikely Duke Richard will be feasting, his brother so lately dead.'

Again he reminded her of her lack of sensibility and she felt a stab of anger. He made her appear shallow, without finer feelings, interested only in the fripperies Court life could provide.

She said, chastened, 'I understand Duke Richard was extremely fond of his brother, the late King.'

'Aye, he was only seven when his father, York, was killed at Wakefield and, since Edward was ten years his senior, I imagine he took the place of father in Richard's life.' He seemed about to add some further comment but changed his mind.

Margaret wondered if Sir Guy did not share Duke Richard's blind devotion to the late King but did not care to reveal his thoughts to her. King Edward had become pleasure-loving in the extreme during these latter years while Gloucester, well away from Court intrigues, had continued to keep peace in the troubled areas of the realm. She remembered her father's amused comment that Duke Richard had not been pleased, after their invasion of France, that the King had been content to make peace, accepting rich gifts rather than go to war over what Duke Richard had stated openly to be a matter of honour—the English King's right to the French throne. After all, the Duke of York, their father, had fought honourably in France during the minority of King Henry VI. They had not always agreed then, those royal brothers, and it was open knowledge that the younger brother had disapproved of the King's hasty marriage to Elizabeth Woodville, or the widowed Lady Grey, as she had been then. If that was so, how did he now consider the fruits of that marriage, the late King's children?

Abruptly Sir Guy pushed back his stool. 'You will want to get to bed. The journey will not be long, but arrival at Crosby Place and introduction to new people may well prove exhausting. Try to get a good rest.'

Despite their earlier antagonism, he had proved a considerate travelling companion and had not once abused his position of authority. She felt an urgent wish to thank him. It might be that she would not see him again and, if Smallberry's plans succeeded, he might well come under the Duke's extreme displeasure for failing to guard her adequately. Could Gloucester become so angry that he would imprison Guy Jarvis or even condemn him to death for dereliction of duty? She had not considered that until now. They were on opposing sides, but she could not wish him harm. She had an uncontrollable desire to warn him, but held it back.

She offered him her hand. 'Sir Guy, as you say, our arrival in London may mean that I will have little opportunity to speak with you again. Though I have resented your curtailment of my liberty, I must thank you for your care of me and your continued control over your men so that neither my person nor my house suffered any serious inconvenience during this difficult time.'

He looked surprised and not a little embarrassed. His fair skin darkened with crimson colour. He was not, she thought, often in the presence of ladies other than the Duchess of Gloucester and his friend's wife, Lady Allard, neither of whom would expect pretty speeches from him nor offer him any form of coquetry. He bowed and, lifting her hand to his lips, kissed the tips of her fingers.

'I wish we could have been friends,' he said gruffly. 'My father would have wanted it so, but I wish you well, lady, and hope that these matters at Court will be speedily concluded, without harm to those you love.' Then he bowed again and took his leave.

He sat brooding over his wine cup in the inn's taproom. Margaret Rushton was right. He would be relieved when this difficult task the Duke had laid on him was finally concluded. Not only had it been embarrassing to be in such a position over the woman who had so rudely shattered his pride so many years ago, but he had also found the last weeks more and more galling. He had found it impossible to see her as a potential enemy. For so long he had chafed under the memory of her childish scorn. He smiled cynically at the thought. She *had* been a child, of course, and under the direction of her father. He had been a fool to let that memory of her get so firmly under his skin. Now she was a true woman, and one to be reckoned with, and he found her presence constantly disturbing. She was comely, though many would not consider her a beauty, and regal in poise and manner. What a chatelaine she would prove to some gentleman endowed with castles and land and properties far richer than he could ever hope to acquire. Her father had been wise enough to know that Margaret Rushton deserved to aim high. Marriage to her was well beyond his aspirations.

He had found conversations with her stimulating. Stolidly opposed to Gloucester's faction as she was, she was shrewd enough to grasp the implications of this coming fight for control. The younger ladies he had known had been bashful in his presence, had muttered trivialities and banal civilities. He had found them vapid and uninteresting. Margaret had been a worthy opponent in the cut and thrust of argument. He hoped her chosen husband would not make the mistake of underestimating her or even deliberately excluding her from his business affairs. Other women of his acquaintance he had taken for his pleasure, though he had chosen carefully and never wilfully hurt one of them deeply. Now he found himself anxious for Margaret Rushton, praying that her father would not be so firmly enmeshed in this treasonous business that he must finally come to trial and execution. Margaret would be devastated, would grieve deeply, and would most probably be handed over in marriage to some man of the Duke's choosing. This she would find so humiliating. He wished fervently that he could have spared her, but he had no alternative but to carry her to London as he had been bidden.

He felt little inclination to sleep, though he should try to. Near two of the clock he must relieve young Owen's guard over the lady's doorway. He trusted no others in the company for this intimate duty. This would be the last night of his vigil. He wondered why he did not view the thought with enthusiasm.

Margaret was uncertain whether she should undress or not. She needed to be ready if Smallberry should summon her, but if for some reason Sir Guy should choose to make a last visit she would be hard put to it to explain why she was still fully clothed. She decided, come what may, that both she and Jonnet would remain dressed and lie upon their beds beneath the coverlets.

The waiting strained her nerve to the limit. Jonnet had blown out the candles, and Margaret lay in the dark listening acutely for every stray noise from the inn corridors or the street outside. It was noisy for some time until the sound of the last, scampering run up the stair told her the weary inn wenches had sought their beds. She could hear Jonnet stirring restlessly by her side but felt it pointless to engage the girl in conversation. It must be well past midnight and the blackness was almost complete, the dark grey square of the window not yet illuminated enough for her to see the room well.

How could Smallberry possibly manage their escape? She was sure, without looking, that one of the men was guarding her door and it was certain that others would be watching the gateways and doors of the inn. Would he attempt to bribe one or more of the company? Surely Sir Guy's men would be too afraid of swift retribution to risk discovery of such a betrayal. Was Smallberry alone in this ploy? She had had no opportunity to question him. Others might be implicated with him. He had promised he would release her. He must have thought out some workable scheme.

Outside the door she heard a faint mutter of voices,

possibly a change-over of the guard, then a sudden thud and a strange, half-stifled, high-pitched cry. She listened, tensed beneath the coverlet, waiting for Jonnet to make some comment, but the girl made no move. Probably she was too frightened to do anything. The silence descended again so that it and the darkness appeared to press down on the wakeful Margaret. She turned awkwardly. That cry must have been from some stray cat in the street or the courtyard.

She had almost given up hope when she heard a scratching upon the door which brought her instantly sitting up in the bed. Jonnet gave a frightened cry, immediately stifled by a hand to her mouth.

'Mistress?' The whisper was very faint but urgent.

Smallberry! Margaret waited for no more prompting but sprang to her feet, stopping only to put a warning hand on Jonnet's shoulder.

'Come now, at once.'

She reached beneath the truckle for the packed saddle-bag and took up the cloak she had secreted under the covers throughout the night. A faint beam of light came from the slowly opening door and Margaret could see the dark shadow of a man framed in the opening.

She joined him, knowing Jonnet was hard on her heels.

He carried a dark lantern, the shutter only partially open so that she could only see dimly, but sufficient to light her way down the stair.

Smallberry's voice was a warm breath on her ear. 'We must go at once. The man on the gate is in my pay but we must walk awhile. I could not hide horses too near the inn.' She gave a brief impatient nod then stepped across the threshold. Her foot caught on something soft and yielding and she gave a quick murmur of alarm. Of course, he must have given some drug to her silent watcher. Smallberry held up the light and, with a feeling of sick shock, Margaret stared down at Owen Lewis's body, slumped against the doorpost. An ugly trail of blood trickled stickily down to the floor. Her gaze went to the boy's head and, even in the very dim light, she saw that he was bleeding heavily and his breathing was stertorous and laboured. Despite Smallberry's urging hand shaking her shoulder, she stopped on the landing and knelt to examine the injured youth.

'Sweet Virgin, you've half killed him,' she whispered, striving to hold back her panic and rising horror. 'I wouldn't have wished him harm. . .'

Smallberry's voice was commanding now. 'Lady, there was no other way. How else could I free you? Do you think he would have stooped to take a bribe? You must hasten or we'll all be taken.'

'He needs help.'

'Sir Guy will arrive soon enough.' Smallberry was gazing huntedly round in the confined space. 'What does it matter if the lad lives or dies? He will be one pursuer out of action. Come now, mistress, or must I render you unconscious too and carry you out of the inn?'

Owen stirred and moaned and Margaret remained, half stooping, her thoughts painfully searching for some way to help the stricken boy and yet prevent their own capture. Jonnet whimpered behind her and she stood up uncertainly. To stay here would mean that she would endanger all of them. She must act and not remain squeamishly by while time ran out for them. Once free of the inn, she would insist that the man in their pay return to Owen and pretend suddenly to discover his plight. . .

'Owen?' There was no mistaking the imperious call from below and Smallberry cursed beneath his breath and covered the light from his lantern.

'Get back into the room, mistress,' he whispered hoarsely. 'I must deal with this before the whole company is on us.'

Margaret scrambled fearfully to her feet. Her tortured brain tried to rationalise her situation. She knew, instantly, that Smallberry's only hope now was to render Sir Guy helpless—kill him. . . The ugly images jarred her consciousness and she gave a warning cry before she was aware of the consequences of her act.

The steps ascending the stair stopped, fractionally, then came on more cautiously. The call to the squire was not repeated and Margaret knew she had been successful in alerting Sir Guy to his danger. Her foot slipped in something sticky—Owen's blood? She gave a little sob. Smallberry gave a harsh, rasping snarl of fury and swept her behind him. She felt rather than knew that he had drawn a weapon, possibly a dagger. A sword would have impeded him in his quiet movement earlier through the passages of the inn.

Margaret's eyes were blinded suddenly by the light from the lantern Sir Guy carried as he rounded the bend in the stair. She was totally unprepared for his actions, unable to see what occurred. Smallberry had crouched for a spring on the unsuspecting man before Margaret had given her warning cry.

Sir Guy's voice, harsh with anger and anxiety, cut across the whiteness of the lantern's glare.

'God's blood, you murdering traitor. A hangman's noose is too good for you—you die by the knife.'

Jonnet had fallen in terror across Margaret's feet and was clutching desperately at her skirts. The blinding light had shifted and Margaret could hear the approaching run of Guy's light steps up the remaining stairs and Smallberry's hard breathing as he sprang at his opponent. They closed and scuffled. Margaret strove desperately to reach Smallberry's discarded lantern near Owen Lewis's sprawled body. The noises were animal-like and Jonnet was screaming now in panic. Sounds erupted all over the inn. The terrible rasping and snarling stopped and Margaret reached the lantern and illuminated the scene. The two men were tangled together like rag-dolls she had been given as a child, for a moment neither moving, then one figure stirred, still breathing hard, and stood up. Margaret gave a sharp exclamation as she saw the bright blood on Sir Guy's dagger. He rose fully to his feet and regarded her; his gaze then moved swiftly to his injured squire.

'I thought you courageous, madam, loyal to your cause and resolute,' he said contemptuously, 'not treacherous. Owen is little more than a youth and too trusting.'

His men-at-arms were mounting the stair now, Will Scroggins calling urgently for attention.

'Are you injured, Sir Guy?'

'Merely scratched.' His tone was scathing. 'See the men are up and alert. There must be more traitors among us.' He kicked at Smallberry's lifeless form. 'Dispose of this carrion, and get me some apothecary from the town or an infirmarian from the abbey. Owen is sorely hurt.'

Two men passed him on the stair and made to lift the squire between them.

Margaret said commandingly, 'Do not attempt to

take him down the stair. Lay him on my bed,' and, surprisingly, found herself hurriedly obeyed.

Without stopping to see what Sir Guy's attitude to this would be she hastened to the bedside.

'Jonnet,' she ordered, 'get some water, straight from the well if possible, as cold as you can get.'

The maid scuttled off to do her bidding, relieved not to face the full torrent of Sir Guy's fury. The men had laid Owen down carefully and, at Margaret's signal, withdrew. Gently she drew up the coverlet and felt for the pulse at his neck. His breathing was still bad but the bleeding appeared to be easing already. Turning to the saddle-bag Jonnet had dropped in her haste, she tore up strips of linen from one of her clean undershifts, then, making a pad of the rest, waited for her maid's return.

A voice from behind her said icily, 'Don't you think you've done him enough harm? Rough handling will only make the situation worse.'

'And you think your handling would be gentler?'

He said evenly, 'I've had the care of wounded men before, after battle,' then, through his teeth, 'I would to God I had the services of one of our army surgeons now.'

Jonnet returned with a jug of cold water, a frightened serving wench peeping anxiously from the doorway.

'Is there—anything else you want, sir?'

Margaret replied for him. 'No, simply send up the monk when he arrives.'

She had dipped a strip of linen in the water and, lifting the young squire's head, began to examine the open wound carefully. It looked clean enough when she cleared away the still oozing blood. There were no signs of jagged shards of bone which could indicate severe head injury, but the lad had sustained a savage blow to the back of the head and it would be hours before they would know if the brain had been harmed.

Sir Guy moved purposefully to her side and took Owen's head between his two hands while she continued to bathe the wound, then waited while she applied the linen pad and wound the strips about his head to hold it in place. The youth moaned and his eyelids flickered as he was placed gently back against the pillows, but he did not regain consciousness.

Sir Guy looked down at Margaret's bloodied hands as she moved slightly away from the bed, her brow creasing in alarm.

'He should be coming to by now, if this were not serious. What was the weapon used, do you know?'

'A weighted cudgel, lead, I imagine,' Sir Guy said grimly. 'The fellow came prepared.'

Margaret gave a shudder. 'You must believe I meant him no serious harm.'

'How did you think to make your escape without injuring or killing one or more of my men?' he snapped. 'I was to blame. I should have realised how much peril Owen might be in. I trusted him implicitly, knew he was the one man I could trust to serve my interests. I forgot how young he was. Smallberry came up openly and the lad would simply think he came with some message from me.'

'I did not think,' she said, her eyes turning back towards the bed.

He looked down again at her hands. 'I see there is more to you than I believed. I had not thought nursing to be one of your skills.'

'Do not be foolish,' she rejoined tartly. 'As you are used to battle casualties, I am used to dealing with accidents on the manor land. My mother taught me to dispense herbs and salves as part of my housewifely training. We had a child once who disobediently mounted one of my father's destriers and was thrown. He suffered a similar injury.'

'And he recovered?' The question was eager.

She avoided his gaze. 'No, he did not.'

'Ah.' The sigh carried a note of desperation.

She said quietly, 'You are deeply attached to the boy.'

'He is my squire. I'm used to his service. Replacing him would be inconvenient, especially at this time.' It was briskly uttered. He would not admit to affection for Owen but she read it in his eyes.

'The monks are very skilled,' she offered as comfort. 'The infirmarian will know what to do.'

He made no answer and she returned to the bedside and dipped another strip of linen in the water, folded it and laid it across the boy's brow. Despite her avowed skill with herbs she felt peculiarly helpless, had no knowledge of what to do in a case such as this. If bone had been shattered and pierced the brain, even if Owen were to live, he might well become hopelessly disabled or paralysed. She prayed silently that her fears were groundless. Her thoughts went to the dead Smallberry. She was responsible, yet it had been her duty to rejoin her father. The man had known the risk, had probably been well-paid. For the first time she considered the possibility that it might have been Bennet Hartwell who had made the attempt and suffered the dire fate of his menial. Another shudder shook her frame, and Sir Guy pushed her almost roughly on to a stool.

'If you feel faint, put your head down low for a while.'

'I shall not faint, Sir Guy,' she said coldly. 'I was merely regretting that my need to escape has cost one man his life and put another in peril of dying.'

He snorted. 'If you think I feel any compassion for that villain you're wrong. The fellow was a spy in the Duke's company, the kind of riff-raff who will take on any treacherous task for money.'

'I do not blame you,' she said tonelessly. 'He would have killed you if he could.'

He made some inarticulate sound as if to remind her that she had warned him, but fell then to silence.

Jonnet sat by the bed on a stool and replaced the bandage with another cold one on the boy's brow. It was all they could do to keep him comfortable.

It seemed an eternity before skilled help came. Soon after daybreak one of the men returned with the infirmarian from the nearby famed abbey. He was tall and almost emaciated, in middle age or possibly younger than he looked, prematurely aged by the responsibilities of his office and hours of prayer and fasting. He examined the wound, his lips pursed. Then he turned to Sir Guy. 'All has been done that can be. When the light is better, I'll sew up the wound. We must pray that he recovers his senses soon.'

'Can he be moved?' Sir Guy barked.

'By no means. That would be dangerous in the extreme.'

Again Margaret heard Sir Guy sigh, whether with exasperation or sincere regret she could not tell.

'I must leave for London in the morning. I am on the Lord Protector's business and cannot delay.'

'That need not concern you, sir. I will send a young monk here to stay beside him for a couple of days until it is safe for him to be conveyed by covered cart to our infirmary. He will have every care.'

Margaret said wistfully, 'Could I not stay with him?'

'No.' The reply was uncompromising. 'To London you go in the morning, before any more—accidents occur. I want no argument and no difficulties along the way. You have caused enough harm, mistress.'

She nodded, biting her lip hard, as he turned his back on her and left the chamber.

CHAPTER FIVE

MARGARET insisted on remaining with Owen until the infirmarian monk had stitched the wound. She stood quietly, holding the injured youth's head clear of the pillow, while the work was done. Sir Guy remained in the room but it was clear to Margaret that he wished he were miles from the place during the torturous proceedings. Soon after Owen had been laid down again he gave a louder moan and the monk turned instantly. This time, to Margaret's great joy, the youth's eyes flickered fully open and he gazed wonderingly round the chamber. Before he could struggle up on the bed the monk had held him firmly down.

'Lie still, my son. You have suffered a grave hurt and must lie quiet for a while. Can you tell me your name?'

Owen's eyes opened even wider and his face contorted in sudden agony as the pain of the wound and its recent stitching made itself felt.

'My name, brother? Of course. I'm—I'm Owen Lewis, squire to Sir Guy Jarvis. I. . .'

'Steady now, Owen, I'm here.' Sir Guy came to the bedside to grip his squire's hand. 'You must do what the infirmarian tells you. You suffered a heavy blow to the head last night and it will pain you for some time.'

'Last night?' Owen became plainly agitated. 'I was on guard—Mistress Rushton? She is safe. . .?'

'Yes, I'm quite safe, Master Lewis,' Margaret said quietly, coming within his line of vision so that he might be reassured he had not failed in his duty. 'Brother

Ignatius here says it is absolutely necessary that you lie still.'

'But we must get on to London, sir.' Owen appealed to Sir Guy. 'What happened? I was attacked, you say?'

'Aye, more about that when you're stronger.'

Owen was frowning in his attempt to remember the events which had laid him low. 'I was here outside Mistress Rushton's door. I wasn't sleeping, sir. I saw Smallberry coming up the stair and thought you had sent him to relieve me. . .'

'And he struck you, rendering you instantly unconscious. It's a mercy he didn't kill you. That weighted cudgel was murderous.' Sir Guy leaned across the bed. 'Thank God you have your full senses, boy. All is well. I dealt with Smallberry and will leave for London very soon now. You must stay here in Brother Ignatius's care until you are well enough to follow us. Rest now. I'll see you before we go.'

He led the way to the landing, out of Owen's earshot. 'Well, Brother Ignatius? Will he recover fully?'

'Praise the Virgin, I believe he will. He appears to have the use of his limbs but he will need complete rest for a while. Sudden movement and the wound could open again.'

'Of course, he must stay with you. My Lord of Gloucester will be grateful for your services.' He took from his hanging purse several gold rose nobles towards the upkeep of the abbey and handed them to the monk, and signalled to Margaret to go below stairs.

'See that your maid is packed and ready now within the hour. Already we are late.'

In the taproom a table had been set with ale, bread and meat. Margaret felt sick but Sir Guy insisted that they eat.

'You will be glad of sustenance once we are on the road.' He leaned across the table to carve for her and she drank thirstily from her ale cup.

'I have to thank you for your care of Owen,' he said stiffly. 'You were not squeamish in there. I confess the sight of a surgeon's ministrations to me or another leaves me dry-mouthed with apprehension.'

'My father is so inclined. My mother was gentle and timid but when it came to the care of the sick she became the stronger one. I'm—I'm very relieved that Owen regained consciousness before we left. I was very afraid for him.' She drew a hard breath.

'Just so.' He was not looking at her but frowning with concentration, his teeth worrying his nether lip. Will Scroggins entered the taproom and saluted his captain. He was ready for instant departure.

'The men wait only for your order to mount, Sir Guy. I hear Master Owen has come to. We're all right glad to hear that.' He looked pointedly at Margaret. 'What of the lady, sir? Is she to ride her own palfrey?'

Margaret's head jerked up and Sir Guy glanced at her sourly. 'Go outside and wait, Will,' he ordered curtly, and waited until they were alone again. He played for a moment with the hilt of his knife.

'As Will rightly says, Mistress Margaret, can I trust you to ride your own palfrey or must I carry you before me to London?'

Margaret's colour had flamed into throat and cheeks. She was breathing shallowly. The thought of being ingnominiously carried before Sir Guy on his saddle alarmed her. Nearness to him during the long hours of the journey would not only be uncomfortable but decidedly unnerving. She waited anxiously for him to come to a conclusion. Obviously it was this doubt which had been troubling him throughout the meal.

At last he pushed his stool back across the rush-strewn floor. 'Can I trust you? Will you give me your solemn word not to try to escape again?'

Margaret hesitated. It was her duty to try to elude his watch, but she was exhausted and sick at heart at the terrible consequences of last night's occurrences. She would be surrounded by men-at-arms. It would be impossible to break clear and ride off.

'Yes, Sir Guy,' she said in a voice which was scarce above a whisper. 'I give you my oath that I will ride with you to London and give you no trouble nor try to get free. After our arrival, that will be another matter.'

He held her steady gaze with his own, then he nodded. 'Good. Then we will go and mount. Grimshaw will follow with your maid and baggage.'

The journey proved uneventful, though Sir Guy seemed unusually watchful, as if he feared, even now, some last-minute attempt to take her from his care. Because they had delayed until Margaret's concern for Owen had been allayed, it was quite late when they arrived in the capital. Margaret's curiosity about the great city remained unsatisfied. Although the streets were relatively quiet, her escort did not relax its guard, and they proceeded through the darkened streets lit by torches above houses and at gable-ends. The leading men-at-arms in their company also lit flaming torches, mindful of the need to guard their lady against footpads who often emerged from sanctuary to attack unsuspecting persons during the night hours. From time to time doors of inns burst open and she caught the sounds of raucous laughter, and, occasionally, the sight of groups of men issuing forth with doxies in their distinctive rayed hoods hanging on their arms. Sir Guy had fallen back in line now to ride very close to her, while Will Scroggins took his place in the van.

She had little opportunity to view Crosby Place, the Duke's recently acquired town house in Bishop's Gate Street, before they had entered the courtyard and grooms hurried up to take her reins and those of Sir Guy. She was stiff from the ride and made no objection when he lifted her down, nor when he took her hand and led her into the lighted hall.

She saw at once that this house, though tastefully appointed, was no palace, and was surprised. She had expected the Lord Protector to take up residence in some state. A door into the hall was flung open and she saw the Duke himself framed against the lintel.

'Guy, at last—we had expected you long since. Mistress Margaret, you must be very wearied. Let me present you at once to my Duchess and then you must be shown to your chamber and refreshment provided. Everything has been made ready for you.'

Margaret curtsied dutifully. The Duke was still in mourning, but rubies gleamed dully in the gold of his neck-chain and his doublet was of the softest Italian cut velvet. He was treating her as if she were an honoured guest rather than his prisoner, and, though she resented such behaviour, she was also somewhat relieved. She had not known quite what to expect now that she was far from her own home territory.

The room was a pleasant solar, not large, the walls oak-panelled, and relieved by colourful French tapestries. Underfoot they trod on woollen rugs. There was the gleam of candlelight on pewter laid out on a fine court cupboard and tapestried chairs as well as cushioned window-seats and carved stools.

A woman sat in a tall-backed chair and held out a welcoming hand to the newcomer.

'So this is Mistress Margaret Rushton. I am so pleased to see you at last. My Lord Richard tells me you are a woman of spirit and I see you are lovely too. Welcome to Crosby Place, my dear. I hope you will not find your stay here too restrictive, but times are so difficult that we all need to be guarded closely.'

Margaret had wondered about this woman for so long that, after she rose from her curtsy, she could not prevent herself from staring quite hard. As Sir Guy had said, there was no trace of hauteur in the Duchess's manner. She was quite small and looked younger than she probably was. Like Duke Richard she was dressed in black mourning, a brocade gown, relieved only by a silver vest within the deep V of the neckline. She wore the fashionable butterfly hennin, draped in black veiling, and an enamelled reliquary showed at her throat. She was very slight in build, ethereal, and her features were small and neat, her mouth generous. Only the slightest trace of fair hair showed beneath her veil. Her voice, like her expression, was sweet and low-pitched. Though she could not be termed beautiful, no man could fail to be charmed by the Duchess's gentle demeanour. Remembering Guy Jarvis's avowed admiration, Margaret could not forbear a slight touch of pique. So this was the mistress Guy honoured in the lists of honour and in daily service.

She found herself answering meekly, 'Thank you, Your Grace, I am a little stiff but not too weary. I shall endeavour to be no trouble to you or your household.'

She thought she caught the faintest snort of amusement from the Duke, who took up a position behind his wife's chair and smiled fondly down at her. Margaret met his eyes challengingly.

'I see your father prefers to keep himself from my presence,' he said, his grey eyes mocking her, though smilingly. 'I'm sure he will soon come to realise where his duty lies and, once the realm is quiet, you will be able to return to your estates.'

Again she curtsied and, as he signalled dismissal, she turned awkwardly for sight of Sir Guy. But the Duke had summoned him to his place by the Duchess's chair and Margaret found her own hand taken by the other lady obviously in attendance on Lady Anne.

'I am Aleyne Allard,' the second lady explained. 'My husband, Dominick, is Guy's friend. Allow me to escort you to your chamber.'

This woman was tall, more sturdily built than the Duchess and about the same age. Her golden-brown eyes, alight with intelligence, were appraising Margaret as if she would gauge how worthy an opponent she would be both for Sir Guy and the Duke and also her own husband, but Margaret liked what she saw. Lady Allard was also in mourning, relieved by a golden linked chain belt. Her expression was friendly but determined, and Margaret judged her a fair mate for the Wolf, her husband, Sir Dominick Allard. She saw now that he too was in attendance, seated on one of the window-seats in the candles' shadow, his hand caressing the grizzled fur of an elderly wolfhound. He rose and bowed.

'Greetings, Mistress Margaret. I believe we have met only once before.'

Margaret's lip compressed tightly as she recalled that he had accompanied Sir Guy on that fateful visit to the manor so many years ago. He was a big man, wide-shouldered, heavily muscled, his broad, open face crowned with a shock of thick brown hair, going only faintly grey at the temples. She curtsied in answer and he nodded, then indolently moved to join his friend by the Duke's side. The Duchess had already turned her attention to an illustrated hour book and the men had moved to the oriel window embrasure, apparently to receive Guy's report. Margaret flushed darkly as she thought they must be hearing of her part in Owen Lewis's injury.

'Mistress Margaret? Shall we go?' Lady Allard was obviously waiting to see her to her chamber. Margaret turned in the doorway to give her final curtsy to the Duke and Duchess before she withdrew and allowed Guy's former mistress to lead her towards the newel stair-foot.

She found herself wishing that Sir Guy would be following to ensure her comfort as he had done repeatedly during the journey south. Lady Allard caught her backward glance and her mobile mouth twitched a little.

'You will find your chamber very small. As you saw, Crosby Place is not large and we are somewhat cramped.'

The room *was* small, at the top of the house, the walls whitewashed, with one small tapestry, and plainly furnished with a bed, a truckle beneath for Jonnet, a prie-dieu and a curtained alcove for Margaret's clothing with a small chest for her other possessions, but perfectly clean and fresh-smelling, a long way from the dungeon her imagination had caused her to fear. Lady Allard sank on to the bed and regarded her thoughtfully.

'So, you were naturally fearful, but Duke Richard

would never dream of harming you or causing you bodily discomfort.'

Margaret coloured hotly at the other woman's accurate reading of her mind.

'And you are already missing Guy. I see he has proved a chivalrous escort.' Lady Allard chuckled as crimson colour again flooded Margaret's neck and cheeks. 'He will be quartered very near, so you will see him often. It is just that Crosby is no castle like Middleham and cannot house all of Duke Richard's household. I live here at present as one of the Lady Anne's gentlewomen, but Dominick is quartered elsewhere and I miss him sorely.'

Margaret said shortly, 'I'm sure Sir Guy will be glad of his relief from this distasteful duty and not in the least anxious to renew our acquaintance.'

'And you, will you be pleased to be rid of him?'

There was nowhere to go to move from Lady Allard's close scrutiny and Margaret could only shrug and turn her gaze aside.

'I have no wish to be here at all, Lady Allard, as I'm sure you are aware, and will be pleased to be with my own people again.'

'But in the meantime you must make the best of things, see as much as you can of London and allow me to befriend you. You will do that, won't you?'

The words were so beguilingly uttered that Margaret could only blink away tears of relief and offer her hand, somewhat grubby from the dust of travel.

'Good. I'll leave you now and send up your maid. I think you would rather eat here alone with her tonight than endure the scrutiny of other members of the household, so I'll arrange for that too. Once you have slept, things will look brighter.'

In the doorway she paused. 'Richard is anxious only to ensure the peace of the realm. He will order no executions which are not absolutely necessary. I know you look at these happenings through your father's eyes, but if he were to come and surrender himself I'm sure he would merely be returned to his manor with grave warnings about future conduct. If you are in communication with him you would do him a favour if you could inform him of what would be in his best interest.'

Margaret sighed and shook her head. 'I assure you, Lady Allard, I have no idea of my father's whereabouts, though, if I had, I am not sure that I would advise him to do as you suggest. I am fearful for his safety.'

Aleyne Allard nodded gravely. 'I understand. I'll see you tomorrow. Do not hesitate to send for me if there is need.'

Jonnet was ushered in a few moments later by one of the Duke's guards, clad in the Yorkist livery of murrey and blue and bearing his device of the white boar. The maid was clearly over-awed by the nearness of such exalted company and made no complaint about their cramped accommodation. Margaret had noticed that, over these last weeks, her maid had become far more assured and less clumsy. It seemed that the coming of romance into her life had matured her. She wore an expression of quiet contentment and Margaret was glad for her. Jonnet had ridden pillion behind her man to London and it appeared that her happiness was in no way threatened by their move from the manor. Sir Guy had chosen Grimshaw as one of their escort, though the man might well have been left in Northamptonshire with the other men-at-arms who had stayed on the manor in order to secure the person of Sir John Rushton should he return to his home. Margaret wondered if Sir Guy had considered the feelings of her maid and hoped that he had done so, and that that had been his reason for including Grimshaw in the company.

Jonnet told her of what life was like in the servants' quarters of the house. The cook, she said, had been brought from Middleham and was said to be constantly complaining of the lack of facilities and the outrageous prices charged by London merchants, to say nothing of the continual noise and stinks of the capital. All the Yorkshire servants were anxious to return north, though Margaret believed that that was very unlikely if they intended to remain in Gloucester's service. While the young King remained a minor, the Protector must stay in London. Would the Duchess also pine for her home in the Dales? Guy had said her son, Edward, was to remain there and she would miss him sorely.

When questioned, Jonnet had heard nothing more of the fates of other members of the royal family. The Queen was still in sanctuary with her daughter and her younger son, the Duke of York, Dorset had fled to France, and the King had now taken up residence in the grim Tower. Margaret shuddered at this news, but Jonnet informed her that, apparently, it was customary for the King to stay for a while in the royal apartments there prior to his coronation, which probably would be quite soon.

'The Londoners are already preparing for the ceremonies,' she said excitedly. 'Do you think we shall be here to see it, mistress?'

Margaret, sadly, had nothing to say on this score and had decidedly mixed feelings about such a possibility.

She lay for long hours sleepless, listening to the unfamiliar sounds from the London streets. Iron-wheeled carts rattled along the cobbles throughout the night, the Watch called out his reports at frequent intervals and, at first light, the bustle began again as country people came through the gates to sell their wares.

She thought of Guy Jarvis. Lady Allard had said he was quartered near by and would present himself soon, but would he? He had fulfilled his task and surely it would be assigned to someone else now to guard the Duke's hostage. Margaret fretted at the thought and castigated herself. What could it matter if she did not ever set eyes on the man again? Punching her pillow aggressively, she realised that it *would* matter, a great deal. She had come to rely on Sir Guy utterly. He had protected her from harm and inconvenience; indeed, despite her haughty manner to him, he had been ever courteous, distant, it was true, but definitely chivalrous, as Lady Allard had said. He had declared he had no interest in marriage, but why? He was handsome, not wealthy certainly, but now, in the Protector's favour, would make some noble lady a desirable husband. Her father had, unfortunately, made the wrong move in so quickly repudiating that match.

Looking back, Margaret saw that the fair-haired young man had never been far from her thoughts, not even during the short days of her first betrothal, and now she hardly gave a thought to Bennet Hartwell, except as the man she expected to come to her rescue with her father. Would Gloucester allow the betrothal to go forward, if her father were arraigned for treason? It would depend on Bennet Hartwell's involvement in the Dorset faction, or evidence to prove it. Margaret gave a premonitory shiver. It would be best for both men to leave England while they had the chance, and leave her to Gloucester's mercy.

What would that be? Both Lady Allard and Guy Jarvis had assured her that Gloucester was a kindly man, but he did appear to find some source of amusement in her discomfiture. He had been mocking her again this evening in his wife's presence. If her father should die, and she could not bear to face this terrible possibility, his estates could be sequestered and she would be penniless. Would Gloucester then concern himself about her helpless state and arrange some marriage of convenience for her, or would he decide that a nunnery would be the ideal place in which to confine her, so that he might wash his hands of her? Yet even a nunnery required a dowry, and she would possess no money of her own. In that event would Guy Jarvis give so much as a passing thought to the long hours of boredom and frustration she would endure for the rest of her days?

The morning, Lady Allard had said, would bring a rosier hue to her worries. It did bring Sir Guy to her door. Confused, in a flurry of excitement, she asked Jonnet to show him in. The breakfast dishes had just been cleared away by one of the serving maids.

He looked round at the room and nodded his approval. 'All things considered, it is the best that could be provided. Did you sleep well after your long journey, Mistress Margaret?'

Margaret promptly lied to him that she had.

'The Duke has requested that I escort you to some of the sights of the town. You will wish to see St Paul's, I am sure, and perhaps visit the shops in the Chepe.'

Margaret would certainly like to do so, but forbore to say so.

'Surely you have duties of a higher priority, sir?'

'No duty has a higher priority than the Duke's command,' he returned coolly.

Margaret was forced to agree and, with Jonnet in attendance, issued forth with him into the wonders of the crowded, stinking but fascinating city.

Margaret had accompanied her father into Northampton frequently, but even that bustling market town had not prepared her for the noise and confusion of the capital. She had expected the overflowing gutters which ran through the streets, was not dismayed by the carcasses of rats and larger animals abandoned there, moved hastily but readily out of the way of carts and the trampling hooves of knights and mounted men-at-arms. What amazed her was the sense of excitement and urgency which imbued the people. The apprentices were intent on scoring off their neighbours, the inn-keepers seemed truly anxious to please their customers, the owners of the shops and booths in the Chepe genuinely interested in what she wished to buy. She knew well enough that much of it was business practice and nothing else but it amused her and, as she caught snippets of talk from around her, she realised that the Londoners were as alarmed by the present unsettled state of affairs as she was herself. One fat bookseller within the church of St Paul's was heard to say to a wealthy client that he hoped the young King was still well and would soon be joined by his brother. If Sir Guy overheard the remark he made no comment.

'Are you tired?' he questioned suddenly, and Margaret confessed that she was. The paving stones of London appeared unaccustomedly hard to her feet.

He led her to an inn near St Paul's Cross and called imperiously for a seat apart from the other customers and the provision of good malmsey.

They were conducted to a high-backed settle near a window and a serving wench scurried to attend to their needs.

Margaret noted the admiring glance the girl gave her escort and, finding Jonnet's eyes questioningly on her, looked hurriedly away.

Indeed, Margaret had been watching the women and their openly appreciative response to Guy Jarvis throughout the morning's many encounters, though he, it was true, paid them scant attention.

'Well,' he said, cutting across her thoughts, 'you have said little during our outing. How do you find London?'

She shook her head. 'It surpasses all my expectations. I had known how huge and bustling it is—my father told me so often—but it is overwhelming. The houses and shops almost blot out the sky and I should be very frightened and confused if I were not so well guided. You have been here many times, I suppose, with Gloucester.'

He made a deprecating gesture. 'Several times when it was necessary for him to come south, but we are both always heartily glad to feel the fresh, invigorating air of the Dales again.'

'But he will be forced to remain here for some time now, surely.'

'Yes,' Guy sighed. 'That will not please Lady Anne, nor, I think, will Richard like it well either, but he was never a man to shirk his duty.'

'Lady Allard was praising him too. What is it about this man which makes those who know him well fly so quickly to his defence?'

'Perhaps because they *do* know him so well. I hope that your first glimpse of Lady Allard pleases you. I know she will befriend and be ever ready to help you should you require it.'

'She seems very kind, and the Duchess, too, was welcoming—considering my situation in the household.'

'Aleyne has known such problems in her time. Her father died just before the battle of Tewkesbury and she was forced to flee her manor to avoid being pressed into an abhorrent match.'

'It was then she met her husband?'

Sir Guy looked somewhat uncertain. 'Well, yes. I was present, in service then to Dominick.' His lips twitched suddenly, remembering something which amused him. 'He took her in charge when she was caught in the very act of stealing his favourite horse.'

'Stealing his horse? Sweet Virgin, what did he do?' Margaret was horrified, knowing only too well how grave the offence was.

'He was not best pleased and threatened to hang her associates, for he was convinced she was in league with some of his men who were engaged in pilfering supplies.'

Margaret listened entranced as he explained how Aleyne had become Dominick's prisoner, had been entrusted to him by the King and how they had fallen deeply in love.

'I do not think I know two people who suit so well as they do,' Guy finished enthusiastically, 'save perhaps the Duke and Lady Anne.'

During the telling Margaret had glimpsed yet another side to Guy Jarvis. His grim demeanour and constant air of reluctantly enduring a spell of unpleasant duty had made him a hard man in her eyes. Now she saw that he had a sense of fun too and was truly affectionate towards those he admired. He would be a good man on whom to lean in trouble, she thought with a sudden pang. She had known few such in her short acquaintances with her father's cronies. Their attitudes were affected only by their abilities to gain preferment in their associations. Men like Dominick and Guy Jarvis were rare, and gleamed as priceless emeralds amid dross. Gloucester was well served.

Guy reached out to take her wine cup as they prepared to leave, and his touch sent a tingle of warning through her body. She pulled away sharply. This man was still her gaoler; she must not find attributes in his personality which would make it hard for her to trick him if she must.

On their return to Crosby they found an atmosphere of suppressed excitement. Sir Guy was informed that Sir Francis Lovell required his presence in the hall and he excused himself to Margaret at the stair-foot. She mounted to her chamber, fearful of the news which clearly had the household in a ferment.

Aleyne Allard joined her as she was about to consider where she should take dinner.

'You are requested to join the other ladies in attendance in the hall,' Aleyne informed her. 'The Lady Anne will be glad of all our company and support today.'

Margaret turned towards her new friend, her eyes troubled.

'What has disturbed Her Grace? No harm has come to the King?'

'No, no—' Aleyne frowned doubtfully '—and none threatened, but something unexpected *has* occurred. The Duchess has been told that Lord Hastings and several prominent members of the Council have been placed under arrest.'

Margaret's eyes widened in shock. 'Lord Hastings? But I thought he was one of the Duke's most loyal supporters.'

'Indeed, we all thought he was but, apparently, it has been revealed that he has been meeting secretly with Mistress Shore and sending messages through her to the Dowager Queen in sanctuary.'

Margaret was aware of the late King's proclivities. Mistress Shore, the goldsmith's notorious wife, had been dubbed the King's Merry Mistress because of her talent to be witty and entertaining. Queen Elizabeth, perhaps wisely, had decided from the first not to antagonise her husband's favourite and the two were understood to be companions, if not firm friends. Margaret had heard that the royal mistress had accompanied the Queen to sanctuary. So she had emerged from time to time and met with the late King's dearest friend and his chamberlain. Will Hastings had spent his youth drinking and whoring with Edward of England, had served him loyally and been rewarded by grand offices and grants of extensive properties. He was one of the richest and most powerful men in England—and he had been the first to inform Gloucester of his brother's death and anxious to warn him that the Woodville faction was intent on jockeying him from power. If Gloucester trusted him and relied upon his support, why had he now imprisoned him? Were Hastings' meetings with Jane Shore tantamount to treasonable acts? Again that deadly sense of chill invaded Margaret's body. If so powerful a man as Lord Hastings had been accused, how could her father be excused in a like situation?

As if in explanation, Aleyne Allard said thoughtfully, 'Of course, Will Hastings was known to be in love with

Jane Shore. She was, I believe, his mistress and he reluctantly surrendered her to his sovereign.'

Margaret stared at her, bewildered. 'How could he do that?'

Aleyne shrugged. 'The King was the King. Edward could be vindictive when he chose and Hastings had his future prospects to consider.'

'And you think he has continued to love her all this time?'

'Possibly, except that. . .'

Margaret waited for further revelations in this passionate tale of intrigue and blighted love.

Aleyne gave her shoulders an irritated shake, as if reproving herself for senseless and unproven gossip. 'I heard that the merry lady was also enamoured of the handsome Dorset, would do anything to have her love returned. Perhaps she has prevailed upon our Will to further her *new* lover's affairs.'

'But Dorset is the King's stepson?'

'True, and very handsome, though not to my taste, I have to confess.'

Margaret drew a hard breath. The very stones of this city spoke of treachery and death.

'You think the Duke would bring Hastings to trial, his brother's most faithful servant?'

'If Hastings has betrayed Richard he deserves to die.' Aleyne's tone was hard. 'That is the one crime Richard will never forgive. His motto has always been "Loyalty binds me" and he has never swerved from it himself, not even when he might have lost the love of his life from a sense of duty to the crown. He will not accept disloyalty in those he considered his friends. Anne says Hastings' man, Catesby, revealed his duplicity and Richard has accused him in open Council. We yet have to hear the outcome, but Anne is deeply distressed and, since there is much talk of dissimulation and intrigue, is in need of the backing of her ladies now. Please come, and do not show too openly your sense of outrage.'

Over the next days Margaret was to hear far more of the fated Council meeting at the Tower which doomed Lord Hastings, for he was executed very hastily following it. His fellow conspirators were also arrested and, while Richard pardoned Lord Thomas Stanley, he imprisoned the Chancellor Archbishop of York, Rotherham, but kept him incarcerated for only a few days while Morton, the Bishop of Ely, who had been in prison with him, was put into the Duke of Buckingham's custody and sent off to his Castle at Brecknock in Wales. Margaret was shocked by the rumour that Lord Hastings had been beheaded summarily upon a rough block of wood left by workmen and had had scarce time to make his confession to the priest hastily summoned for the purpose. More and more her forebodings grew concerning the possible fate of her father, and she was partially relieved that she heard no more from him, believing that it was now more than probable that he had escaped overseas.

She saw nothing of Sir Guy, who was occupied on the Protector's business, and thought it likely that he had gone north again, since she was informed by Aleyne that Duke Richard had sent to Yorkshire for reinforcements from the men loyal to him there.

'The city is in a disturbed state,' she murmured, glancing hurriedly back towards the Duchess seated in the window embrasure. Anne of Gloucester was looking more and more pale and haggard as day succeeded day. She was reunited with her husband but saw little of him now that he was constantly engaged with members of the Council discussing preparations for the young King's coronation. Hastings' man, Catesby, came more and more frequently to Crosby, and Margaret surmised that the man had betrayed one master to obtain greater favours from another more highly placed.

Since Guy was not near to escort her, Margaret found herself feeling stifled within the walls of Duke Richard's town house and confessed as much to Aleyne as they sat early one Sunday after mass, trying to occupy themselves with embroidery.

Aleyne looked up thoughtfully. 'There is no reason why we should not walk in the town. Will Scroggins will find me two good men for escort and I'm sure the Duchess will excuse us from attendance. I've a fancy to visit St Paul's and look through some of the newly printed books. One would make a fine gift for the Duchess, and I would like a bestiary for my children before going north again. I have seen one Lady Scrope had for her little daughter with the most beautifully drawn animals.'

Margaret was delighted when the Duchess gave her permission gladly, and the two women set out with Jonnet and the two Allard men-at-arms in attendance.

The usually busy streets round Bishopsgate seemed oddly deserted and it was not until the party was approaching the great cathedral with its famous cross that they realised why. Here a large crowd had collected and the men-at-arms found it necessary to enforce their authority to push their way through for their ladies' passage. The street leading to St Paul's Cross was lined on both sides by chattering, expostulating townsfolk, held back by soldiers in a livery Margaret could not identify.

One of their escort explained. 'They're the Bishop of London's men keeping the way clear for Mistress Shore's public penance. I think we should try to return home, my lady.' He addressed Aleyne respectfully. 'I had forgotten that this was the day appointed for it, and I do not think Sir Dominick would wish you to be present.'

Aleyne frowned in concentration as Margaret was jostled roughly against her. Both women were aware that Duke Richard had placed Mistress Jane Shore under arrest in the Bishop of London's palace, for her complicity in the Tower plot. It had been whispered that the late King's Merry Mistress had been accused of dark practices, of witchcraft, of ill-wishing the Protector in order to render him helpless to counter the Queen's machinations. Margaret had scoffed at the notion but Aleyne had soberly reminded her that the Queen's mother, Jacquetta of Bedford, had been called a witch and that many in the realm believed the Queen had shackled King Edward to her by her witchery. This accusation would be sufficient to place Mistress Shore under the jurisdiction of the church and, if tried and found guilty, she would be hanged. Surprisingly, the Duke had not pushed the charge, and Mistress Shore had been found guilty of harlotry only, and condemned to make public penance.

Both women would willingly now have extricated themselves from the avid crowd could they have done so, but they appeared to be trapped and could only wait until the Bishop of London's procession had passed and the crowd dispersed. The two men-at-arms moved in as near to their charges as they could, and the frightened

Jonnet stared wide-eyed about her as Margaret caught at her maid's arm to keep her close to her.

The crowd seemed in holiday mood, most good-tempered, though Margaret knew that as the condemned woman was brought near they would likely abuse her with missiles as well as shouted insults. The sound of tramping feet came nearer and soon Margaret was able to glimpse the leading men-at-arms. The people became more excited and craned their heads to gain a better look at the prisoner. Between armed men Jane Shore walked alone. Margaret was shocked to see that she wore only a simple white sheet, her brown hair streaming past her waist, and she stumbled awkwardly as her bare feet caught the rough edges of stones and cobbles. The lighted taper wavered in her grasp and she stopped, until one of the men near her urged her on, not brutally but firmly. She was not beautiful, quite small-made, her figure and comely features well-rounded, but Margaret could understand how her good-natured face would appeal all too well to men, particularly those nobles who dealt daily with more haughty and unapproachable females. Even now the woman was smiling gamely as she pressed on to the Cross itself where she was to make a full confession of her sins. Margaret thought angrily that it would be more appropriate if those who had shared her favours could be condemned with her, but both her noble lovers were dead and Dorset fled to France. No man of lesser state would dare to stand up for her now and, as most abandoned women, she was left to bear her shame alone.

The muttering of the crowd grew louder. One or two women shouted filthy names but another, more loudly, proclaimed, 'Let her be. She was never one to abuse her position and ever willing to listen to the poor when they begged her for help.'

At this the crowd became strangely silent and the procession moved on. As Jane Shore passed close by her, Margaret could see that she was weeping now; the brave smile had disappeared. Were the tears for Hastings, already being carried to St George's, Windsor for burial, or for her own suffering? What would happen to her after this? Would she be returned to the Bishop's prison? Likely her possessions had been seized as forfeit. How would she exist without a rich protector, and who would dare to care for her now, disgraced as she was and with the whispered stigma of witchcraft levelled at her?

The procession had reached the famed Cross now and Margaret strained to hear what was being said, but the late King's mistress was so soft-voiced that no words carried to her. So intent was she that she failed to notice the man who rudely pushed Jonnet aside until he urgently tapped on her arm. Angrily she swung round, then peered hard at the hooded face and gasped as she recognised her betrothed, Bennet Hartwell. Momentarily she had been separated from Lady Allard by the movement of the impatient crowd. Hartwell briefly placed his finger on his lips, warning her not to cry out or catch the attention of her two escorting men. She nodded and inclined her head to catch his whispered words.

'I wanted you to know we are still near you in case of need. It is better that you stay where you are at present, until we are able to send word again and manage to free you. Your father is safe and can be reached at the Saracen inn in the South Wark. It is very near the bridge. Send to us there if you feel in any danger.'

She nodded again and before she could say anything in answer he had pulled away and was immediately lost in the crowd which quickly swirled round her again. She stood, bemused. How had he known he could find her here? Was she constantly watched or was there still some traitor in Duke Richard's service who was always ready to inform on her movements? She was unsure what to make of the situation and looked round anxiously for Aleyne and Jonnet.

She could see no sign of them. Somehow she had become totally separated from her escort and could only hope that Lady Allard and Jonnet were still being guarded by the men. Finding it impossible to press her way through the crowd—in any case she did not, at present, know which way to go—she decided to stay where she was for a while and await events. Surely this public event would soon be over and the crowd would disperse. There was no way to catch even a glimpse of the Cross now; she couldn't see over the heads of taller members of the crowd and had no way of knowing how things were proceeding.

Suddenly that knowledge made itself painfully clear. The mood of the crowd turned decidedly ugly. There were catcalls and shouts and men began to press towards the Cross. Margaret found herself jostled and crushed until she could hardly breathe and feared that if she should stumble in this press she would be trampled underfoot.

'Let her go free; ain't she done enough?'

'What call 'as that there Protector with his high and mighty ways and principles to judge our Jane? The way I 'eard it 'e's got bastards of 'is own.'

'That's right enough,' a shrill, woman's voice took up the cause. ''Is brother would never 'ave treated 'er so.

What call 'as His saintly Grace to turn his nose up at our Jane's services to the crown?'

There were a number of guffaws and giggles at this sally but many of the people were in no good humour. Margaret heard cries and grunts and shouted commands from the sergeant-at-arms, and guessed that people in the front line of the spectators were pitting themselves forcibly against the crossed pikes of Jane Shore's guards. There would be real trouble soon and heads broken with staves if order wasn't quickly restored. The excited London crowd was rebelliously showing its displeasure at the way this Duke from the north was treating one of their own favourites.

Margaret imagined that the trouble had been sparked off when the soldiers attempted to return Jane Shore to her prison in the Bishop's palace. Though she had felt a distinct sense of pity for the shamed woman, Margaret thought that Jane herself must now be feeling frightened. She would be far safer within the prison's stout walls than caught in the fury of this London crowd. Rabble-rousers would inflame passions and no one would be safe. About her, nervous husbands were trying to extricate their wives and children, and Margaret had all she could do to stay upright.

There was another authoritative shout and the sound of running feet, men's booted feet, and Margaret was unsure whether to be pleased or sorry that reinforcements were being brought in to assist the beleagured men of the Bishop's guard. She struggled to find some nearby support and managed to reach safety against a house wall behind her, but still found it impossible to move clear of the street while the angry crowd clawed and screamed and fought around her. She saw one old man knocked to the ground by a pike borne by a liveried man-at-arms, this time wearing the distinctive colours of the Duke of Gloucester. A woman screamed and fell on her knees beside him, desperately trying to shield his head from further punishing blows. Margaret clung wildly to the extending lead of a window embrasure. It was the best she could do now, to keep tight hold, prevent herself from being swept into the thick of it again. The soldiers would soon prove victorious, as they were armed and well-disciplined, but there would be innocent casualties before the business was ended.

Not daring to relinquish her hold, she could not hope now for sight of Lady Allard. She would be missed, of course, eventually, and someone would quickly return her to Crosby Place, once she was able to identify herself to one of the officers.

Someone caught at her arm and jerked. She fought desperately to thrust him from her until an angry voice yelled, 'What in God's name are you doing here? They told me at Crosby you had gone out and I've had the devil's own business to find you.'

Guy Jarvis was in a towering rage and Margaret surrendered herself to his grasp as he forcibly swept aside those who would impede him and pushed her before him to safety in a quieter alley near by.

The sounds of battle still reached them here, even in this backwater, and he muttered a sturdy, soldier's oath beneath his breath.

'Lady Allard and Jonnet?' Margaret demanded breathlessly.

'Safe on their way back to Crosby. Dominick commanded that one of the companies be sent to quell that mob. Now, will you tell me why, today of all days, you chose to go out without my escort?'

Winded and bruised, Margaret wrenched her wrist

from his hold and pushed herself free of him, breathing hard. She had been in peril of her life and knew it and, now that she was safe at last, was in no mood to be scolded as if she were a foolish child.

'The Duchess gave permission. We had two men as escort. We knew nothing of the Jane Shore penance, at least *I* knew nothing and neither did Aleyne, or else she forgot it. You are no longer my gaoler, sir. Do not dare to treat me like a half-witted prisoner. I assure you I had no wish to witness that poor creature's shame if it could have been avoided. We got caught up in the press, as you very well know.'

'That "poor creature",' he mimicked her, 'was involved in a plot to bring down the rightful government of this realm.'

'I'm sure she was very dangerous indeed,' Margaret mocked him back, equally fiercely. 'I'm sure His Grace of Gloucester must think himself very brave indeed to bring down the might of his authority on such a powerful enemy.'

He stopped suddenly and, facing her, took her again by both her elbows and shook her. 'So you think dangerous enemies are only men? What of Jeanne d'Arc and her witchery? Did she not put enough iron into those cowardly French almost to defeat our regiments?'

'Witchery!' Margaret scoffed. 'I thought you a man, sir, not some credulous child to believe such superstitious nonsense.'

'I did not say I believed it, madam,' he snapped. 'It is enough if other, more credulous folk believe such tales. It is fact that there are godless people who perform sacrilegious rituals for their own ends, and Jane Shore and the Queen are rumoured to be of their number, like it or not. Mistress Shore is fortunate she is not hanging from a scaffold at Tyburn this very moment and, but for the forbearance of His Grace of Gloucester, she would be.'

Margaret was breathless again from her shaking. His words had astounded her.

At last she found her voice. 'You really mean that Jane Shore and the Queen attempted to bring harm to the Duke by dark, evil practices?'

'I don't know,' he said gruffly. 'That is what they were accused of and naturally it is easier to bring such charges against Mistress Shore than the Queen herself, though that Woodville bitch is capable of anything, in my estimation.'

'And the Duke spared Jane?' she said wonderingly.

'He has never been one to war against women, though he needs to watch his back. That Woodville woman brought the mighty Desmond down for daring to insult her. Do you think she will be more circumspect with her brother-in-law who she knows will curb her ambition?'

Margaret had heard the tale that the Irish lord had called the Queen 'the King's Grey Mare' and she had never forgiven him.

'The Londoners dislike these soldiers from the north and distrust them,' she said quietly. 'You cannot blame them.'

He shrugged. 'Times are unsettled and there are always men to inflame such mobs for their own purposes. We must hope that only heads are broken and no lives lost. Now let us get back to Crosby.' He was still holding her fast and said harshly, 'Swear to me that you will never venture into the city again without me.'

She said hotly, 'Why should I do that? Has the Duke appointed you my gaoler permanently?'

'This has nothing to do with the Duke. You were in real danger out there. Don't you realise that yet?'

'And why should you be concerned?'

He shook her again, his face so close to hers that she could smell his faintly wine-fumed breath.

'Damn it, you are mine, Margaret Rushton, meant to be mine from the beginning, and I'll surrender you to no one, do you hear me?'

Her eyes widened in shock. 'You are out of your mind, sir. Our betrothal was broken years ago. I am promised to someone else. You are mad to talk so to me.'

He bared his teeth in a fierce grin. 'Promised you may be, but not bound by holy church. I still have the advantage. I want you, and I'll have you. Do you think the Duke will deny me if I ask him? Now do me the favour of preserving your pretty skin until this business over the regency is decided.'

She backed away from him, her hands defensively behind her, but he made no move to come any closer, remaining facing her, that blazing blue gaze fixed on her, unblinking. Then he said sharply, 'Come, let us get back to Crosby. Lady Allard will be concerned for your safety.'

He put out one hand to take her arm again but she shrank back and he shrugged and waited, arms folded, until at last she came slowly forward, and they walked side by side back towards Crosby Place. The crowd was already being forcibly dispersed and there seemed little danger now that Sir Guy would be attacked but, grimly, he continued to keep one hand on his sword-scabbard.

Margaret's thoughts teemed. How was it possible

that she should be caught in this trap? For trap it was in truth! He was confident that the Duke would not refuse him her hand, yet her father still lived. She was not a ward of court. She drew a hard, shuddering breath. If her father was to be attainted as a traitor, the Duke would certainly have the power over her to grant Guy Jarvis's request. Why, why did he want her? If her estates were sequestered she would be no wealthy heiress. On the contrary she would be a landless beggar, reliant on charity for her daily bread. Of course Gloucester could then grant her estates to Guy Jarvis, but, in the event of attainder, the lands would revert to the Crown. He would be able to do that if he so wished and without the need to encumber his young captain with a disgraced ward of the Crown. Guy had shown no desire for her. Not by the flicker of an eyelid had he revealed the slightest interest in her as a woman. He had hardly appeared to notice her, other than to report to her concerning manor affairs. Then why, now, had he stated his intention to possess her? Because she was promised to Bennet Hartwell? Was his announcement simply based on a wish to oust his rival purely as a dog-in-the-manger reaction? No, she did not believe Guy Jarvis harboured that kind of petty resentment—except against her.

As on so many occasions, she lived again through that highly embarrassing encounter five years ago. Her behaviour had been inexcusable. Was his wish now to subject her to the humiliation he had felt then?

She stole a hasty glance at his averted face but his expression revealed no trace of malice, appeared merely impassive.

A rush of warmth swept through her body. What was her reaction, now that the initial shock of his disclosure was over? Her eyes half closed as she visualised, vividly, herself helpless in his arms, naked in the marriage bed. She told herself stoutly, I am not afraid of this man's threats. He cannot force me to accept him. At the altar steps I will steadfastly refuse to accept him. I would rather starve in the streets. It was an impassioned and over-dramatic inner declaration and she swept the thought aside as unworthy, typical of some foolish maiden with an over-worked imagination and ridiculously romantic bent. She, Margaret Rushton, was not so foolish as to give way to such whimsies. She had a mind of her own. She was still free to give herself. Only an hour ago—less—she'd had word that her father was near enough to offer her a way out, protection from such threats as these.

Her thoughts strayed to Bennet Hartwell. He had risked himself to meet with her in that mob, knowing the Protector's men would be on the alert for trouble. She strove to bring to mind his frank, good-humoured face, his sturdy form—and could not. The mind picture of him was thrust aside by the reality of the man beside her, who even now stood aside, scowling, for her to precede him into the Duke's lodging.

CHAPTER SIX

MARGARET was desperately anxious to reach the sanctuary of her chamber but was forestalled in the entrance hall by Aleyne Allard who rushed forward at sight of her.

'Sweet Virgin, I had feared you lost. We had such trouble pressing through that mob that I thought you must have been trampled underfoot.' She looked hastily at Guy. 'Thank God you found her in time. You are not hurt, Margaret?'

'No,' Margaret mumbled, conscious that her encounter with Bennet Hartwell had been the principal cause of their separation. 'I'm sorry you were so frightened. I was pushed away from you and took refuge by a house wall.' She was terrified that Aleyne might have caught sight of her in talk with her betrothed and, unwittingly, reveal the fact to Sir Guy. She glanced down at her dust-stained gown. 'I—I must hurry to my chamber and change. The Duchess may have need of my services.' She glared pointedly at Guy who continued to remain stolidly at her side.

Aleyne took her arm and moved with her to the stairfoot. 'The Duchess is with Duke Richard and will not need us for a while. Let me help you. That maid of yours was so distraught I sent her to the servants' hall. She'll be little help to you in her present state.'

She glanced back towards the screen door to the main hall and gave a nod in Sir Guy's direction. 'The Duke may have need of you, Guy. Have you heard that the young Duke of York has at last been surrendered by his mother into the Protector's care? He will join his brother immediately. Edward must have missed young Richard sorely and will welcome his company.'

Guy's intense blue eyes darkened in surprise. 'No, I hadn't heard. How was the Woodville woman persuaded to part with him?'

'It's said the Archbishop went with His Grace of Buckingham to the Westminster sanctuary and convinced the Queen that she had nothing to fear for her sons.'

'I hope he is right.' Margaret's intended mutter emerged much louder than she had expected and she stepped back, startled and not a little embarrassed, as the Duke of Gloucester swept into the entrance hall attended by his closest friend, Sir Francis Lovell.

That the Protector had heard her ill-chosen words was only too clear. His dark brows moved fractionally towards his hairline and he paused for a moment, his hand on his sword-hilt.

His grey eyes glittered strangely and instinctively Margaret drew closer to Aleyne. There was a short silence, then Gloucester said mildly, 'Ah, I see you found Mistress Rushton. My Lady Anne will be greatly relieved.' He inclined his chin and Margaret knew she was being dismissed. She curtsied low and Aleyne drew her up the stairs hurriedly. Margaret caught only the tail-end of Gloucester's words to Guy.

'. . .want you to see to it that the prince is escorted to the Tower safely.'

Once the door of her chamber was latched, she turned shakily to face Aleyne, blinking back frightened tears.

'Dear God, he must have heard me and thought. . .'

'Indeed,' Aleyne said grimly. 'What possessed you to speak so foolishly here, at Court? This is not Northampton, you know. It is unwise to reveal to anyone, and I mean *anyone*, even your closest friend, what you are thinking about the motives of those in power.'

Margaret moved to the bed and sat down, giving way to helpless tears. This well-deserved reproof brought home to her the precariousness of her position here at Crosby.

'I meant. . .'

'Whatever you meant, I think the Protector believes you are questioning his guardianship of his nephews.' Aleyne's comment was dry, and she lifted the lid of Margaret's travelling-chest to find her a clean gown.

'But don't you, in your heart, question his need to have them securely within his hands?'

Aleyne turned back and, for once, Margaret saw that her friend was truly angry with her.

'I certainly do not. I would rather question the guardianship of their own mother. Elizabeth is ambitious and conniving and will do anything at this stage to further her own interests even if it would mean sacrificing her sons.'

'You cannot believe that.' Margaret was appalled.

'I do. I have lived at courts, Margaret. I know what people will do when ambition rules. Of this I am sure: Richard would never harm his brother's children, and if he has placed them within the walls of the Tower it is because that is the safest place for them.' Aleyne's eyes were snapping with fury and Magaret shook her head weakly.

'Forgive me, Aleyne. I cannot doubt your faith in the

Protector.' She drew a hard breath. 'It was the last straw to hear that. I was already—upset.'

'Yes, of course, you must have been terrified. The mood of that crowd was positively menacing.'

'No, no, it wasn't that. . .' Margaret's voice trailed off miserably as she realised she had begun to divulge more than she meant.

Aleyne sat down beside her on the bed. 'I think you had better tell me,' she suggested, the cold note in her voice giving way to one of concern.

Margaret swallowed. 'He—he said things which. . .'

'By "he" I take it you mean Guy Jarvis.'

'Yes.'

'Improper things? Guy Jarvis insulted you? I can hardly believe that.'

'No, yes—he said—he said he was determined to. . .'

'Well?'

'To marry me.'

'Ah.' Aleyne's lips twisted slightly and Margaret waited for her reaction.

'I am betrothed already,' Margaret said hotly. 'He has no right. . .'

'You have feelings for this man, your betrothed?'

'I don't know him, have only met him—once—' the hesitation was only fractional '—but he is my father's choice for me,' she ended stoutly.

'And you always accept your father's wishes tamely?'

Margaret considered that carefully.

'I have never consciously defied him,' she said at last. 'He has always had my best interests at heart.'

'Has he?'

'Of course.'

Aleyne thoughtfully stroked the silk of Margaret's

CASINO JUBILEE
"Scratch 'n Match" Game

DETACH AND POST CARD TODAY!

CHECK CLAIM CHART BELOW FOR YOUR FREE GIFTS!

YES! I have placed my label from the front cover in the space provided above and scratched away the silver box. Please send me all the gifts for which I qualify. I understand that I am under no obligation to purchase any books, as explained on the back and on the opposite page. I am over 18 years of age.

1A5M

MS/MRS/MISS/MR ______________________________

ADDRESS ______________________________

____

______________________________ POSTCODE ______________________________

CASINO JUBILEE CLAIM CHART

			WORTH 4 FREE BOOKS A FREE FLUFFY DUCK AND MYSTERY GIFT
			WORTH 4 FREE BOOKS
			WORTH 3 FREE BOOKS

CLAIM No 1528

Offer closes 30th June 1995. We reserve the right to refuse an application. Terms and prices subject to change without notice. Offer not available for current subscribers to Legacy of Love. One application per household. Offer valid in UK and Eire only. Overseas readers please write for details. Southern Africa write to IBS Private Bag X3010, Randburg 2125.

You may be mailed with offers from other reputable companies as a result of this application. If you would prefer not to share in this opportunity please tick box. ☐

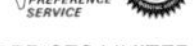

clean gown which she had withdrawn from the chest ready for her change.

'But you were once betrothed to Guy. Didn't your father then think that was in your best interests?'

'I suppose he did. Then—then the Jarvis fortunes foundered and. . .'

'And now, with the rise of Gloucester to the supreme power of Protector, I imagine the Jarvis fortunes will rise again since Guy is in his favour. What if your father should change his mind?'

'No, he wouldn't, couldn't—*I* couldn't.'

'Well, you appear to have definite feelings about Guy at any rate. You have certainly made up your mind about that.'

'I detest the man. Is it any wonder when Gloucester has appointed him my gaoler?'

Aleyne's lovely lips curved in a smile. 'Perhaps Gloucester has as much care for your safety as he has for his nephews. Have you considered that?' She rose and moved back to the chest for a hennin and veil. 'Come, we must get you ready to wait on the Duchess and, please, no more unfortunate remarks at supper.'

There was a note of suppressed laughter in her friend's voice but Margaret was aware of the very real warning, for all that.

During the next few days Margaret feared reprisal from the Protector, or at least some strong reproof, but he passed no comment. Once or twice she saw his grey eyes dwelling on her sardonically as she went about her tasks waiting on Lady Anne. She dreaded to find Guy at her elbow and started whenever someone entered the Duchess's solar, expecting to meet the calm, possessive gaze of those cold blue eyes, but he appeared to be busy on some errand for the Duke. She did not venture again into the London streets, mindful of his warning and fearful that new speculation concerning the struggle for power would again send the Londoners into a frenzy of rebellion.

Shocked, she heard that Lord Rivers, Sir Richard Grey and Sir Thomas Vaughan had been executed at Pontefract castle but, before that information could have effect, another, greater scandal was to rock the capital.

For days the Duchess of Gloucester saw little of her husband. He came and went to various Council meetings at the Tower. Aleyne supposed the nobles were continuing to discuss the date and elaborate preparations for the young King's coronation but once, when she remarked on this, Margaret noted a strange expression cross the features of Sir Dominick. Guy Jarvis returned to court and was once more in constant attendance upon the Duke. Gloucester now appeared abstracted, a frown habitually drawing his brows together, unlike his usual teasing self. He seemed not to notice Margaret as she curtsied low in his presence, always watchful of his attitude towards her. She had not spoken to Aleyne Allard again about Guy Jarvis's declaration of intent to wed her. She tried to thrust that thought aside and with it the temptation to send Jonnet to the South Wark with a message for her father. Rumour grew that the Protector had sent north for yet further reinforcements and Margaret thought that Sir Richard Ratcliffe, now free of his onerous task of overseeing the trials and executions of the King's kin at Pontefract, would be in charge of raising the levy. This would be no time to risk her father's withdrawal from hiding to get in touch with her. She must bide her time.

She had not yet been threatened with unwanted attentions. Sir Guy, like his master, seemed too busy to notice her.

The news broke finally when Aleyne and Margaret sat with the Duchess in the solar sorting silks for her embroidery. The Duke entered abruptly and, with little of his usual courtesy, dismissed her two attendants. Aleyne found her husband striding restlessly across the fine new carpet in the hall.

'Dominick, what is it? The Duke's expression is thunderous. Is more trouble threatened in the city?'

Margaret, about to withdraw, saw, with a slight start, that Guy was slumped in a window-embrasure seat, moodily staring down into the depths of a wine cup. She murmured an excuse to leave Aleyne with her husband, but he halted her in her tracks.

'No, you had best remain and hear this. It will be all over the house within the hour and the Duchess will be glad of your support when it breaks. I have the Duke's permission to reveal the gist of the latest tidings from Council.'

Guy turned and fixed Margaret with a direct stare and she came slowly nearer to Aleyne.

'There is news of my father? He has not openly joined a rising. . .'

'No, no. This does not concern your father, though it may affect his decision to act.' Dominick gave a harsh sigh and motioned both ladies to stools.

'We have been aware for some time that there was trouble in the wind. Then, this morning, Duke Richard summoned us to attend him at Council as Buckingham informed him that there was some weighty matter to be discussed. I believe Richard would have preferred to consider it in private but apparently he was forced to hear it in open Council. Stillington, the Bishop of Bath and Wells, was hurriedly admitted and came before the Duke. The man looked very white and frightened, as well he might be. Buckingham stared him out and imperiously ordered him to reveal what he had already told him. Then the man stunned us all by saying, in so low a voice that we could scarce hear him, that he could not in all conscience allow the coronation of the late King's son to proceed, as he knew the children of the marriage to have been conceived out of wedlock.'

'What?' Aleyne was about to accept a cup of wine from Dominick, but her hand stayed frozen while she stared at her husband. 'But that is arrant nonsense. We all know His Grace was married to the widowed Lady Elizabeth Grey, as she was then, secretly at Grafton. Unpopular as the marriage was, everyone accepted it, even the Earl of Warwick. Is Stillington saying the marriage was unlawfully celebrated, that there was some impediment?'

'Stillington avers that there was indeed—that the late King had already been contracted in marriage to Lady Eleanor Butler, the widowed daughter of Talbot of Shrewsbury, a marriage which had been kept strictly secret but was, none the less, legal, and that it was for this reason that the King had not proceeded with the plans made for him to contract himself to the Princess Bona of Savoy.'

'You are saying that the lady was still living when the King married the Lady Elizabeth?' Aleyne's tone was incredulous. 'Two secret marriages? It is past belief.'

'Lady Eleanor Butler died in a nunnery in 1468, therefore——' Dominick drew another hard breath '—was still alive when King Edward went through this empty ceremony with Elizabeth Woodville.'

'Then all the children are—illegitimate?' Aleyne said wonderingly. 'Why did the Bishop keep silent so long? Is the Duke convinced of the facts?'

'Buckingham, apparently, investigated the claim before announcing the Bishop's statement to the Council. Richard seemed stunned, as we all were.'

Margaret's thoughts raced, and she bit her lip. Of course the Protector would appear stunned. Clearly this fabrication had been made to oust the boys from their inheritance. That must be it but—and the thought nagged at her mind—was it also the reason why the Dowager Queen had been so anxious to have the boys in her control, not subject to the guardianship of their uncle? The Woodvilles had been so determined to have the boy crowned. Once crowned and anointed he could not have been set aside.

Aleyne was demanding urgently, 'But what will Richard do? The heir is now young Edward, Clarence's son, I take it, but. . .'

'The Council will never accept the boy. He is said to be slow-witted. Since his father's execution he has been kept closely mewed up, often in Dorset's charge, never prepared to fill such a position.'

'So the Council will likely offer the crown to Duke Richard. How very convenient for his hopes.' Margaret's tone was hard, jeering.

Sir Guy got to his feet, scarlet mottling his smooth, tanned cheeks. 'Have a care for your unwary tongue, madam.'

Margaret also had risen, knocking over her stool in her clumsy haste, and he crossed to her and snatched at her hand.

'Isn't this plan what this farrago of innuendo is about?

Stillington has, like as not, been bribed to tell this tale—'

'Stillington was imprisoned by the late King soon after Clarence's execution for, and I quote "he uttered words prejudicial to the King and his state".' Sir Guy's words were equally chilling. 'How dare you suggest that our Duke would stoop to such knavery? I know for a fact that Stillington's tale was as shocking to him as to us. It brings into disrepute the good name of his dead brother. Do you think Richard would have allowed such a slander were it untrue and he allowed to quell it? Buckingham faced him with it in open Council so that Duke Richard had no choice but to accept the tale. The truth was out. Why do you think George of Clarence was executed secretly in the Tower? He was given no opportunity to speak to the crowd from the scaffold, mind, as was customary. We all wondered, and now we know the reason for it.'

'Anne will be distressed,' Aleyne murmured. 'Poor soul. She, of all people, was praying that Richard's sojourn would not be long in the capital.'

Margaret was sure of that. If this tale had been concocted between Buckingham and Gloucester it certainly had been kept from the Duchess. Anne's whole life was bound up at Middleham in Wensleydale with her young son. If her husband was to be offered the crown and accepted, it would be a terrible blow to her peace.

A servant entered the hall and Dominick motioned that they should all now remain silent. Sir Guy masterfully took Margaret's arm and led her back to the window-seat he had recently vacated. She looked round desperately for Aleyne but Dominick was ushering his wife from the hall.

Guy said in an urgent whisper, 'It is imperative that you keep a still tongue concerning your opinions. Gloucester is in no mood to be conciliatory.' He still held her arm, keeping her seated as the servants began to prepare the trestle-tables for supper.

She remained stiffly still, having no desire for anyone to witness an undignified struggle. His grip was not hurting her yet she had an overwhelming desire to snatch her arm free. They were much too close in the oriel embrasure. Men watching might think they were lovers stealing some illicit time together. Her face flamed. Nothing could be further from the truth.

She said between her teeth, 'Of course I shall be careful. It would not pay me to be otherwise. To speak openly against the Protector is dangerous in the extreme, as Lord Hastings and Lord Rivers found to their cost.'

'Neither spoke openly but plotted in secret. Both of them might well have known more about the business we have recently been discussing than they cared to impart.' Guy glanced cautiously back towards the door of the Duchess's solar.

Margaret made no answer but Guy's words gave her further food for thought. Had her father been aware of the bastardy of the late King's children when he agreed to support the Marquess of Dorset? If so, he had placed them all in jeopardy by this ruthless bid for power.

Guy said softly, 'I hope you have given some thought to what I said to you the other day.'

She turned the direct gaze of her dark eyes on him. 'I consider your conduct beneath contempt,' she said without obvious heat, so that no one could guess that their conversation was anything but the lightest of

Court gossip. 'My betrothed is Master Bennet Hartwell and soon we shall wed.'

'I think not.' He bent and imprinted a kiss on her upturned palm. Margaret felt the very flesh burn and pulled her hand away.

'You are impertinent, sir. If my father were here to protect me, you would not dare.'

'But he is not,' he replied equably. 'If he were as concerned about you as you claim, he would be here now to champion you, as would Master Hartwell. In all events I heard the betrothal was not celebrated.'

'It was delayed. It *will* take place,' she replied fiercely. 'My father will come. He waits only the best time. . .'

The blue eyes were mocking. 'Do you think I would consider my own skin if you were held against your will?'

Her eyes clouded and she lowered her head. There was no reply to that. He would, she knew instinctively, come to her side if he wished to, though hell should bar the way.

'Excuse me, sir,' she murmured thickly, tears threatening to choke her. She made an ineffectual movement to rise and he stood up at once and made to escort her to her chamber.

She walked, spine erect, refusing to meet his gaze, but at her door he checked her again, a gentle hand, this time, on her arm.

'You must trust me, Margaret. I will let no harm come to you; believe me in that at least.'

'I do, sir, but I cannot give you the hope that I would ever consent to our—our union, not even,' she said huskily, 'if Gloucester, as king, should command it.'

'Then you know he will be our king.'

She bowed her head again. 'Yes. The Council will not wish to place the safety of the realm in young Edward of Warwick's hands. Duke Richard is a soldier, experienced in warfare and in ruling. There will be many relieved that England will be in his care.'

'But you will not?'

'I did not say that,' she said uncertainly, 'but there will be others, and many of the common people, who will distrust this testimony of the Bishop. They will say it is a ruse to steal his nephews' heritage and many will fear him.'

'He knows that,' Guy said quietly, 'but he will do what he must.'

'As *I* must. My loyalty must go to my father and I will hold out against any coercion to do what he would condemn.'

Guy's lips thinned and his eyes narrowed in thought.

'I understand that. There will come a time when you will accept the Duke's will because you will know then that it is the right course for you—aye, and for your father too.'

He bowed courteously and stood back as she made to enter her chamber.

The following day, June the twenty-second, Margaret heard that Friar Ralph Shea, brother of the Mayor of London, preached a sermon at St Paul's Cross, taking as his text 'Bastard slips shall not take root'. He spoke of the Protector's many qualities and reminded the crowd that, of all the late Duke of York's sons, Richard of Gloucester was the only one to have been born within the realm, at Fotheringhay. He revealed the story of the late King's bigamous marriage and explained that the children of this illicit union must be set aside in the succession, urging that, since the Duke of Clarence's heirs and properties had been placed under attainder, the Duke of Gloucester must now be considered the rightful heir to his brother. Margaret knew that Gloucester had ridden out to the Cross attended by his friends and several Yorkist supporters. She surmised that Guy must have been in the company. The Duke had appeared pale and grave-featured when she had seen him at mass and she wondered what his innermost feelings were. The Duchess's reddened eyelids showed signs of her extreme disquiet at the way events had shaped themselves. What were Guy's convictions? Did he, in his heart, distrust the motives of the master he had served since boyhood? Margaret found herself deeply troubled for him. Despite everything, she knew Guy Jarvis to be an honourable knight and his loyalties would be stretched to breaking-point if any doubts were to surface.

That very evening Gloucester commanded her presence within a small room which constituted his study and where his secretary worked upon his correspondence. She found Guy present and even as she curtsied low before the Duke there came a light tap upon the door and the Duchess entered.

'You wanted me, Richard?' She glanced enquiringly at Margaret.

'I did. Considering what I was about to say to Mistress Rushton, I thought she should have someone of her own sex present, someone whose counsel she could trust.'

Margaret stiffened, but Anne of Gloucester, looking somewhat troubled, took her seat on a chair by her husband's side. Margaret remained standing facing him, her fingers resting lightly on the edge of his desk for support. Guy stood, ramrod-straight, some paces from the Duke's chair. One hand played absently with his sword-hilt while he regarded Margaret steadily with that piercing blue gaze.

The Duke turned briefly towards him then back to Margaret.

'Your father has decided not to come to your assistance, Mistress Margaret, and these are trying times. Sir Guy has requested that I give him permission to wed you. Since you were formally betrothed, I see no objection to the banns being called immediately, signifying intent to marry within the next few weeks.'

She had expected it but still felt her knees threaten to give way beneath her and caught at the hard wood of the desk to remain upright. The Duchess gave a little concerned intake of breath and half rose as if to give her support.

Margaret said more harshly than she meant, 'You cannot give me into the hands of a husband, sir. I am not a ward of the court and my father still lives.'

'And I think you will wish him to continue to do so,' the Duke replied suavely.

The tone was bland but Margaret sensed there was a hardness of purpose in contrast with his former mocking sparring with her. He was England's future king and he knew his power. Even were her father to come forward now, and this calling of the banns openly was an invitation to him to surrender himself if he had his daughter's best interests at heart, would he dare to defy his sovereign? She felt trapped. Avoiding Sir Guy's eyes, she strove to speak again, her traitorous tongue cleaving to the roof of her mouth. Determinedly she forced speech.

'Sir, I am promised. . .'

'But not officially. There can be no need of a dispensation. That need not delay us. Sir Guy was once considered a suitable husband, therefore your father could have no real objection to my choice. It will please me, Mistress, if you will give your consent. Sir Guy has given me true service and will not lose by his continued loyalty to me. He asks no dowry but I will see to it that you do not go to the altar empty-handed, whatever fate befalls your father.'

Margaret blenched at the implied threat. Her father could still be proclaimed traitor and his estates sequestered. Once she was married to Sir Guy Jarvis, it might be within her passionate persuasion to save her father from the direst consequences of his actions. She swallowed any further pleas. Tears were pricking her lashes but she fought them back and curtsied low.

'I am sure Your Grace has my well-being at heart,' she murmured, refraining from voicing her consent but forbearing to give offence by further outright refusal to accede to Gloucester's wish.

Anne said quietly, 'Sir Guy has been in our service at Middleham for many years, Margaret. I have always known him to be honourable and true. I am sure he will make you a strong and considerate husband.'

Guy had said nothing throughout the interview, clearly leaving his Duke to present his case. Only now did Margaret find herself looking full at him as if to challenge this 'honourable' man to refrain from pressing her to a consent so abhorrent to her own desire, but he inclined his chin very slightly, the clear gaze of his blue eyes never wavering.

'I swear I will defend Mistress Margaret with my life if necessary and be to her a true and gentle husband,' he returned woodenly as the Duchess smiled in his direction.

Margaret was by no means certain she could rely upon his promise to be gentle if she proved obdurate, but she could see there would be no point in crossing swords with him now. Gloucester was determined. Guy was his vassal and he would need the support of all his friends in this bid for supreme power. If Guy wanted Margaret, why then he should have her, with the blessing of his sovereign.

Margaret curtsied again, her head lowered to hide the glint of the further onrush of tears, and whispered a plea to be excused.

'Certainly, my dear,' Gloucester said expansively. 'The Lady Anne will excuse you from attendance, I'm sure, while you go in search of Aleyne and discuss with her arrangements for your wedding-gown.' He waved his hand in dismissal and Margaret stumbled from the room, to lean against the closed door, one hand held against her heart as if she could steady its rapid beat by the very pressure of her fingers.

She recovered quickly and natural anger returned. Talk of her wedding-gown indeed! Arrangements for the actual ceremony would be decided by Gloucester and Guy. She would be allowed no part in that. How dared they treat her so? She had accepted her father's choice because she knew it was required of her but this interference by another, no matter how royal, infuriated her. Lady Anne had not intervened; of course not. She would support her husband in his decisions, even in this most vital one of acceptance of the Crown, and she knew and liked Guy Jarvis. She could not be expected to recognise Margaret's dire need. Slowly she went up to her chamber, silencing Jonnet's wish to question her with an upraised hand. The girl was clearly very upset by her mistress's appearance. Margaret was composed now, marks of her tears gone, but she was still trembling and her face was unnaturally pale.

'Will you find Lady Allard, Jonnet, and ask her to come to my chamber? Tell her my need is urgent.'

'Yes, mistress.' The girl scurried hastily by her and down the stair. Margaret moved to the window and stared down over the bustling scene below. Days ago this clamour and confusion had been strange to her; now it seemed that she had always lived here in this tension-ridden city.

Aleyne arrived very quickly and came to Margaret's side. 'What is it? The Duchess was dispatching me when Jonnet arrived and begged me to come. You haven't received bad news? Your father. . .'

Margaret uttered a jarring laugh. 'My father is safe and well as far as I am aware. The ill news is that Gloucester has commanded me to wed Guy Jarvis as I feared he would. He gives me little time but orders the banns to be read immediately.'

Aleyne pulled her friend down on the bed.

'What did you say?'

'What could I say? I protested, said I was promised to Bennet, but, since vows between us were not said before a priest, the understanding does not count. The Duke prefers, for his own purposes, to believe that our old, former betrothal still exists, ignores the dispensation which was obtained by the Bishop of Salisbury.'

Aleyne was silent for a moment. 'You said, the other day, that you could never bring yourself to wed Guy Jarvis. Why? He is presentable, and many would envy you, he is so handsome, honourable. . .'

'Everyone is anxious to assure me that he is honourable,' Margaret stormed. 'If he is so honourable why does he not refrain from pressing a maid who is so clearly unwilling for the match?'

'But you know so little about Hartwell. You confessed you held no deep feeling for him.' Aleyne's golden-brown eyes were troubled. 'I know how you feel. I was myself pressed into a match, coincidentally by Gloucester. Oh, it was the late King who commanded the marriage, but at Gloucester's request, I'm convinced.'

'Were you not very angry?'

Aleyne sighed. 'Very,' she admitted, 'but I was already being pressured by another man whom I detested and. . .'

'And?'

'I learned to love Dominick. It is the lot of all women to be given in marriage without their consent, Margaret.'

'Yes, but by their fathers. Mine would vehemently oppose this arrangement. Do not tell me he should come and do so openly. You know he would be immediately arrested. If I allow Gloucester to force me into this, I play into his hands. My father will lose either way unless. . .'

Aleyne's apprehension was growing now as she eyed the deepening determination in her friend's expression.

'You are planning escape? Margaret, you must not. Don't you know how angry Gloucester would be? And he will shortly be our king, make no mistake about that.'

'I am convinced of that,' Margaret said bitterly. 'My only hope is to reach my father and wed Bennet Hartwell before I can be recaptured and forced to the altar with my persistent gaoler.'

'Even if you could leave Crosby unseen, how would you find your father?'

Margaret hesitated. Could she trust even Aleyne, who had proved herself a generous companion since her arrival in London? But Aleyne adored her husband who was pledged to Gloucester's service and Guy's greatest friend.

'I know where he can be reached,' she confessed finally, and Aleyne gave a gasp of surprise.

'But how. . .?'

'Bennet Hartwell came to my side during the confusion near the Cross the day Jane Shore made her penance. He told me where my father was hidden.'

'Ah, so that is why you were separated from the rest of us.'

Margaret nodded. 'I'm sorry, Aleyne, I would have confided in you but I was afraid. . .'

'Naturally you were,' Aleyne returned drily. 'I would have done the same thing in your place. Do not tell me now. No,' she added, putting light fingers across her friend's lips, 'it is unwise to reveal it. Later, if ill comes to your father, you might believe, with good reason, that I betrayed you.'

'But you would not?'

'Not purposely, no. Good, you know where he is, then, and can reach him, if we can get you out of Crosby without being observed. The Duke will leave tonight to join his mother at Baynards Castle. It is likely both Dominick and Guy will be in attendance, considering the importance of the next few days' activities, but we must remember that the Duchess will want us near her.'

'She will watch me closely,' Margaret said fretfully. 'She was present, knows my opposition to the match.'

'She is gentle and understanding but loyal in all things to Richard,' Aleyne mused, 'and by no means so ineffectual as one might suppose by observing her open admiration for Richard. She is as strong-willed as I am and that is saying something,' she added with a half-laugh. 'The place crawls with self-seekers and spies. We must make no sudden moves. There is still time to escape your fate, Margaret Rushton, but you must be patient tonight. Do not dispatch your maid to your father. She will undoubtedly be followed. At supper appear composed but upset—that will be expected—and try to avoid Guy. There must be no quarrel observed.'

'You will not speak of this to Sir Dominick?'

Aleyne made a comical grimace. 'Sweet Virgin, no. He will support Guy and in no way oppose Gloucester's will. Trust me, child. Sleep as best you may. Tomorrow I will think of some way of getting you out of the house.' She gave another heavy sigh. 'The men will be well occupied. I wish to God King Edward still lived and we could hope to ride north within the foreseeable future.'

Margaret glanced at her quickly. Here was yet another wife who had no pretensions to high office for her spouse.

She slept only fitfully, desperately seeking some way out of her dilemma. As Aleyne had warned, if she alerted her father to her plight, he could be discovered and immediately arrested, but were she to wait until the banns were said her father would then be forced into a decision either to rescue her or abandon her. She would not be the tool in Gloucester's ploy to bring him into the net, but how could she avoid the constant watch of Anne of Gloucester, who would be unwilling to allow her from her sight?

As she expected, she was summoned very early to attend the Duchess. Anne's own favourite ladies usually prepared her for the day and Margaret was surprised to find Her Grace still undressed. As she entered and curtsied, Aleyne followed her in.

Anne thrust herself up against her pillows and beckoned for the two to approach the bed.

'Richard is with his mother at Baynards this morning,' she announced crisply, 'so we must devise a way to get Margaret clear of the house.'

Margaret stared at her dumbfounded until Aleyne gave a little delighted laugh and clapped her hands.

'Then, Your Grace, you will not stand in the way of any attempt we make for Margaret's escape?'

Anne thrust an impatient hand through her curling fair hair which fell, free and lovely, to her shoulders.

'Aleyne, have your forgoten how necessary it was for someone to have a care for *my* future? I felt just as trapped as Margaret does now. Both of us know how terrible this is for her. Though both of us have discovered great joy in the men whom we were, in the end, forced to marry, that may not happen in Margaret's case. Guy is a good man, and I applaud Richard's assessment of his character, but Margaret must have her choice. I considered trying to change Richard's mind but decided against it. He is Plantagenet and most royal at times—' she dimpled happily '—and I love him in his stubborn moods as much as in his kindly ones, but were he to know I am on Margaret's side in this I should have no opportunity to be of help now.'

She drew Margaret down to sit upon the side of the bed. 'Can you see any way out of this? Is there anywhere you could go for a while—not to your manor, alas, but somewhere where you could stay safely hidden? The Duke will soon be engaged in weightier matters——' she gave a heavy sigh '—and will have little time to speculate about your whereabouts. He may be angry for a while, but it is never his way to make war upon women and he will forgive you eventually.'

Margaret exchanged a wary glance with Aleyne and, on her nod, told the Duchess of her need to reach her father in the South Wark. Anne considered for a moment, then nodded.

'Then we must get you close to the bridge. If you were to accompany me, then no member of the household guard will dare to stop or hinder you. You will take your maid——No, that might not be wise. It would suggest you did not intend to return to Crosby. She must go separately, but with an escort. No woman is safe alone in these troubled times. Is there a man you could trust or bribe to do that without betraying you?'

Margaret nodded vigorously and blushed. 'Jonnet has a suitor, Will Grimshaw, in Sir Guy's company, but he may be in attendance upon Sir Guy at Baynards.'

Anne grimaced. 'In Guy's company? The man could find himself in grave danger of severe retribution if he is discovered to have broken his captain's trust. He will have to love your little maid a great deal to dare to risk himself so.'

'I belive he does,' Margaret said quietly. 'I think he will be prepared to forsake that service and join my father's household but. . .'

'Does Sir John intend to leave England?'

'Your Grace, I know nothing of my father's intentions, but I do not think he plots treason. He supported My Lord Marquess of Dorset before there was any question of disloyalty to the Crown and has become embroiled in this quest for power. . .' Her voice trailed off miserably as she thought how her words could be judged insulting to Gloucester's ambitions.

The Duchess looked at her intently and gave a little inclination of her chin. 'My dear, we women find ourselves so often caught up in these machinations without knowing how they can happen. I was scarcely more than a child when my own father decided to use me as a pawn in his bid to make himself kingmaker. I was betrothed to a young man whom I loathed and who terrified me. I have never dared to confess fully my fears of Edward of Lancaster, and my desperation, to my husband, then another, who I thought was bound to me by ties of family—sisterhood—stood by while her husband. . . sought to have me murdered.' She spoke steadily through her teeth but Margaret glimpsed a tear pricking her lashes. She shook off her morbid remembrances of Clarence and her sister, Isabel, both in their tombs now in Tewkesbury Abbey, and returned to the problem in hand. 'I will do my best to plead your cause with Richard when I think the time is right, but now I will try to help you reach your father. Aleyne, you had best help to dress me, otherwise my other women will be suspicious.'

The two robed the Duchess and arranged her hennin and veil so that she was ready to hear mass in the small room used as a private chapel. While they were occupied Anne revealed her plan.

'I shall visit my nephews in the Tower and make the journey in my chariot. You, Margaret, will ride inside with me and Aleyne. When we alight at the Tower you will don a dark cloak, wait in the carriage for a moment while I hold the sergeant of my escort in talk, then you can slip out and cross the bridge.' She bit her nether lip uncertainly. 'It is certain the men will be watchful but I must try to find some slight ruse to keep them occupied till you are clear. It is not the best of plans but it will have to serve.'

Aleyne said doubtfully, 'Will Scroggins is in charge of escort duty today and he is no fool, Your Grace. Margaret will be missed within the Tower and certainly by the time we return to the chariot. Scroggins will immediately inform Sir Guy and, possibly, the Duke of her escape and—' she hesitated '—I fear you could be questioned, madam, and accused of complicity.'

'True,' Anne mused. 'Also it is hot for the wearing of hooded cloaks. Well, then, Margaret must be hidden within the chariot before we begin the journey, preferably dressed in her maid's clothing. That way she will not excite notice when walking alone from the Tower.'

Margaret's thoughts raced hopefully. 'If Will Grimshaw is here at Crosby, he could possibly smuggle me unseen into the chariot while it is being prepared for Your Grace. Perhaps I could then hide on the floor near your feet, unnoticed by the men of your escort. I would not be missed then at the close of the visit.'

Aleyne's eyes revealed her eagerness to begin to put into practice their plan. 'Your Grace must excuse Margaret from attendance at mass. . . No, better still, you can show dissatisfaction of her service to you so that she will flee to her chamber in disgrace and will therefore not be expected to accompany Your Grace to the Tower. She will be believed to be closeted within her chamber, in fear of your further displeasure, and undisturbed until there is a genuine outcry later in the day when she will be discovered to have absconded.'

'Brilliant,' Anne breathed. 'Aleyne, go and discover, if you can, if this Grimshaw is available. You and I——' she favoured Margaret with the warmest of smiles '—must find some reason for my acute displeasure so that I can dismiss you with a flea in your ear from my presence.'

Aleyne hurried off and Anne paced her chamber, looking round for anything which might give her inspiration. Her eyes finally alighted on her jewel-box and she gestured for Margaret to bring it. Pushing back the velvet-covered lid, she picked her way through necklets and rings, reliquaries and bracelets.

'Here,' she said triumphantly. 'The necklet my Lord Richard bought me for my last birthday. He will be expecting me to wear it on the very next official occasion.'

Margaret watched in horror as the Duchess wrenched hard at the gold fastening until it broke, and winked in her attendant's direction. It was so beautiful, a cabochon-cut ruby, set in an oval of pearls suspended from a very heavy chain.

The Duchess pointed to the bell on her night-table. 'Ring it, Margaret, and try to look suitably chastened.'

'Madam,' Margaret murmured brokenly, 'the Duke's latest gift! It must be very precious to you. . .'

'Of course it is, you goose, and easily repaired, and one over which my ladies will most expect me to repine.'

Two of her older ladies burst into the chamber at the bell's urgent summons to find their mistress in an unaccountable spasm of weeping. It was not Anne's way to rage at her ladies so tears were her best way of assuming distress and anger.

'Look,' she said tragically, holding up the damaged necklet, 'just look what this stupid girl has done. I was wearing it and changed my mind. It caught on my veiling, and could this fool patiently work to undo it? No, she must wrench at it and now it is broken. What will My Lord Richard say? He is sure to notice I am not wearing it at the banquet for the city's dignitaries. Oh, go to your chamber, girl, and stay there until I can find some simple task for you to do, one which will not tax your intelligence.'

Lady Cecily Scrope gazed, astounded, at her usually kindly mistress. Never had she known Anne to be so vituperative. She sighed. All this intrigue and menace in the air was upsetting her mistress, who was anxious, as they all were, to be in her usual comfortable surroundings at Middleham. She waved testily at Margaret who stood uncertainly hovering near the doorway.

'Go on, girl, do as the Duchess commands.' She turned back to the still tearful Anne of Gloucester. 'There, there, my dear. Richard will not be angry. When have I ever known him to be so with you? We will send immediately to the goldsmith in Cannongate and it will be expertly repaired and back in your jewel-case by supper.'

Margaret slipped out of the chamber thankfully. The Duchess's ruse appeared to be serving them well. No one, during the rest of the day, would comment on her absence from Crosby's public rooms. She lowered her head as if tears were threatening and made for the stair. She was about to place her hand on the newel-post when her name was called, and she stopped, uncertain whether to ignore the summons and dash on up to her chamber or turn to acknowledge the speaker. She decided it might be safer to do the latter and turned, her eyes genuinely reddened now, for she was growing more and more excited by the moment, to encounter the smiling, ingenuous gaze of Owen Lewis.

'How good it is to see you again, Mistress Rushton,' he said warmly. 'They told me at the abbey how well you had cared for me after the attack, even bravely stayed in the room while the wound was stitched. I trust you are well, as I am now.'

Margaret's hands were trembling and she was now close to tears of real frustration at this sudden and unaccustomed interruption to their plan. She forced a smile and he noted, ruefully, the marks of her distress.

'Is something wrong, Mistress Rushton? You are not ill or have heard bad news?' He hesitated as if recognising that the possible source of her distress might be the arrest of her father and she was embarrassed by it.

'No, no,' she reassured him. 'I have angered the Duchess and she has dismissed me to my chamber. It is nothing serious. The matter will soon be mended, but naturally I am upset.' She lifted a handkerchief to her eyes. 'The Duchess has been untold kind to me since my arrival in London and I am deeply sorry that my clumsiness has brought me into disgrace. But how are you? Recovered fully? You look very well.'

'Oh, yes,' he smiled. 'The infirmarian pronounced me fit to travel and I arrived at Baynards late last night. I came with Sir Guy to fetch some papers required by the Duke for today's Council meeting at the Tower.'

Margaret stared at him aghast.

'Sir Guy is here, at Crosby?'

Owen nodded, smiling. 'He is with the Duke's secretary now. We must return to the Duke immediately.

I understand the Duchess has ordered her chariot to be prepared to take her to the Tower to visit the late King's sons. Sir Guy will be able to escort her most conveniently.'

Margaret's fingers clawed blindly at the newel-post once more and Owen looked grave. 'Do you feel faint, mistress? I could call your maid.'

She checked him hurriedly. 'No, no, it is nothing. My chamber is very near. I shall go and lie down for a while. This—this business with the Duchess has upset me.' She forced her feet to climb the first two steps and looked down at him gamely.

'You must get back to your master, Owen. He will be impatient of delay. I—I am so glad to see you well again.'

Head down to hide from him her sense of fear and shock, she mounted the stair and reached the refuge of her chamber.

CHAPTER SEVEN

ALEYNE was in Margaret's chamber when she burst through the doorway. Jonnet was already packing garments into a saddle-bag. A fustian gown, Jonnet's best, was laid out on the bed.

'I found that Grimshaw fellow and he has agreed to do all we ask. You must come and change quickly—the Duchess should not delay her departure; that might cause suspicion,' Aleyne said, then stopped and stared at Margaret's shocked face and wide eyes as she moved slowly towards the bed. 'Whatever is it? You've been crying. The Duchess did not slap you too hard, did she? It was a mistake. She would not mean to hurt. It is just not like her.'

Margaret waved away the suggestion. 'No, no, it is nothing to do with the Duchess. It is Guy Jarvis. He is here at Crosby and intends to ride as escort to the Duchess's chariot to the Tower.'

'What?' Aleyne stared at her friend unbelievingly. 'I thought he was at Baynards with Dominick.'

'I've just seen Owen Lewis. Apparently the Duke sent them back to procure some papers he needed for a Council meeting—*at the Tower*.' She emphasised the last words grimly.

Jonnet stared at her mistress open-mouthed, checking in her folding of a cloak. Aleyne sank down on the bed, for the moment totally nonplussed.

'Owen is back from St Albans,' Margaret said evenly,

as if that piece of information could be important, then she added, 'What can we do? We can't proceed now.'

'Will could be discovered and punished,' Jonnet whispered piteously. 'He is in Sir Guy's service and he will not tolerate disloyalty. Will 'as said as much scores of times.'

Margaret watched Aleyne anxiously as if her friend possessed a charm to ward off disaster.

'This could be embarrassing for Lady Anne,' Aleyne said at last, frowning, 'but I do not think she would counsel us to abandon the plan.'

'But I can't,' Margaret said emphatically. 'I couldn't stay hidden in that chariot while he was—so near——' She broke off and shuddered.

'Can you think of a better plan?' Aleyne demanded bluntly. 'Think, Margaret. You have this one chance. Guy may very well decide to put Owen here to watch over you now that he is back on duty and,' she added meaningly, 'at any moment Gloucester will be proclaimed our king. Any act of defiance would be regarded as treason. We have some slight excuse at present if we are caught, but not afterwards. Do you want to reach your father? More than that, do you wish to be given willy-nilly in marriage to Guy? Is this worth the risk?'

Margaret swallowed. 'Yes,' she said very softly, 'but I would not have you and Lady Anne involved, let alone Will and Jonnet here.'

'Will Grimshaw must decide for himself,' Aleyne said briskly. 'I am willing to speak for myself and the Duchess. What about you, girl?' She turned to Jonnet. 'You mustn't be afraid to speak out. Will you risk yourself with your mistress?'

Jonnet turned appealingly to Margaret then, seeing

the torturing doubt in her mistress's face, nodded tremulously.

'I can't see 'as how this changes aught,' she said at last. 'If the mistress be well hidden, Sir Guy'll know no diff'rence. But I should get down to the courtyard and warn Will.'

'Can you find him before he goes out to the vehicle?'

Jonnet made a hurried and clumsy curtsy. 'That I can, my lady, then I can bring him up to lead Mistress Margaret down by the back way. He's already fixed it so the other men-at-arms'll be kept away for a bit.'

'Then you must hurry, Margaret. Go, girl. Have you got what you'll both need?'

'Yes, my lady.' Jonnet snatched up the saddle-bag.

'Good girl. Off with you.'

Aleyne reached up to lift free Margaret's hennin. 'Come on, now. No time for further talk. We must be ready when Grimshaw comes for you.'

Jonnet and Margaret were of approximately the same size. If anything the maid was a trifle plumper than her mistress and the gown hung on Margaret, although not so much that it would excite notice, but Jonnet was considerably shorter, so that the hem was well above Margaret's ankles. Aleyne tugged at the thread which held the hem and thus let the skirt down more than an inch.

'That should serve,' she muttered as she rolled up the thread and made to dispose of it. 'Hide your hair under that white cap. So, you look well enough. There are so many maids dressed like this, you will not be noted in the courtyard. I doubt even Sir Guy would recognise you. After all, he doesn't expect to see you in the Duchess's chariot.'

She lifted her head as there came a cautious knock

on the door and the whisper, 'Mistress Rushton. It's Will Grimshaw. You must come quickly.'

Just for a moment Margaret hesitated. Once before she had been moved to attempt an escape after just such a summons and Owen Lewis had almost been killed. She glanced back hurriedly at Aleyne, who smiled reassuringly.

'All will be well. Even if the worst should happen, no one will blame you for trying. As for the Duchess and me——' she shrugged '—trust us to handle our own menfolk. Before you go, one more thing.' She pressed a small leather purse into Margaret's hands. 'One or two insignificant pieces of jewellery, just in case of dire need.'

Margaret's throat was beginning to close with emotional tears and she flung her arms round her friend's neck.

'I shall never forget you,' she murmured brokenly. 'Tell the Duchess I shall pray for her every day of my life.'

Aleyne tilted up Margaret's chin with a gentle finger. 'She knows that. Now, go with God, my dear. I shall pray you find your happiness as I did mine.'

Margaret stopped only to secure the little purse by a string beneath her skirt then she smiled gamely, pressed back the pricking tears at her lashes, and moved to the door.

Grimshaw hurried her down the rear stairs and out towards the entrance court which opened into Thames Street. He paused in the doorway and gestured her to remain behind him for a few moments while he surveyed the court.

Over his shoulder she whispered, 'Surely there will be men-at-arms round the vehicle.'

He shook his head, not turning. 'Not yet, mistress, I've arranged to keep them occupied for the next few minutes in the buttery.'

She did not enquire how he had managed to accomplish that. Possibly a friend had offered to persuade the men of the escort to take ale before they mounted. That would not prove difficult, but she chafed against the delay, however short. At any moment Sir Guy Jarvis would leave the Duke's study and instantly command the men to line up in readiness for the Duchess's departure.

The chariot was a great, lumbering, unwieldy contraption, open at both sides to the elements but for leather curtains which could be rolled up and secured to the roof. It was once owned by the Duke of Clarence. In Yorkshire the Duchess of Gloucester always rode beside her husband unless either she or her young son, Edward, felt unduly wearied, and travelled between the castles of Middleham and Sheriff Hutton in a horse litter, but the Duke had acquired this vehicle soon after his brother George's death and kept it in case any one of the household at Crosby should have need of it. Margaret wondered what excuse the Duchess had given to require it now, since it would have been simpler to reach the Tower by river barge.

Grimshaw pressed her arm gently. 'Now, mistress. Walk without haste. In these clothes you will not be noticed by any of the grooms.'

The horses had not yet been harnessed and Margaret could hear the men talking and guffawing in the stable. She crossed the court with Grimshaw, outwardly calm, but in a state of emotional turmoil. How could she be hidden in this vehicle which was so open to public view? Fortunately there had been a light drizzle earlier and the Duchess would be able to request the letting down of the curtains. Since the general unrest occasioned by the Jane Shore penance, nobles riding about the city had encountered hostile receptions, so it would not seem strange that the Duchess would not wish to be seen by the citizens at large, at least not yet, until the business of the succession had been finally decided and announced.

A clattering of hooves told them the horses were about to be led out, and Grimshaw impelled Margaret towards the chariot.

'Inside, mistress, right in the corner. Crouch down beside the seat and cover yourself with the fur rug I've put ready.'

She had no time to thank him, no time for second thoughts that she was imperilling all of them. She obeyed him immediately and stepped up into the musty-smelling interior. The vehicle was rarely used and had been so hastily wiped and dusted that dust motes still hovered in the air, and Margaret feared she might sneeze and betray them all, but she identified the rug Grimshaw had mentioned and took her place near the cushioned seat, sitting with her back right up against it, her knees drawn up, sufficiently withdrawn into the shadows for her not to be seen when the Duchess entered with Aleyne. She did not immediately cover her face but put her hand ready on the fur to do so when it became necessary.

She could hear Grimshaw strolling towards the grooms now, and the snorting and movement of the horses as they were led to the traces. She let out a pent-up breath. Now there would be an agonising time of waiting before the party could leave. It was hot and there was little room for her limbs, but she had no intention of dwelling on her bodily discomfort. She must pray that she manage to escape notice and in a matter of hours she would be with her father again—and Bennet Hartwell. She found, surprisingly, that that thought gave her little comfort, though the man had seemed personable enough, and brave to risk arrest when he had brought her her father's message.

The voices of the men came to her and the vehicle moved on its clumsy leather springs as the horses were backed up. Her spine was sorely jolted and she clenched her bottom lip with her teeth. Soon now the Duchess would arrive and with her Guy Jarvis.

Booted feet and ribald comments could be heard emerging from the buttery as the men of the escort began to assemble with their mounts in the courtyard. Margaret tensed again. Was Guy Jarvis even now taking his place with them?

But no, it was some time later before she heard his clear, crisp tones addressed respectfully to the Duchess as he walked with her to the chariot and assisted her into the shaded interior.

'I hope you will not be too uncomfortable, Your Grace. I was assured the vehicle has been thoroughly cleaned.'

Lady Anne glanced round cautiously and, seeing Margaret's crouching form against the far opening, inclined her chin very slightly and took her place, accommodating Margaret's head and shoulders close to her feet. Aleyne scrambled in beside her.

'This is quite pleasant, Sir Guy. I had a fancy to use the chariot this morning. It is too drizzly for the river passage and I wish to make some purchases at the book stalls in St Paul's on the return journey. Will you lower the curtains on my side and partially on Lady Allard's?

I've no wish to be recognised by the crowd this morning.'

Margaret held her breath again as someone moved to her side of the vehicle to do as the Duchess requested. She was able to glimpse fine leather riding boots and judged that Sir Guy had taken this duty on himself.

He moved away. There came a word of command and the men-at-arms mounted, then the chariot began to trundle ponderously towards the archway into Thames Street. Margaret's body quivered slightly and the Duchess bent to touch her lightly on the arm.

'All is well,' she said soothingly. 'Aleyne saw your maid and her man move off with your possessions. They will meet you outside the inn in the South Wark. When we arrive I will call Sir Guy to me again and request that the men escort me right into the Tower precincts. You must choose your opportunity then and get out on the far side and make for the bridge.'

'Your Grace risks your husband's anger for me.'

'What he does not know he cannot complain about,' Anne returned cheerily. 'When you are married, Margaret, you will discover that however much you may come to love your husband there will be matters which you will endeavour to hide from him, some of them quite trivial, of a domestic nature, and others——' She paused, then added, 'Of much greater moment.'

Margaret pondered in the grey dimness about the time Anne Neville had been her father's pawn and quite what her relationship had been with the man she had said earlier she had detested, her first husband, the young Prince Edward of Lancaster. There were some who murmured that the Duchess might well have borne

Edward a child while in hiding during those dark days of 1471. If he suspected so, the Duke had chosen to ignore the possibility. Margaret had seen plenty of evidence that Gloucester truly loved his wife and she him.

It seemed an eternity before their destination was reached, though in reality the distance was quite short. The vehicle jerked to a halt, Aleyne murmured an annoyed comment as she was almost thrown from her seat, and the Duchess turned her face towards the leather curtain on her side. Almost instantly it was rolled up and Guy Jarvis presented himself to hold out a hand in readiness to assist her from the chariot.

As she stepped out Margaret froze into immobility but Guy did not look within. Anne's clear voice came to her, requesting further protection from his men, and his faintly muffled reply as they moved slightly away from the vehicle. Aleyne was assisted down by another of the men and she had only time to whisper a word of encouragement before Margaret was left alone. She waited for a moment, straining her ears for sounds indicating that men might return, but of course there was still the coachman and his assistant. After a few moments she heard the man talking to his fellow and Margaret feared they might move the chariot on so that the horses would be kept on the move. She took her courage in both hands, stretched awkwardly in the confined space, and managed to scramble towards the half-curtained opening and peer out. There was no one her side and she seized her opportunity and slipped from the chariot. It was quite a drop, since no steps had been placed her side, and she was momentarily winded. Biting back a shocked gasp, she straightened up warily and looked about her. She was standing shadowed by the massive bulk of the vehicle and she now saw that the two men had stepped down from the box and were standing talking together near the horses' heads. Cautiously Margaret began to move away but no one turned.

The high outer walls of the Tower with its gigantic gatehouse loomed above her and she gave a shiver of apprehension. She knew well enough that the old castle was a luxuriously appointed palace as well as a prison, but she was glad she was not to enter. The ancient fortification would have oppressed her spirits, and she wondered how the late King's sons felt now that they were sheltered behind its stout walls. Did they see themselves as prisoners—or honoured guests?

The river ran slow and oily grey, and she hurried along now to reach a more busy thoroughfare where urchins, apprentices, merchants in furred robes and grey-clad friars mingled. She was relieved to see that women clad as she was—servants, inn wenches and wives of craftsmen—walked freely seemingly without the need for escorts. No one appeared to notice her and she joined the great crush of people wishing to cross the bridge to the South Wark. Here her progress was delayed by a press of horsemen and carts whose passage was, of necessity, slow, for the bridge was narrow, shops and houses along its width towering above the wayfarers and appearing to shut out the light. She wrinkled her nose against the variety of stinks that assailed her nostrils from the closeness of humanity and the many and varied contents of the carts. Some farm vehicles were returning home from the city markets carrying the remains of rotting vegetables and rancid butter and cheese that had stood over-long in the earlier heat.

She was across now and, for the first time, allowed herself the luxury of feeling safe. Surely Jonnet and Will would soon be able to join her. She had heard talk in Crosby Place that the South Wark was the haunt of pimps and prostitutes. Here the men of the great sprawling city on the north bank came for their nightly entertainments in the taverns and brothels. Already she could see that many of the buildings appeared seedy and in need of repair, though others, more gaudily painted, robustly proclaimed their attractions from the swinging signs. She peered anxiously for one which depicted a Saracen warrior and was gratified to discover that the inn she sought was near the waterfront and one of the less dilapidated buildings.

All the buildings in this vicinity looked sleepily deserted and Margaret judged that they came to life during the evening hours, their denizens taking their opportunities to rest after the activities of the previous evening's debaucheries. She hoped fervently that her father would be at home. A lone woman would feel vulnerable indeed without a stout protector. Her mind flew to the occasion when Guy Jarvis had come to her aid near St Paul's Cross and she wondered how long it would be before he discovered that his prey had flown.

In her own village she would have walked boldly into the inn and demanded service but here she thought it more prudent to knock and await instructions.

It was some time before a woman with tousled hair answered her knock and stared at her truculently.

'We're not open for business yet,' she said rudely, then her eyes opened wide at sight of Margaret's neatly attired form and prim white cap. 'And I can't think what you'd be doing 'ere if we were. Be off with you, wench. This is no place for the likes of you.'

Margaret refrained from replying in similar vein and telling this harridan just what she thought of her. If her father was staying here she would not wish to antagonise the household servants.

'I was told Sir John Rushton was staying here for a while,' she said coldly but politely. 'Would you inform him that his daughter is here and needs to see him urgently?'

The woman gave a gasp of surprise. Her eyes narrowed as she peered again at Margaret's shabby but discreet gentility, then she snorted.

'You'd best come in, then, 'adn't you,' she said reluctantly, adding belatedly, almost as an insult, 'mistress?'

The place stank of stale ale. The rushes on the floor of the tap-room had lain for weeks, possibly months. Unwashed tankards and wooden platters littered the stained tables and Margaret frowned her distaste. How could her father stand living in this frowsty inn? At home he would have stormed at servants—aye, and even cuffed one who had dared to leave kitchen or solar in this state. Disdainfully she followed the woman up the rickety stair, drawing her skirts aside to avoid contact with the filthy and grease-stained woodwork.

The woman knocked politely enough at the chamber door on the landing and there was a slight wait until the door was opened by Bennet Hartwell. He was clad in dark worsted hose, riding boots and stout leather jack as if ready for travel or recently returned from a journey. Like the inn wench, he started at sight of Margaret and, before the woman could explain, he stepped out on to the landing to take her hand in his.

'Mistress Margaret.' He glanced hurriedly down the stair as if he feared she might have been followed by some enemy. 'We—that is I—had not expected you so soon. Come in, please.'

He drew her into the chamber and firmly closed the door against the obvious attempt of the inn wench to see or hear what might transpire between him and his visitor. Once inside he bolted it firmly and drew Margaret to a joint-stool near the table. Some attempt had been made here to clean the place and Margaret saw that, though stained and dented by knives, the surface of the table had been wiped down and the dishes apparently collected for there was no evidence here of the untidy disorder below. She looked anxiously round for her father.

Bennet made no comment on her dress but poured her wine from a jug, wiping the rim of the tankard carefully before proffering it.

'He's not here,' he said in explanation. 'I was to join him at Blackheath this very night. It was as well you caught me when you did.'

'Blackheath?' she echoed blankly.

'Your father has gone to meet with a messenger from the Marquess of Dorset. He's on his way to Canterbury. I was to have accompanied him but something delayed me.'

Margaret drank thankfully and looked up to see him eyeing her gravely.

'Is something wrong, Mistress Margaret? You have not been ill-used or offered insult? Why did you come here before we sent for you?'

'Is my father on his way to France?' she enquired evasively. 'Why did he leave me here in London? Surely——'

'No, no,' he interrupted. 'He will be returning within

a few days. He merely acts as a courier. He would not have left you to your fate.'

She gave a relieved sigh. 'Surely he would be safer in France, and you too?'

He nodded regretfully. 'Very true. Our usefulness here will soon be concluded and it is just as well you are free now to come with us. I cannot leave you here in this place.' He sniffed, then reddened as if his meaning might not be quite clear to her and would need explanation.

She smiled her reassurance. 'No, I understand, but when must we leave? I arranged to meet my maid and one of Sir Guy's men here. There is no need for alarm. The man loves Jonnet and will come with us.'

'A couple of hours, but we can wait longer. Sir Guy? You mean Jarvis, Gloucester's captain?'

'Yes. He is escorting the Duchess to the Tower. She helped me to get free of Crosby hidden in her chariot. I will explain more fully to my father why I needed to leave urgently but. . .' She hesitated then plunged on. 'Gloucester intended to marry me to Sir Guy Jarvis. The banns have already been called.'

Hartwell muttered a soldier's oath beneath his breath, then just as quickly apologised.

'Dear God, naturally you were desperate. You will be safe enough with me.' He lifted her limp hand to his lips. 'You must be tired and hot, hidden in that chariot. You must lie and rest on my pallet.' As her eyebrows rose anxiously he waved his hand reassuringly. 'I will go below and see to it that that wench sets about preparing a meal for all of us. You will not be disturbed. I'll see to it.'

He drew her to a curtained alcove where there was a pallet bed covered in coarse sheets and home-spun blankets. 'It's tolerably clean. I found it necessary to kick the innkeeper's behind before he obliged us, but he's well-paid both by us and—others. We're safe here from prying neighbours. Men here keep their own counsel. Rest now. I'll knock when the meal is ready or that maid of yours arrives.'

She looked up at him in shy gratitude. He was solicitous of her comfort, this man her father had chosen. She did not know him well, but in their short acquaintance he had shown her a grave courtesy. She told herself she would be fortunate when they were safely wed and Gloucester helpless to intervene. She would be safe from Guy Jarvis with his cold blue stare which was so intimidating and the meaningful glitter which warned her to beware of retribution for her past treatment of him. Again she gave that odd litle shiver in the frowsty warmth of this stark inn room, telling herself that he could not touch her now. Within hours Bennet would take her to her father and soon they would all be safe beyond the reach of Gloucester's minions.

Guy Jarvis was utterly amazed when Gloucester summoned him to his chamber at Baynards next evening, and even more startled when he saw that the Duke was preparing to ride out. The Duke of Buckingham had only that morning addressed London's principal citizens at the Guildhall, urging Richard of Gloucester's suitability and right to the throne of England following the unfortunate discovery of the bastardy of his nephews. Since it was likely that Richard would shortly be visited by those very dignitaries, it seemed necessary that they should be received at the Yorkist stronghold of

Baynards rather than the luxurious but somewhat cramped conditions of Crosby Place.

'Ah, Guy, I'm glad the page found you quickly. I want you to ride with me to Crosby immediately.'

'Sir?' Guy obviously looked blank and the Duke brusquely explained.

'I have just received a message that Mistress Margaret Rushton is missing from Crosby and I felt you should be the one to investigate the matter with me.'

'Missing? My betrothed? But how, Your Grace? Surely she was under surveillance the whole of the time? Often she was in attendance upon the Duchess and then Lady Allard has formed a strong friendship with her and——'

'Aleyne Allard, just so,' the Duke said grimly. 'Dominick is the one who informed me and I believe he suspects Aleyne is involved.'

Guy blinked rapidly. Aleyne had ever been his friend. She could not have done him so grave a disservice as to help the escape of his betrothed. The Duke was pulling on riding gloves and regarded him thoughtfully.

'Women are queer cattle, Guy. Aleyne is your friend, make no mistake about that, but she has formed a strong attachment to Margaret Rushton—as has my wife.' His grey eyes held Guy's steadily.

The captain's blue eyes were widening further. 'The Duchess?'

'I cannot be sure—yet, but I have grave doubts. It seems the girl has been missing since yesterday afternoon. There was some trifling problem, a broken jewel-clasp or some such gewgaw. Anne was furious with her and dismissed her to her chamber. I'm told she fled in tears. Now that astounds me. It is unlike Anne to be so cruel to an attendant. Afterwards, apparently, Aleyne attended Anne when she visited young Edward and Richard in the Tower. They travelled in the chariot—another unusual feature to this affair. Since then Margaret Rushton has not been seen and both ladies hold to it and stoutly that they were not surprised since Margaret had seemed so distressed by Anne's sharp reprimand.'

'Then Your Grace suspects the three concocted this plot to. . .' He choked on his anger. It would not do to utter any adverse comment on the behaviour of his patron's Duchess, but Richard eyed him sardonically and saved him the embarrassment.

'It was foolish of them in the extreme. I ride to Crosby now to get to the bottom of it. If Margaret Rushton has tried to find her father I fear she has put herself in grave danger.'

Guy's anger changed to a deadly fear. 'Danger, Your Grace? I confess I can see no reason to fear that——'

'Two days ago I was informed of a meeting between one of Morton's creatures and one Bennet Hartwell at some tavern on the south bank. Shorly afterwards Hartwell returned to his lodging at the Saracen near by and an older man, Rushton, no doubt, left with an unnamed serving man for the south. It was my informant's opinion that messages were being conveyed to Dorset or another malcontent. The riders were making for the Canterbury road and were probably *en route* to Dover. If Rushton is seriously involved now in definite treason it would be unfortunate, to say the least, if Mistress Margaret were to be found in his company. Matters could go hard with them both. She must be found and returned to my keeping. I think it necessary for you to follow and try to apprehend her. But first we'll discover what we can at Crosby. One or other of the women should be able to tell us more, I imagine.'

Guy's thoughts were racing. 'She was not alone! If she ventured into that vile hotbed of debauchery she might not survive to join her father.'

'The same thought has occurred to me. It should have occurred to her fellow conspirators, but women think along different lines. Both would see only the necessity of helping one of their number who was seemingly oppressed and forced into an unwelcome match.'

Guy's eyes blazed blue fire and Gloucester put a gentle hand on his arm.

'I know, Guy,' he said quietly. 'I understand how deep your feelings run for Mistress Margaret. I would not have entrusted her to you else, but now we must act quickly and keep cool heads, for her sake.'

Aleyne was pale but composed when she stood before Richard of Gloucester in his private study. Her husband stood at her elbow, his face grim.

Richard said quietly, 'You do Margaret Rushton no good service by refusing to say anything you might know of this.'

For a moment Aleyne's golden-brown eyes flashed up at him and her brow furrowed doubtfully, but she shook her head, her mouth compressing firmly. 'I'm sorry, Your Grace, but I cannot help you.'

Guy's breath escaped in a little angry hiss, then he forced himself to remain calm as the Duchess of Gloucester entered the study and moved to stand beside Aleyne.

'They told me you were angry with Aleyne, Richard. I came to give my support,' she said steadily.

Guy thought sourly that she had not made it plain to whom she was anxious to offer support. He stole a hasty glance at Duke Richard's expression, and an inclination of the chin appeared to be the permission he sought.

'My lady—Aleyne,' he said pleadingly, 'the Duke has explained to me that Margaret could be in grave danger. Please, I was always your friend and helped you whenever I could.' He hesitated then pressed on, avoiding Dominick Allard's gaze. 'Even when it might have placed me under Sir Dominick's displeasure and brought harsh punishment. I love Margaret Rushton with all my heart. I must know where she has gone so that I can do everything in my power to save her from harm.'

Aleyne's lip trembled, but before she could answer, the Duchess put in bravely, her chin uplifted to face her husband's wrath, 'I am to blame, Richard. I had not known—realised——' she turned thoughtfully to Guy '—just how matters stood. I thought this match was one of convenience to you and Guy only. Margaret was so distressed and you know I have experienced something of such sorrow and fear myself. We wanted only to help her. I could not know it would put her in danger to join her father——'

'Where is her father?' Richard demanded impatiently.

Aleyne said softly, 'She met with her betrothed in the crowd when Jane Shore. . .'

'Hartwell?'

'Yes. He told her to bide her time and, it seemed, did not appear anxious for her escape from surveillance then.'

'No, he would not,' Richard murmured beneath his

breath. 'He had matters in hand of a more pressing and dangerous nature. Go on.' He waved to Aleyne to continue.

'He told her that her father was staying at the Saracen inn in the South Wark and that they would send her further word. When—when she found herself in the desperate situation of avoiding—' Aleyne moistened dry lips and moved a trifle from her infuriated husband's side '—avoiding an enforced match—she seemed afraid of Guy here—and we thought—we thought. . .'

'I made the decision to help her,' Anne finished. 'We conveyed her, dressed in her maid's clothes, to the Tower, concealed in the chariot.'

'But I was escorting. . .' Guy's fury choked back further words.

'Yes, Guy. I—I kept you dancing attendance on me to give Margaret opportunity to climb from the chariot and reach the bridge. Since I heard nothing of her recapture I assumed she was sucessful in finding her father. But,' she appealed to her husband, 'surely he means her no harm?'

'Hartwell is involved in treasonous correspondence. There is no doubt of it. My spies were having him watched and were waiting for him to approach his accomplices before arresting him. Now, it seems, he has persuaded Margaret's father to do the dirty and dangerous work for him. Rushton was not at the inn, I know that. Margaret must be in Hartwell's hands and frankly I am concerned for her. The man is unscrupulous and could use her as a bargaining counter.'

'As *you* did,' Anne said baldly.

'As I did,' he agreed, facing the issue squarely. 'But, knowing the situation, I was sure she would be happier as Guy's wife. I still am so convinced,' he insisted as

Anne's blue eyes brimmed with tears and she put out a hand to him, which he squeezed gently. 'Now, now, both of you meant the girl well, I understand that.' He sighed faintly. 'She will have had well over a day's start, Guy. I could have done with you by my side tomorrow, but this is a more pressing need. Take Scroggins and a small troop. Bring her back, lad, as quickly as you can. Put Hartwell under arrest and see to it that Rushton is brought here under guard and is allowed to speak with no one before I have seen him.'

Guy bowed and left the chamber. Outside he found Owen Lewis anxiously waiting for news.

'Find Scroggins for me and tell him to bring four of his most reliable men. I intend to ride south immediately. See to it that I have a good horse ready, lad.'

Owen hesitated only a moment, then, seeing his master's frown of annoyance, said hurriedly, 'They say Mistress Rushton may be in some danger, sir. I take it you are going to search for her. Allow me to go with you.'

Guy's frown deepened. 'Are you sure you are well enough recovered for hard riding? I cannot be delayed, Owen.'

'I'm perfectly fit, sir, I swear it. I would not endanger Mistress Rushton, not after the kindness she showed me.'

'Right, then get yourself ready at once.'

Guy was about to pull on his gloves when Aleyne emerged from the Duke's study. She was so intent on catching him that she almost stumbled over the fashionably long hem of her gown, normally held high to the waist when walking.

'Guy?'

He turned and bowed, though it was clear that he was displeased by the delay. 'Lady Allard?'

'Was it true what you said in there—that you love Margaret?'

His fair skin flushed darkly and he half turned away.

'I am——' he sought for words '—responsible for Mistress Rushton. I have developed some—natural feeling for her. It seemed probable that both you and the Duchess would be more likely to give me more information about her whereabouts if you believed my motive in pursuing her was——'

'Stop hedging,' Aleyne said sharply. 'Do you truly love her?'

He was facing her now and his blue eyes were clouded with doubt. 'I want her,' he said bluntly. 'She was promised to me and I'll have no man taking her from me.'

Aleyne's eyes snapped with impatience. 'That is not what I asked. It is important that I know, Guy. I have become very fond of Margaret.'

He drew a hard breath. 'I don't know if what I feel is love,' he confessed. 'I thought, in the past, she was arrogant and spoilt, but when Owen was attacked I saw what compassion she had for him, and courage too. Few women could have endured to remain while the infirmarian stitched up the wound. I felt queasy myself. And on that day of the riot she showed no panic. I admire strength of purpose in women. I have seen and loved that in you, my lady, but I fear Margaret holds nothing but contempt for me. The fact that I was forced to act as her gaoler has not helped.'

Aleyne nodded thoughtfully, mouth pursed. 'She may well come to thank the Virgin for your help if what the Duke surmises about Hartwell is true. Be gentle with her, Guy. Whatever happens she will be fearful, both for her own happiness and her father's survival.'

He stooped and kissed her hand. 'Be assured, my lady, I will find and bring Margaret back safely and I promise that I will treat her with the respect due to her.'

Aleyne opened her lips as if to offer further advice, then thought better of it, nodded and watched him stride off to the courtyard. Her brow was still creased with concern.

CHAPTER EIGHT

MARGARET stared in wonder at the magnificent jewelled shrine to St Thomas à Becket in the great cathedral of Canterbury. Behind her Jonnet stirred restlessly. Margaret was afraid that the morning's sightseeing had wearied her maid. Even the glitter of gold and the gleam of the priceless jewels adorning the saint's tomb failed to keep her attention. Together they had walked about the lovely city which had been the destination of pilgrims from all over England and Europe for almost three centuries. Like Jonnet, Margaret chafed to return to the inn where her father and Bennet Hartwell were, even now, meeting their contact from France. John Rushton had been determined that his daughter should not even see the man sent by Thomas of Dorset to meet them. Margaret must be kept from this dangerous intrigue which he himself had only agreed to reluctantly. He dispatched her with her maid and Will Grimshaw in attendance to see the cathedral and buy trinkets from the market if she so desired. Margaret felt no wish even to visit the market. Her thoughts were far too troubled to find relief in the feminine pursuit of buying trumpery objects for pleasure.

Her mind went back to the moment, two days ago, when she had first set eyes on her father after their long parting. It should have been a joyous occasion, and he'd greeted her with pleasure, but she'd been aware that there was a reserve in his manner which she had failed to understand. Though she had wanted to ask him outright why he had looked first startled, then alarmed, when he'd come into their chamber at the inn in Blackheath where she'd sat with Bennet and her two servants, she had kept back the words. John Rushton had undoubtedly changed over the weeks since their parting. He did not appear unwell, yet there were signs of strain around the eyes and the hard, strong mouth which she had not noted before, and Margaret believed there were more strands of silver among his dark locks than she remembered. Yet she had not pressed for an explanation. Naturally the events of the last weeks weighed on his mind. His patron, Thomas, Marquess of Dorset, had been forced to flee to France and even now was ensconced within the household of Henry Tudor, the only remaining Lancastrian claimant to the throne of England.

Margaret had found this alliance a strange one. What possible advantage could Thomas Grey gain from an association with the man who challenged the right of his own stepbrother to the crown? Actually Margaret could see little evidence that Henry Tudor indeed possessed a valid claim. He was the son of Lady Stanley, formerly Margaret Beaufort, whose ancestry certainly was Plantagenet, but only from the adulterous union of John of Gaunt, Earl of Lancaster, great-grandfather of the late King Henry VI, with his mistress Katherine Swynford. True, he had later married Katherine, but long after the births of his Beaufort children and, though they had been legitimised by Richard II, only on the understanding that they be barred from the succession. Margaret Beaufort had been married as a child to Edmund Tudor, the elder son of another Katherine, the widow of Henry V, and this Henry Tudor, living as a pensioner of the French

King in Brittany, was her only child, born when she had been hardly fourteen years of age. Now that both Henry of Lancaster and his son Edward were in their graves, Henry Tudor had the support of those disgruntled Lancastrian lords who had fled England after the Yorkist victory at Tewkesbury. Now, it seemed, Thomas, Marquess of Dorset, was of their number and Margaret found that perplexing. Young Edward V had been declared a bastard after the Stillington revelations and it was hardly likely that the Tudor would be persuaded to advance his cause. Yet Dorset had sent messengers to her father and Bennet Hartwell here in Canterbury.

Margaret moved from the shrine of St Thomas to view the tomb of the Black Prince, but her mind was anywhere but on England's history and she signalled to her two attendants to follow her outside into the cloisters. It was another fine day and she rejoiced in the fresher air now that she was free of the noisome capital. She wondered if the Duchess Anne or Aleyne had yet been brought to book because of her escape—and what of Guy Jarvis? Would Gloucester hold him responsible, since he had been in charge of the escort which had accompanied the Duchess to the Tower? Margaret sank down on a stone bench and Jonnet and Will drew together some little distance away to whisper together. A smile glimmered on Margaret's lips. At least Jonnet was happy in the love of her chosen man. Now that she, Margaret, was free of Guy Jarvis, why was she not rejoicing in that same freedom to wed the man chosen for her? She winced from the thought. Chosen for her. Was it her destiny always to be dictated to in matters of the heart by others? Jonnet's lowlier status had given her the right of choice, some compensation, perhaps, for the life of toil the servant classes were forced to endure. Indeed, what was to be Jonnet's future? John Rushton certainly was in no position now to ensure the fortunes of any of them. Will Grimshaw had left his service with Sir Guy Jarvis and must rely on the goodwill of his new master. Margaret shuddered a little, even in the warm air, as she thought what might befall Will Grimshaw if he were ever to cross Sir Guy Jarvis's path.

Worse, what would happen to her, Margaret, if they met again? But she must not fear that possibility. Even if it were to be so, she would be safely wed to Bennet Hartwell. Guy Jarvis could have no hold over her.

She bit her lip as she contemplated her changed circumstances. How soon now before she became Bennet Hartwell's wife? He appeared in no hurry to take her before a priest—in fact her own father seemed to have lost all enthusiasm for hastening the match.

She frowned as, again, that little stab of doubt assailed her when she remembered their meeting in Blackheath.

Hartwell's small company had experienced no difficulty in leaving the capital, though Margaret had noted how watchful he was until they were well clear of London.

'Are you fearful we might be followed?' she'd enquired as his fingers had repeatedly strayed towards his dagger-hilt. He'd glanced across at her, riding close to him, Jonnet riding pillion with Will just behind them, two of Hartwell's men ahead and three more bringing up the rear.

'No, no, just taking precautions for your safety. In these unsettled times who knows what rogues might take advantage of the dubious leadership to attack any unwary traveller? Your father would never forgive me if anything were to happen to you while in my care.'

It had been a most unlover-like speech, and, while she had known from the beginning that the match was arranged, she had experienced a vague sense of disappointment. Most bethrothed men would have found a more gallant mode of address, even if the sentiment had not been entirely sincere. Rapidly she had gone over in her mind the occasions when she had been in Bennet's company. Not once had he uttered one word of admiration. Then she'd seen that his attention was entirely upon the possible hazards of the road and the dangers to his own person.

Guy Jarvis would have been considering her first and foremost. She compared the journey south with him from Cold Ashby and recalled how constantly he had watched her and assured himself of her comfort. But that had been because he was responsible for her safety to Gloucester, she told herself fiercely, as Hartwell was now to her father—but if that had been the only thought in Guy's mind, why had he pressed for the match, why had he told her so commandingly that he would never allow her to be possessed by another? Her body grew hot at the memory. She had been afraid of him then, of the sudden burst of passion. Bennet Hartwell aroused no such feeling of panic—but then, she felt little response to him at all.

Her traitorous mind had dwelt many times on lying with Guy on the marriage bed, had shivered in frightened anticipation of all that consummation would mean. She could picture herself, lying cool and quiet beside Bennet Hartwell, but she could not imagine living with him in amity, bearing his children. In their short acquaintance she had decided that his was a calculatingly cold nature. His mind balanced advantage and disadvantage of this or that action—to himself. He had no thought for others, not even for her father's safety, least of all for hers.

She remembered vividly Guy Jarvis's concern for his squire, his unqualified loyalty to his friends and to Gloucester. Where Guy Jarvis gave his heart, he offered it complete and whole. Yet had he offered her love? He had never spoken the word, only of wanting, of possession. Margaret smothered a sigh. She could not understand the motives of men. Her father had allied himself to that faction he considered offered the better chance of preferment, but now he appeared to be most uneasy at that simple choice. If she had not known him better she would have said he was afraid.

She had noticed how she had rarely been left alone with her father. Always Bennet had seen to it that either he or one of his men was with them.

'As things stand,' he had remarked coolly, 'we are all in danger from Gloucester's creatures. My men are here to give us protection.'

Margaret had seen a sudden and hastily suppressed scowl cross her father's features and she had glanced hastily at Hartwell. Similarly, her father had seen to it that she was not left alone with her chosen husband, not even with Jonnet present. It was as if he was fearful for her. Why? If Hartwell was soon to be her husband, why should her father seek to avoid any chance of her being with him without himself in attendance?

This morning his unease had been most evident and disturbing. They had had only a moment alone together and Sir John had seized his daughter's arm in a bruising grasp.

'I want you to stay clear of this inn until late

afternoon. Do you understand? On no account are you to grow bored or tired and return here.'

'Father, what is it? Surely I have a right to know if something is worrying you, and I can see that all is not well. . .'

His fingers had tightened warningly on her arm so that she'd thought she would scream with the pain as Bennet Hartwell had come back into their chamber. She'd noticed that he rarely did them the courtesy of knocking before entering. She'd had the frightening notion that he was in charge of proceedings, her father merely one of his henchmen. The knowledge had done nothing for her peace of mind.

She sat on the bench now, worrying at her bottom lip, concerned for her father's safety. Yet he had made his wishes very plain. She must obey him. Squarely she faced facts. Was her father now regretting his alliance with the Queen's relatives, wishful to return to his allegiance to the Lord Protector? Did he distrust the motives of Thomas of Dorset? How could that be since surely Dorset was only eager to place his young half-brother on the throne again? Her father had had ample opportunity now to assess more thoroughly the character of Bennet Hartwell and his suitability as a future son-in-law. He had found him wanting. Undoubtedly he had given out sufficient signals for her to realise that was the case.

When she had explained her principal reason for disobeying his first instructions and escaping from Crosby, he had shown no great anger at the revelation that Gloucester was forcing her into a marriage with Guy Jarvis. Though words had been unspoken in Hartwell's company it was as if John Rushton regretted that the marriage had not taken place. It was Hartwell, then that he distrusted, not Dorset, and Hartwell was sufficiently well guarded to make it almost impossible for her father to leave his company. Her father, she knew, was no coward. Despite the threatening presence of Hartwell's men, she thought her father would have broken from this faction had he not feared for her. Had she now become a hostage to the Lancastrian cause as she had previously been for Gloucester's?

Because of her, he was hourly becoming more deeply embroiled in this treason. She shivered again as a cloud crossed the sun. Until this moment she had not been in the least afraid of Bennet Hartwell, merely disillusioned by the facets of his character she had seen recently revealed; now she feared for the safety of all of them—of Jonnet and Will besides herself and her father.

Impetuously she rose to her feet. It would soon be time for the field labourers to return from their work. Surely now she could go back to the inn and find some opportunity to confront her father alone and discover the real reason behind his unwonted alarm.

Jonnet turned at her movement and the two came to her side.

'I'm going back now,' she said, 'but when we get near the inn I want you two to stay outside for a few minutes.'

Jonnet stared back at her, clearly puzzled by this instruction. The young maid had been far too interested in her own growing relationship with Will to be aware of any sense of danger. She knew better than to argue, however. Will looked more anxious but he nodded slowly and his eyes met Margaret's. A silent communication passed between them. If anything at the inn were to alarm him, he would see to it that Jonnet was taken immediately away to some place he considered safe until he could assess the situation.

Margaret hastened up the main street and paused only moments outside the White Swan. There appeared to be no undue activity. Indeed, the place seemed lost in the somnolent warmth of the afternoon, the servants taking the opportunity to rest from their labours before tackling the hectic rush of the evening's activities. Margaret turned back once towards Will, who nodded again and drew Jonnet more closely to him before stepping into the shade of a stable wall.

Margaret paused for a moment on the stair but there was no sound. Hartwell's men-at-arms, then, must be drowsing in the courtyard sleeping off the morning's ale.

Outside the door of her father's chamber she paused and listened. The door was stoutly constructed and she could hear no sound of voices within, so, more than likely, the morning's visitors must have left. Still, she knocked cautiously and waited for her father's invitation to enter.

There was no command and she knocked again. Had he and Hartwell left for some reason? Had their visitors still been present surely someone would have come to the door and asked her to wait. The silence in the sultry heat of the place became oppressive and unnatural. Margaret waited only a moment longer then put her shoulder against the door and pushed, determined to enter despite her father's previous warnings. It gave inwards immediately, so was not barred. No one, then, was concerned at this time for secrecy.

At first she thought the room empty but then her eyes accustomed to the gloom, for someone had drawn the window shutters, and saw the sprawled figure beside the overturned table.

For one second Margaret stood rigid with terror, her hand pressed against her mouth, then she lunged forward and knelt at her father's side. Her fingers sought reassurance that his flesh was still warm, that he lived, though she saw in an instant the handle of the dagger which protruded from his chest.

Stifling the first scream which bubbled upwards, for his enemy might still be inside the inn, she implored him softly to come to his senses. As if in answer to her whispered prayers, his eyes flickered open and gradually sense dawned as he recognised her. His hand clawed at the weapon then reached out and caught at her hand.

'Nay, lass, don't seek to draw it out yet. . .' His words were weak but comprehensible. 'If—if you do—it will be the end of me.'

His eyes turned towards the overturned table and she followed his gaze to a stoppered wine bottle. It had fallen and rolled but remained whole. She scrambled to her feet and retrieved it, looked frantically for a wine cup, and carried both back to her father.

'Lie still now,' she begged. 'I'll go for help. . .'

He clawed at her hand again. 'No time, lass. Give me—give me—some wine. . .'

She found a pillow from the bed and half lifted his head and shoulders then held the half-filled cup to his lips. He drank, swallowed a little, coughed and waved the cup away.

'Come—close—child. Nay——' he coughed again '—don't call out for help. I doubt if there's a soul left alive in the inn. . .'

'Who did this?' she demanded, holding back the rush

of tears while his need to have her close to listen was so obvious.

He ignored that and plunged on. 'Tell—Gloucester—the boys are in peril——' The words were choked off again in a bout of coughing and Margaret gasped as she saw blood trickle from the side of his mouth. 'Tell him—tell him—watch Buckingham.'

'Buckingham?' she echoed blankly. Buckingham was the Protector's cousin and ally. . .

'The—the Tudor plans to wed Elizabeth—if—if she is. . .' His words became incoherent now and too soft for her to catch.

'Father,' she murmured, her voice thick with unshed tears, 'please don't try to talk. I'll—I'll get a doctor. Rest. You mustn't try to talk any more—please. . .'

The grip on her hand tightened as she tried to stand and run to summon help, despite his pleading.

'Dorset—Dorset wants to come back. Tell Gloucester. . .'

There was a harsh rattling sound, a terrible bubbling and his head fell sideways. The final rush of blood from his mouth splashed on to her hand and instinctively she tried to snatch it clear. There was no resistance now. The grip relaxed, the hand became flaccid and fell back.

She sat back on her heels, staring down at him. Still the tears would not come. The horror was too great. She knew he was dead, that there was no longer any need to try to summon help. Will was close by, and Jonnet, but for the moment she could not rise, just sat rocking helplessly in an agony of grief.

Sir Guy Jarvis arrived at the Saracen just before the establishment was about to open for the evening's entertainment. Curtly he ordered the landlord to bar the doors and when the man protested loudly at the prospect of losing valuable custom he ordered two of his men to take him in charge and hustle him into the taproom, where a frightened slattern, who was probably his wife, huddled by the door, watching.

The man was thrust ungently on to the nearest stool and one of the men forced his hands behind his back, holding them in a tight grip. The landlord's nervous gaze flickered from the badge of the boar, the Lord Protector's personal emblem, blazoned on the tunics of his captors, to the hard face of the fair-haired man who hooked forward a second stool, pushed up one leg on to it, and stood, one hand on hip, leaning forward slightly across the bent raised knee towards him.

Guy's voice was deceptively mild in tone. 'You have recently had lodgers, two gentlemen, possibly several henchmen in attendance.'

The landlord nodded, his nervous anxiety growing by the moment. He had been ready enough to keep secret the comings and goings of his guests. The younger one had paid him well for his trouble, but the arrival of the Protector's men was a different matter altogether. If there was the faintest whiff of treason clinging to his former guests he wanted none of it to attach to him.

'Did they furnish you with their names?'

This time the landlord shook his head, then volunteered, 'One referred to the other as Sir John once. I never asked.'

'No, quite.' Guy continued in the understanding tone, which did nothing to relieve the landlord's fears, 'There were other men coming to see them from time to time?'

'No, sir, both men went out a lot. I saw nobody else in their company. There were five henchmen, I think.

Two of them took it in turns to sleep in my taproom. I don't know where they were all lodged.'

'And where are they now, these gentlemen and their—guards?'

The landlord forced an uneasy laugh. 'Bless you, sir, how'd I know? It's best for the likes of me not to ask too many questions.'

Guy ignored that. He pressed on. 'A young lady arrived, with a maid and another man, a soldier?'

The landlord looked blank. 'I don't remember no young lady. . .'

Guy leaned forward and deliberately slapped the man hard across the face with his riding glove. 'Let me refresh your memory.'

'No, sir.' The man's voice has degenerated into a whine. 'I tells you I never seen no young lady, no respectable young lady, that is.'

The woman near the door spoke anxiously, starting forward as if to come to her man's assistance but eyeing the other guard doubtfully as he stood near her with folded arms, impassive.

'I saw 'er, sir. Me man, he was out that afternoon when she comes. She knocks and asks for Sir John Rushton. I didn't know the man's name, sir, but I takes 'er up to the guest chamber where the younger man was. T'other had left already, the man I thought 'ud be 'er father.'

'Ah.' Guy turned his attention to her. The icy tone was still there but he was now, again, studiously polite. 'Mistress, describe the young lady, if you please. She was a noblewoman?'

'She weren't dressed like no noblewoman, but respectable, like. I showed 'er upstairs and then two others come, like you said, another woman—a maid, I reckon—and a soldier. They all went with the younger man and his servants.'

'Went where?'

She shrugged sulkily. 'I never asks no questions—s'not 'ealthy.'

'No,' Guy agreed suavely, 'not when this place could be a nest of traitors.'

'No, indeed, sir,' the landlord blustered. 'I alus been loyal to King Edward, and to the boy, bless 'im. 'Eaven keep him from 'arm now. . .' He trailed off as Sir Guy's blue eyes flashed fire.

'What harm should befall the boy in his uncle's hands? But, no matter, we were talking of your erstwhile guests. Ask questions you do not, listen you do. Where were they heading?' He fiddled gently with the gloves in his hand.

The landlord swallowed hard and blinked. 'Yes, I listens. I 'eard one of the men, soldiers, they was, saying they was going to Blackheath to meet with Sir John. They all left. I wa'n't there when they took off but I reckons as 'ow the young lady must 'ave bin with 'em. There ain't no sign of 'er 'ere now.'

Sir Guy stood down from the stool and nodded to his guard to release the landlord's arms. The fellow rubbed life back into his wrists resentfully but his eyes continued to watch Sir Guy warily.

The guard said, 'Do we leave for Blackheath, sir?'

'Yes, immediately.'

'And this fellow and his wife? Are they to be detained for further questioning?'

The landlord's greasy face blanched.

'No.' Guy looked distastefully round the taproom. 'I think he's told us all he knows. He makes it his business not to enquire too closely into his guests' habits and associates.' He addressed his hapless captive. 'You would be better advised to keep to your principal source of income—entertaining your customers.' The word was uttered with a curl of his lips. 'Refrain from harbouring possible enemies of the realm. You understand me?'

The man's frightened eyes appealed to him for approval. He licked dry lips and nodded obsequiously.

Guy stalked out of the room to Will Scroggins, who was impassively keeping control outside of irate customers anxious for their night's carousal.

'Blackheath,' Guy said tersely, and mounted the moment Owen brought up his horse.

The company clattered out of the street in his wake, heading for the road south-east.

Guy elicited no further information concerning Margaret's destination from any of the inns in Blackheath. He learned only that a man likely to have been Sir John Rushton had been staying at one and had been joined by Hartwell's company. They had left soon after but the landlord knew nothing more and after some thought Guy headed on towards Canterbury and Dover. He doubted that the party had doubled back towards London, and therefore deduced that they must be either meeting with other insurgents from France or were attempting to leave the country themselves.

In Canterbury he detailed Scroggins to make a round of three of the inns and taverns while he himself, with Owen and two of the men, tried those remaining.

At the Swan he drew in his horse with a hiss of relief mingled with anger when he saw Will Grimshaw lingering outside with Jonnet, Margaret's maid.

Thank the sweet Virgin, she had not taken ship for France as he had feared.

He snapped an order to his men to apprehend Grimshaw and himself chased after Jonnet who, on sight of him, took off at a run. It was a simple business to catch her and grasp her firmly by both arms.

'Your mistress,' he barked. 'She is in the inn?'

Terrified, Jonnet looked beyond him to where her Will was struggling in the hands of his guards.

'Please, please,' she begged, 'don't hurt him. He's done nothing wrong.'

'Nothing but helped the escape of the King's hostage, allied himself with traitors. His crimes are considerable, wench.' He gave her a hasty shake. 'Conduct me to your mistress at once.'

As he entered the inn he ordered, 'Keep Grimshaw safe, one of you. Tom, get to the stables and find out where the horses are, and if Sir John Rushton has ridden out, then try and find Scroggins and come to guard the door.'

There seemed to be no inn servants about but he hustled Jonnet before him up the stair, expecting to find Margaret within one of the guest chambers. The open door at the stair-head showed him which one. He thrust Jonnet aside and strode in. The scene of destruction met him and he stopped short in the doorway at sight of Margaret kneeling, her father's head supported against her breast. She was rocking him as she would a hurt child. Guy's shrewd gaze took in the flaccid way the head lolled and he guessed the bitter truth.

He uttered an oath beneath his breath and strode forward. She didn't look up. She must have heard his passage along the flagged hall and his struggle with the reluctant Jonnet up the stair, but he thought she was deeply shocked. Dear God, what in the name of God had happened here?

He dropped to the floor beside her and put a gentle hand on her shoulder. She flinched as if someone had struck her a blow, and turned with vacant eyes to stare at him. For a moment there was no recognition in her dark gaze, then her lips parted as if in wonder and she began to scream and strike at him blindly. Sir John's body fell back on the rush-strewn floor and Guy reached out to take the stricken girl by both shoulders.

'Oh, my dear,' he said very gently, 'let me help you. Here, I'll lift you to your feet.' He looked down at her father's body and tried to draw her up and away.

Still she screamed. 'Murderer, so you have come back to finish your work. Kill me, then. Pity I wasn't here when you came the first time. That would have made it easy for you.' The desperate hate in her voice startled him and the power of the blows she continued to deliver on his shoulders and chest gave considerable pain but he held on grimly and at last succeeded in raising her. There was dried blood on her hands and smearing her gown so he knew John Rushton had been dead some time. Tears streamed blindly down her cheeks at last and he forced her down on to a stool and shouted to Jonnet, who was too frightened to advance into the room.

'Come here, girl. Come and help your mistress. What in the name of God keeps you there useless?'

Jonnet, petrified and sliding horrified eyes from the corpse, came at his call and knelt by her mistress, attempting to take her hand and comfort her. She opened her lips to say something but was apparently too choked for words to form.

The screaming had stopped but Margaret's expression was wild and clearly she was not in full possession of her senses. Had she witnessed the killing?

'What happend here?' Guy snapped at the maid.

The girl lifted round eyes to meet his angry blue ones and shook her head dumbly.

'We—we—weren't here—not—not for most of the day, sir. The mistress took us with her into Canterbury. We—we went to the cathedral. The master—he didn't want us to be here when—when the others came.'

'What others?'

'I—I don't know, sir. Master Hartwell, he arranged it and—'

Abruptly Margaret tore her hand from Jonnet's and fixed her venomous gaze on Guy.

'What harm had he done you? He wasn't a traitor, I know he wasn't, not at heart. . .' The storm of weeping began again and Guy signalled for Jonnet to rise.

'Get some water or good wine if you can find it. The inn appears to be deserted. God knows where they all are, or this screaming would have brought all the servants here by now. Send one of my men up.'

Jonnet scuttled away, glad to be free of the dreadful responsibility of trying to help her mistress, if only for a moment.

Margaret tried to get to her feet but Guy held her down.

'What have you done with his body?' she demanded.

'Do not disturb yourself. I'll make arrangements. Stay quiet now until your maid brings wine.'

Her dark eyes were blank, dulled with grief. 'I shouldn't have left him,' she murmured brokenly. 'I knew something was going to happen and he distrusted—'

She broke off again and stared at him wildly then she lunged at him again, her open hands like claws.

'*He* sent you,' she hissed. 'Sent you to kill my father. Your men came and killed him and went away for. . .'

She stared at the door where one of the guards, sent up by Jonnet, was hovering in answer to Sir Guy's summons. 'Look, he's wearing the Protector's badge. You are all murderers. He killed Lord Hastings and Rivers and now—he sent you to kill my father, kept me with him to lure my father into his net. . .'

He had caught tight hold of her hands again to protect his face from her clawing fingers and now when he released them gently after the first storm of her passion she buried her face in them and sat, her shoulders bowed, weeping helplessly.

'Find the nearest apothecary,' Guy said to the man over his shoulder. 'Tell him I need some valerian, something to calm a distraught lady. Bring the man here. She cannot ride in this state.'

'Yes, sir.' The man ducked back and, in the doorway, was shouldered aside by Will Scroggins who came to Guy's side.

'Saints in heaven,' he said, bewildered, 'there's been some desperate struggle here. Is the lady hurt?'

'No, but in such a state I scarce know how to help her. She accuses me of murdering her father. Have they found any of the others? Hartwell?'

Scroggins pursed his lips, shaking his head. 'Your men have made an extensive search. The birds have flown all right, headed for Dover, I reckon. But why, in the name of the old gods, should they come to blows and murder one of their number? Does she know?' He indicated Margaret's bent head as she rocked blindly in a paroxysm of grief.

'It seems not. The maid says Sir John sent them from the inn while some meeting was to take place between him and Hartwell and presumably one of Dorset's creatures from France.

Scroggins rolled his eyes skywards to indicate understanding of the delicacy of the situation. 'We'll get little out of the lass, then, but Hartwell could not have trusted him for some reason or other.'

Jonnet returned with a ewer of water and a towel and another guard appeared in the doorway with a jug of wine.

Guy was still kneeling before Margaret's stool. He stood up now and surrendered her into her maid's keeping, then crossed to the far side of the room with Scroggins.

'We must take her back immediately. I fear for her reason in this state. She blames herself for leaving him but storms at Gloucester and me. I think she assumes that a company of the Protector's men came across Hartwell's company here, that there was a fight, the Protector's men triumphed, that they took prisoners, but left her father for dead. She babbles about the badge of the boar but to my knowledge none of Gloucester's men is in this vicinity but us. He sent me deliberately to handle the matter discreetly and to see to Mistress Rushton's safety. I cannot imagine him dispatching others and, in all events, no men passed us on the road.'

'She's distraught, poor lass, that's plain enough, and none of this will advance your marriage plans, I'm thinking.'

Guy's eyes caught and held those of his friend and his lips compressed.

'We must have the body conveyed to the abbey. Have masses said for Sir John's soul. Margaret cannot think of anything for now. I'll order him placed in a lead-lined coffin so that, if she wishes it, he can be carried to his own manor and buried in the family tomb.'

Scroggins nodded gloomily. 'I'll get downstairs and put things in motion. Best we move her father before she becomes aware again. Explanations can come later.' He called from the doorway, 'The apothecary fellow is here. I'll send him in.'

The man was a tall, spare individual who looked curiously around at the scene of disorder but, noting the Protector's badge of the boar embroidered on the jacks of the men-at-arms, quickly placed himself at Sir Guy's disposal and went to the help of the stricken girl. Hurriedly he prepared a calming draught which, administered in wine, Margaret was persuaded to take. While the apothecary was busy with his patient, Scroggins returned with two men who reverently removed Sir John's body on a hastily constructed litter. As they reached the door with their burden Margaret gave a great grief-stricken cry and Jonnet drew her back in the chair, placing herself between the sight and her mistress's body.

Guy left the room to assure himself that his men knew what to do in the inn and to issue orders for their departure.

'Do you wish me to try to obtain a horse litter for Mistress Margaret, sir?' Owen enquired.

'No.' Guy shook his head decisively. 'That would only slow us down. Mistress Margaret should be returned to the care of Lady Allard as soon as possible. I'll carry her before me on my saddle-bow.'

None of the inn servants had returned and Guy began to fear that some ill had befallen them. Had Hartwell decided to leave no witnesses to his murder of Sir John? But, if that were the case, his men had discovered no more bodies and it was unlikely that there had been time to bury them, so, presumably, the inn's inhabitants had taken themselves out of harm's way until they deemed the coast to be clear for their return. The sight of more men-at-arms would further alarm them, so they would continue to lie low for a while.

He returned quickly to the guest chamber, to find Margaret much calmer and almost submissive. Her great dark eyes followed his movements imploringly and he came to her side and took her hand. This time she did not seek to withdraw it.

'Lady,' he said gently, 'you are much distressed and will need the presence of your friends to reassure and comfort you. I intend to take you back to London immediately.'

He expected an impassioned outburst but she continued to stare at him dully and he concluded that the apothecary had, indeed, done his work well. The man was even now being paid off by Will Scroggins, who a moment later came back into the room.

'All is ready, sir. Your horse is saddled and stands at the door.'

'Good. One of your men take up Mistress Margaret's maid pillion. Is Grimshaw still under guard?'

'Yes, sir.'

Jonnet had started at the sound of Will Grimshaw's name and she looked anxiously at Sir Guy. She was not reassured by his stern gaze.

'Go now with Master Scroggins and leave your mistress to me.'

She went obediently, looking backwards towards her mistress.

Bending, he lifted an unresponsive Margaret into his arms and prepared to stride out of the room and down the stair.

CHAPTER NINE

MARGARET woke to find Aleyne seated by her bed. She thrust herself up on her elbows, staring round the room wildly in an attempt to discover where she was. She gave a little sigh on finding she was back in her chamber at Crosby Place. Aleyne gently but firmly laid her back against her pillows.

'Rest, my dear. You are quite safe here with us.'

'Does the Duke know. . .? Oh, Aleyne, my father. . .' Margaret broke down, tears of weakness and grief streaming on to the fine linen of her night-shift.

'Hush, dear. We all know. There is nothing to fear. Guy brought you back.' Aleyne hesitated then pressed on. 'He had your father carried to the abbey in Canterbury. All will be done with reverent care. Give your heart peace.'

Margaret lay silent for a spell, the tears, unheeded, continuing to roll down her cheeks.

'He *found* him dead, didn't he?' she said at last huskily. 'Oh, Aleyne, I accused him of such dreadful things and My Lord of Gloucester too. . .'

'The King understands you were distraught.' Again Aleyne hesitated. 'Were you there, Margaret? Did you see who. . .?'

Margaret shook her head. 'No. I—I came too late. My father sent us out to make a pilgrimage to St Thomas's shrine.' The last words were harsh with bitterness. 'He—he must have known it would be dangerous for me to stay. I—I think he knew from the beginning—from the time I joined him—that he was in peril, and feared for me too.' There was another strained silence, and Aleyne bit her lip uncertainly and waited. Margaret resumed. 'It was Bennet Hartwell who killed my father, I am sure of it, and, like the coward he is, he rode away. I knew it in my heart even when—even when I said such harsh things to Guy Jarvis. He came on us, you see, some time after I found Father dying. I was—holding him in my arms.' She gritted out the last words through her teeth. 'And then—and then Guy came and I saw Gloucester's men and I thought—I thought that they had come back after dealing with the rebels—but of course they had only just arrived. . .'

Aleyne had grasped her friend's hand and was squeezing it tightly.

Margaret mastered her tears. 'It was a mercy in a way,' she said slowly. 'My father had become a traitor. If he had lived he would have been arrested and——' she gave a terrible shudder '—and died horribly—at Tyburn.'

There was a stir behind Aleyne, the door opened and Lady Anne entered. She came hurriedly to the bed.

'How is she? Ah, I see she has wakened.'

Margaret gave a smothered sob. 'Your Grace, have I caused you trouble with your lord? I pray not. . .'

'No, no,' Anne assured her, seating herself on the bed. 'It was just that when Richard explained to me that he feared for your safety we told him what had happened and our part in it. He dispatched Guy immediately to try and find you—and your father. Unfortunately he came too late to. . .' She glanced hastily at Aleyne who shook her head mutely.

Anne continued more briskly this time. 'You must stay abed until you feel more recovered. You have had a terrible shock, Margaret. I know what it is to lose a father dearly loved.' She paused and looked deep into Margaret's dark eyes which were still brimming with tears. 'This is a bad time to ask these questions but I feel I must. While you were with your father did you—did you become betrothed to Bennet Hartwell or was there anything between you which could constitute a binding tie? My Lord the King has charged me to ask this. Forgive me, Margaret.'

Margaret shook her head decisively. 'No, thank the Virgin, for I now believe he was responsible for the murder of my father. It was murder, foul, despicable murder—of a man who believed himself a comrade.'

The Queen and Aleyne exchanged glances and this time the Queen squeezed Margaret's hand.

'We feared—— But no matter.'

Margaret said quietly, 'Does the. . .King——' she hesitated slightly at the use of the Protector's new title '—still wish to arrange my marriage, Your Grace?'

Anne's gentle face clouded and she sighed. 'As I have said, this is a bad time to broach such a sensitive issue, but times are uncertain and soon——' again she uttered a heavy sigh '—my lord will be over-busied with state affairs. He would have you safely wed, Margaret, and under the protection of a man he trusts.'

'Guy Jarvis?' Margaret's pale cheeks flushed with scarlet as she recollected how she had berated the man—and unjustly.

'Yes, Guy has asked for you and is anxious to conclude the match without delay. I am sure he will be considerate about your loss and treat you accordingly. You are an heiress, Margaret, and now it is doubly necessary that your interests should be safeguarded and your lands in the hands of a trusted—king's man.'

A faint smile curled Margaret's lips, but she nodded submissively. 'I—I am prepared to obey the King, of course, Your Grace. I know now he had done all things to assure my welfare.'

Anne bent and kissed her on the forehead. 'I will inform the King of your acceptance. I know he will be relieved, as will be—Guy.' She smiled then warmly. 'Guy is very anxious to know all is well with you. You were unconscious in his arms when he brought you in. He was fearful that the drug the apothecary administered had been too strong.'

She withdrew as Aleyne rose and curtsied and Margaret struggled up to offer a suitable obeisance.

Margaret sat back against the pillows. 'So Richard of Gloucester is now truly our king?'

Aleyne nodded. 'You know how the Duke of Buckingham urged Richard's right to the throne? On Wednesday July the twenty-fifth, Parliament was assembled at Westminster. Not all members were present since the summons was so sudden, but it was a legal assembly, a true Parliament in all but name. There was a great deal of talk about the bastardy of the Woodville children, of the plot to unseat the Protector, and the desirability of placing the realm in the hands of an experienced warrior and ruler, and a petition was drawn up begging Richard to take the throne. Nobles and citizens came to present it next day at Baynards Castle and, after much persuasion, Richard acceded. He then proceeded to Westminster Hall and was formally seated upon the marble bench of sovereignty where he took the oath of kingship. He will be crowned on July the sixth.'

'And the young King?' Margaret breathed softly, then corrected herself. 'The late King's son and his brother?'

'Still in royal apartments in the Tower. They are quite safe, have been seen in the gardens, practising at the butts.'

Margaret looked away from her friend's questioning gaze. She had seen so much of treachery and death over these last hours that she dared not think what might befall those innocents who came to be in their rival's way.

Aleyne said softly, 'You have decided to obey the King without further argument? Can it be that you have changed your mind about Guy Jarvis, Margaret?'

Margaret's lips trembled and still she kept her eyes averted.

'What can I do? If I refuse I anger the King and—and I could find myself promised to some stranger who only covets my land and property. The Queen spoke of my inheritance, but you know, Aleyne, it is well within the power of the King to deprive me of my lands and property, should my father be formally declared a traitor and under attainder. Do—do you think Guy would still want me—if this is the case?'

'Yes,' Aleyne avowed stoutly. 'I'm sure he would. He was prepared to wed you five years ago when you were not an heiress and your father might well have then produced a male heir. Why should he jib at the match now? He wants you, Margaret. I heard him say so when he came with the Duke to Crosby to discover what had happened in your escape.'

Margaret made no answer and Aleyne wriggled closer on the bed and placed a hand on her friend's shoulder.

'Had you any real feelings for Hartwell? I know you now think he was responsible for your father's death but you may well still harbour thoughts of love. . .'

'Do not speak to me of that man,' Margaret hissed. 'I have nothing but contempt for him.'

'And Guy? Do you still hate Guy?'

'I have never said I hated Guy,' Margaret said defensively.

'You had hard things to say about him after your encounter at St Paul's Cross.'

'Yes, I know, he was—very forceful.' Margaret dabbed at her brimming eyes with a corner of the linen sheet. 'I was confused and. . .'

'Frightened?' Aleyne suggested.

'I am afraid of no man.' Margaret's dark eyes flashed angrily and Aleyne gave a little laugh.

'Then you are like no woman I ever met. There is no disgrace in admitting that a man like Guy frightens you. He is strong and courageous and domineering and haughty. Believe it or not, Margaret, but those are the very traits which have made him attractive to all of the Queen's unattached ladies, and many who are wed besides.'

'Oh?' The single syllable was decidedly waspish and Aleyne laughed again.

'So you are somewhat jealous; that is good. It bodes well for the marriage.'

'How should I be jealous? This is not a marriage of lovers but one arranged by His Grace the King and. . .'

'Who would not have done so had he not believed that there will be a measure of affection between you two. Guy asked for you. He truly wants you. He is in the King's favour and could have asked for lands and gold and possibly some other heiress. Why do you think he asked for you if he has no love for you?'

'Love? He has shown me precious little attention, except to keep guard over me as his duty.'

'And what feelings have you revealed to him, Margaret? Disdain, anger, untrustworthiness. . .'

'I have never been untrustworthy. . .' Margaret's voice trailed off as she recalled the scene in St Albans when she had indeed deceived Guy, and almost cost young Owen Lewis his life.

Aleyne pressed her gently, 'Do you say you have no feelings for Guy Jarvis?'

'I believe him to be what you say, brave and honourable and—proud. His pride was hurt—that time, five years ago. Now he is determined to take what was denied him.'

'And that is acceptable to you?'

Margaret turned the full gaze of her luminous dark eyes on Aleyne and said huskily, 'Yes, that—is—acceptable to me.'

'You could come to love him?'

Margaret's lips parted slightly and her gaze softened. 'I think I have thought of no one else all the time we have been parted.'

'Ah.' Aleyne sat back, satisfied. 'Then I am content. I have deep affection for Guy and I want him to be truly happy. I have known you only for a short time, Margaret, but I believe you are the woman to grant him that happiness. As the Queen says, the time is bad for you, but you will need someone to care for you now, more than ever. Do not hold your longings at bay, Margaret. Give yourself time but allow yourself to love as you were made to love. I know how it can be. There is no miracle in heaven or earth to compare with a loving surrender to your heart's love.'

Though the Queen excused Margaret from her duties until she felt fully recovered, she was determined to rise and fulfil all her usual tasks after dinner had been served in her chamber. The Queen was to depart for Westminster Palace in the afternoon to oversee necessary changes, for she and King Richard would move into the royal apartments now, until the customary night they must spend at the Tower before their coronation.

Margaret and Aleyne accompanied her and marvelled at the warren of buildings which made up the ancient palace. There were rooms of state superbly furnished, solars and bedchambers, but the place was like a small town within a town. Around the palace quarters were outside kitchens, offices, stables, armouries, blacksmiths' quarters, courtyards and passages, thronged with nobles, clerics and officials, so that Margaret thought she would never find her way about the place. She wondered how the Queen would view these sumptuous, scented but oppressive quarters after her wistful talk of Middleham Castle, her favourite dwelling in the Dales of Yorkshire.

She was delighted at last, after her duties for the day were ended, to seek a breath of air, tainted though it might be, from the gardens near the river. Even here the atmosphere was heavy and noisy as she could see and hear the bustle from the King's steps to the barges and ferry-boats which carried the royal servants home to their residences. The river was still packed with traffic but here, at least, she was clear of the suffocating odours of musk and sweat, wine and roasted meats and rich sauces which threatened to turn her sick in the banqueting hall. Jonnet had followed at her signal and stood some little distance away, her eyes stretched wide with astonishment at the crush of humanity below them. Margaret drew in a breath of river air and wrinkled her nose doubtfully. Would she ever become accustomed to the varied stinks of the capital? The thought struck her that Guy had once said he was hoping soon to be released from attendance upon the King. Would he wish to take her north, or to his manor in Gloucestershire or, she thought hopefully, to Rushton and the rolling green farmland of her dear Northamptonshire?

As if in answer to her thoughts of him, he appeared suddenly at her side.

'Aleyne told me she thought I would find you here.'

He bowed and she curtsied formally. There had been no lack of suitable black mourning for her to borrow, since the Duke of Gloucester's household had only just emerged from mourning King Edward. Margaret wore one of Aleyne's gowns, of black silk adorned with silver and with a simple white silk vest beneath the deep V of the neckline. She looked dignified and yet very vulnerable, and Guy's fierce blue eyes softened at the sight of her.

He was keeping close hold of her hand and she glanced down awkwardly at her imprisoned fingers. Swiftly he released them with a muttered apology.

'They tell me the King's physician says you have taken no great harm from the drug administered so that I might bring you home without further distress.'

'I have to thank you, sir,' she said softly, 'for your care of me on that journey and—and I must express my sorrow for—for the way I treated you at the inn.' She was rushing her words, avoiding his gaze and he waited courteously. 'I—I was very foolish—out of my mind with grief. I know you were not responsible for—for what took place. I should not have left him.'

He said gravely, 'If you had been present you might well have died with your father, Mistress Margaret.'

'I know. He—he thought of that—and saw to it that I was well away.'

'You loved him very much?'

She was not sure if the words constituted a question or a statement.

She said firmly, 'He was not a man to show affection. He inspired obedience, respect, rather than demonstrations of love. My mother was always a little afraid of him, I think. I—I always obeyed what he demanded of me.'

Again he was silent for a moment. They were both considering that repudiation of his claim five years ago and he acknowledged that this was the nearest approach to an apology he was ever to get from her.

'The Queen gave me leave to speak with you.'

She inclined her head. Tears were pricking at her lashes and her mouth was very dry. She was very aware of his nearness, of the masculine smell of him, clean, tanged, mingling with the faint smell of leather, soap, the merest suggestion of lavender and rosemary which she believed emanated from the linen cloths in which his fine velvet doublet had been wrapped within his saddle-bag. For the first time she saw him out of mourning. He wore dark blue doublet and grey hose. The simple gold chain at his neck was unadorned with jewels, as was the studded leather belt at his waist. The garments sat on him elegantly. No other man would have worn such simply cut clothes at Court with such grace.

'We have to talk.' He indicated a marble bench near

by and she went willingly, his hand gently upon the crook of her elbow.

'They have told you that it is my ardent wish that our marriage should take place as planned, despite your recent loss?'

Again she inclined her head.

'I know the arrangement is not ideal but His Grace is to be crowned on July the sixth and will shortly afterwards leave London on royal progress. I do not know what tasks he will then have for me, and where he sends me I wish to take you.'

'Yes.' The word was a slight sigh.

'You are not afraid of me, Margaret?'

This time her smiling dark eyes met his anxious blue ones.

'Certainly not, sir.'

'The thought of the match is not still—repugnant to you?'

The reply was unhesitating. 'No.'

'Then you agree to the celebration of our marriage in St Stephen's chapel, two days from now?'

She gave a slight gasp as if she had not fully understood the shortness of time left to her, but she swallowed and said quietly, 'Yes, I agree.'

'They told you what arrangements I had made for your father's conveyance to Northampton?'

'Yes, for that too I have to thank you.'

'The King has agreed that we will have some time at your manor to allow you to attend a solemn requiem and interment before I am dispatched elsewhere.'

For the first time she allowed herself the relief of a slight sob. 'I—I appreciate that. Despite his rough way with me I did love him dearly.'

'I am sorry that you are bereft of both parents within

so short a time. One day soon, I hope, I shall take you to see my mother. She is a gentle, loving lady who will be delighted to see you. It is unfortunate that there is not time for her to travel to London for the ceremony, but she will understand the need for haste and you will have Aleyne to attend you and the presence of the Queen to give her blessing.'

He stood up, ready to escort her back to the royal apartments.

'I will not impose my presence on you while you are still in a state of grief and shock. I'm glad we have had this quiet talk together.' He hesitated. 'Can I claim a chaste bethrothal kiss?'

Margaret looked huntedly towards Jonnet who was hovering a little closer, uncertain whether her mistress wished her to intrude on this meeting or not. She felt unaccountably breathless, unsure how to answer him. One part of her wanted to refuse, to hold this barrier between them until the very last moment, yet another wanted to draw closer, to bind him to her so that he would not change his mind and request to be free of this match. He represented her one hope of security. She had glimpsed a terrifying chasm stretching before her, the moment she had realised her father was gone. There was no one to protect her now from the grasping claws of self-seeking men but Guy Jarvis, yet why was she so convinced that he himself was not one of them? She swallowed hard and forced a smile.

'Of course, sir. It is your right.'

He drew her close so that she could feel his heartbeat against her own, and she experienced a panicky desire to pull away violently before she was drawn into some uncontrolled vortex, then she allowed her body to relax against his and he tilted up her chin with one gentle finger and tenderly kissed her upon the lips. His breath was sweet, his touch firm but undemanding, and she resisted a sudden wish to respond, to crush her own lips on his possessively and draw him back to her, even as he released her. Her disappointment was strong, because she felt as if this surrender of herself at last should give her some sense of belonging, but in fact she felt little more than the feeling of relief experienced on a handshake when a bargain was struck, for this was a bargain, nothing more. By this marriage she would keep her own lands and property and in return she would warm his bed and, if God was kind, provide him with children. There was no suggestion in any of this that there should be love between them, certainly not passion. She had always been practical, she told herself fiercely, and she had never expected more, certainly not from Bennet Hartwell. Why should she hope for more from Guy Jarvis?

They walked together through the garden and he bowed again as he released her arm near the entrance which would lead to the Queen's apartments.

'Till we meet again in the chapel. Please send for me if you have need.'

She bowed her head in acceptance. As he turned to leave, she said a trifle breathlessly, 'Have you—heard news of Bennet Hartwell?'

He turned instantly and his face now appeared as an inscrutable mask. 'Nothing,' he said crisply. 'Men have searched the district round Canterbury but it seems that he had ample opportunity to get clear away. He's probably with Dorset in France even now. Are you concerned for him?' The final question was bluntly put.

She hid her eyes from his penetrating stare. 'No,' she

said dully. 'Master Hartwell is capable of looking after himself; it is—just that. . .'

'Quite,' he said grimly and, before she could explain herself further, he had turned again and walked quickly away.

Margaret woke suddenly during the night to the sound of sobbing. She sat up instantly in the bed and peered over to the huddled form of Jonnet on the truckle-bed beside her.

'Jonnet, is that you crying?'

The sobbing hushed abruptly and there was a little silence, and then a gulp and the whispered words, 'Yes, mistress—I'm—I'm sorry.'

'Child, what is it? Are you ill?'

'No, mistress.'

'Light the rush dip and come to me.' Margaret's tone was kindly but nevertheless commanding.

The maid scrambled about and soon the pallid light of the dip illuminated the little room and touched on Jonnet's features, blotched and swollen with weeping.

Margaret patted the side of the bed. 'Sit down, Jonnet.'

'Mistress. . .'

'Come, child.' The old note of asperity was there. 'Come and do as you are bid. We have to get to the bottom of this. Has someone hurt you or threatened you?'

Awkwardly Jonnet perched on the rim of Margaret's bed and tried to sniff back the tears which were threatening to pour down her round cheeks again.

'It's—it's Will,' she got out at last.

Margaret's frown deepened as understanding dawned. 'Will Grimshaw? Oh, my dear, in all this turmoil of events I forgot. . . What has happened to Will?'

'That's just it, mistress.' The words fell over themselves now in Jonnet's eagerness. 'They won't tell me. No one'll tell me. I—I 'aven't seen 'im since Sir Guy. . .'

Tears choked her again and Margaret leaned forward and took her shoulder in a gentle grasp.

'When we came back to London, he was brought with us? I remember so little about what happened. . .' Her own distress for the events of that night was beginning to overwhelm her too, but she took a firm grip on her own feelings for Jonnet's sake.

'Yes, mistress, they bound 'is 'ands behind 'im and made 'im ride, then when—when we got 'ere they hustled 'im away and I 'aven't seen 'im since. That man who took me up behind, he said—he said they would 'ang 'im.'

'What? Oh, surely not.' Margaret's thoughts were racing now and she began to fear that there might well be some truth in what Jonnet was fearing. Grimshaw had become embroiled in her escape and her father's business and it could go hard with him.

'Since we arrived, you have heard nothing further?'

'No, mistress. I tried to talk to one of Sir Guy's men but he just laughed and said Sir Guy was a hard man and. . .'

'But you have not heard that he is—dead?'

'No, mistress,' Jonnet said miserably, then, with a pitiful note of hope, 'Someone'ud 'ave told me if he was dead, don't you think that?'

'I'm sure of it,' Margaret assured her stoutly, though she was by no means convinced in her own mind.

'And, mistress,' the maid added timidly, 'you won't let them send me away, will you?'

'Send you away? Of course not. Where did you get such an idea?'

Jonnet gulped again. 'That Mistress Isabel, of Lawton Manor, when she married and went to her husband in Leicestershire he sent all 'er servants 'ome.'

Margaret blinked rapidly. She had not considered this possibility. It was not unusual for a husband to dismiss his new wife's servants and replace them with his own. It was often deemed politic to do so and Jonnet had doomed herself in Sir Guy's eyes by attending her in the escape. It would be unthinkable to be parted from Jonnet now. The girl's earlier awkwardness had been replaced by a deep devotion and Margaret could not face the future in some remote Yorkshire home without her familiar presence.

'You must try to sleep now,' she said gently. 'I will see Sir Guy in the morning and get this matter straight and—and I will try to discover what has happened to your Will and—if I can—do my best for him.'

'Oh, mistress.' Jonnet's gratitude was pathetic and Margaret waited until the weeping stopped before ordering her to extinguish the dip and lie down again.

As she lay in the darkness she thought wryly of what her promise entailed. Guy had instructed her to send for him if she had need. She had not then contemplated the necessity of asking favours of her betrothed.

Indeed she felt even more awkward the following day when she dispatched a royal page to find Sir Guy. It would not have been appropriate to receive him in the chamber allotted to her and she waited in a window embrasure of the great hall, conscious that the eyes of all, from the ladies-in-waiting down to the most youthful of the pages, were fixed upon her in avid curiosity. Aleyne was in attendance upon the Queen in her private solar and Margaret was glad of it. The last thing she wanted was to be seen to be beholden to Guy, yet this could not be avoided.

He came at last, fair brows contracted in surprise, but his bow was as courteous as ever as he led her to one of the window-seats a little apart from the throng of courtiers ever present now and anxious to secure the goodwill of the new King.

'The boy said you had urgent need to see me. There is nothing wrong? You have not decided at the last moment to oppose the match?'

'No, no.' She bit her lip uncertainly. 'It was just that I had to see you on another matter.'

'Oh?' The fair brows rose in puzzlement again.

She rushed in before her courage failed her. 'What—what has happened to Will Grimshaw?'

'Grimshaw?' He looked even more bewildered, as if the fate of one of his men-at-arms could hardly be expected to concern him now. 'He is still under guard, I imagine.'

'Has—has he been tortured?'

'No,' he said shortly, then, 'Since under question he revealed everything he appeared to know concerning the Hartwell affair, it was hardly deemed necessary.'

'Will they—hang him?'

'I would think that highly likely.'

She gave a little gasp of pity. 'Is—is the sentence within your authority?'

His blue eyes narrowed as he regarded her thoughtfully. 'Since the fellow is one of my men, it will certainly be up to me to decide his fate. He has been cleared of plotting deliberate treason. There remains the crime of negligence on duty and flouting my express orders. It would be unwise for me to countenance such behaviour without severe penalty.'

'Yes,' she said unhappily, 'but I beg you to be merciful for the sake of my little maid—and for mine. He was only anxious to serve me.'

He was silent, considering, and his gaze did not falter, then he said abruptly. 'Did you bribe him?'

'No.' She looked alarmed. 'No. He—he loves Jonnet and, since she was prepared to accompany me into possible exile, he was persuaded to go with us as escort. Would you not have done as much for someone you love?'

Still his blue eyes did not turn from her. 'It would depend on whether I believed such conduct could secure my love's safety and happiness.'

She flushed unhappily, avoiding his stare. 'Then—if you do not accept the excuse I am—trying to put forward for him—I beg you will show mercy. I feel responsible for his plight. . .'

'You are,' he said bluntly.

She bit her nether lip so that she could feel the salt tang of blood.

'Then I can only ask you to reprieve him—for my sake.'

'Naturally I am prepared to do anything you ask of me.'

The capitulation came so quickly that she could not at first believe it, and stared at him blankly.

'You will release him?'

'I did not say that. You asked me to reprieve him, I suppose from the sentence of death?'

She nodded dumbly.

'Then so be it, but I shall exact punishment. No man

of my company disobeys me with impunity. They all know that. To excuse the crime completely would create a precedent for further insurrection.'

'Yes, I understand that. Will you—dismiss him from your service?'

He smiled grimly. 'I take it you would wish me to keep him with us. I suggest a more appropriate punishment would be a thorough flogging.'

Her lips parted as if she would plead further, then she nodded in reluctant acceptance. 'I suppose that is just, but—I still feel I am to blame.'

'Then perhaps your unhappiness at knowing his suffering is, to some extent, punishment for you too.'

Tears pricked at her lashes but she nodded again gravely. 'It is just—and merciful.'

His smile was still a trifle grim. 'Is that all? All you want of me?'

'Well, yes, that is, no—I—I would like to keep Jonnet in my service.'

His head shot round then in utter amazement, then his smile deepened. 'Ah, you think I shall play the heavy-handed husband and dismiss the girl for her complicity in this affair.'

'She is—afraid you will.'

'And quite right too. Most men would decide she is unreliable, worse, a likely accomplice in further foolish adventures. I hope that is not to be the case.'

'I assure you I will not involve Jonnet in any future wrongdoing—I mean,' she floundered helplessly, 'I haven't the slightest intention of embarking on any such misconduct.'

'That relieves my mind.'

His lips twitched slightly and she stared at him

accusingly. 'You had no intention of hanging Will or of dismissing Jonnet. You are deliberately baiting me. . .'

They were seated close on the window-seat and he took one of her hands in his own, his blue eyes sparkling with amusement now.

'No, I was not baiting you. Grimshaw is in severe trouble and I had every intention of punishing him, but I knew you would be distressed if he were to end on the scaffold so I begged the King for his life. I do not think a few awkward moments on your part too high a price to pay for the trouble you gave all of us, Grimshaw and your maid in particular. You could all have lost your lives—if you had been present when your father died.'

Her lip quivered and she dabbed at her brimming eyes with her linen kerchief. 'I know.'

'Swear to me you will act more cautiously in future.'

'I swear it. When I am your wife I will do nothing you would disapprove of. . .'

He laughed out loud. 'Do not go too far, Margaret. I know you too well to believe you will become a docile wife. I'm not sure I would have it so.'

He rose and drew her to her feet. 'You are content, your mind at rest before the ceremony tomorrow?'

She inclined her chin. 'I'm sorry I had to incommode you. . .'

'I shall ever be at your service, Margaret. From the moment I was old enough to understand the responsibilities of our bethrothal my only wish was to prove myself a good husband. I have not changed.'

They were hidden slightly within the embrasure and he bent and kissed her full on the lips. 'Until tomorrow, then, keep this as a promise of what is to come.'

Her body tingled half in dread and half in excitement

despite the hurried nature of the embrace, and she was still trembling when he took formal leave of her.

Aleyne sought her that evening to discuss what she would wear for the wedding ceremony. The court had put off mourning in celebration of the new King's accession and coming coronation. Aleyne pursed her lips thoughtfully.

'Though you are in mourning for your father, I think we can dispense with that for your wedding. You are about my size. I'm sure I can find you something suitable in my travelling-chests, if you will accept the offer.'

Margaret allowed herself to be persuaded. She understood that the King, who had already declared his attention of leading her to the altar, would not wish to be reminded at such a moment of her father's recent death and treason. Neither, she thought, with a pang of doubt, would Guy.

'Of course I would be only too grateful,' she assured Aleyne.

With Aleyne's maid, Kate, and Jonnet in attendance, they rummaged through Aleyne's travelling-chest which, with the Allards' saddle-bags, had been brought from Middleham.

Aleyne gazed disparagingly at the assorted gowns arranged on her bed. 'I brought mostly drab gowns for the mourning and my best must be worn in Westminster Abbey for the coronation, but we must make do.'

She draped one or two experimentally against Margaret. 'I do not think you should wear scarlet; it becomes you well, but it might be—unsuitable. Ah, perhaps this.' She held forward a gown in apricot silk damask trimmed with cloth of silver at the hem and sleeve cuffs and a cloth-of-silver vest within the deep V of the neckline. 'What do you think?'

Margaret fingered the beautiful cloth reverently. 'It is so beautiful, Aleyne, it must have been a costly gift. I think it too fine for—'

'Nonsense,' Aleyne declared briskly. 'Do you like it?'

'Of course, but what will Sir Dominick say. . .?'

'It was not a present from Dominick but given by the Queen last Christmas. She is ever most generous, as you know. She will be delighted, as I will be, to see you wear it in the chapel tomorrow. Then we must fashion you a garland for your hair. Thank the Virgin it is high summer and there will be roses in plenty in the palace gardens.'

Kate and Jonnet added their agreement to the choice and, after Margaret had tried on the gown, began to make the necessary adjustments.

She had been excused attendance on the Queen and returned to her chamber to sit, dreamily thoughtful, while Jonnet put the final stitches into the hem.

'You need have no further worries about your Will,' she assured her maid. 'He will be punished but he will live and continue in Sir Guy's service, as you will.'

Jonnet was tearfully grateful and went about preparing her mistress for bed in a considerably more cheerful mood.

It would be the last time she slept alone, Margaret thought as Jonnet was about to extinguish the dip. She was not even sure where she would spend her wedding night—within Guy's chamber, she supposed—but she asked few questions about the arrangements, allowing herself to be guided by others as if she had no will of her own. In this matter, she concluded, she had not.

She had been destined for Guy Jarvis's bed from childhood, she knew that now. He had stated it baldly. 'You were meant for me, and I will have you.' Surprisingly, she had no fears for her future. She had seen him in action, knew she could rely on him to protect her interests. Would he prove a passionate lover? She thought perhaps not. He was always so quietly efficient and self-contained. Oh, he would consummate the match, she had no fear of that. It would be necessary, and she doubted if he would use her selfishly for his own pleasure, but would he give her joy—and could she satisfy him? Her pale cheeks flushed crimson at the thought. She was not ignorant of what was expected of her but she had no skills. Her gentle mother had explained that such accomplishments were taught by husbands, otherwise only acquired by whores. She would be eager to learn. She knew now that she loved Guy Jarvis, had only resisted the idea of marrying him because she'd had a perverse feeling that her father had objected to the match. She gave a little shudder when she thought of Bennet Hartwell. Personable he might be, but she would have found him icily unresponsive to her helpless desire to please, and she thought now that she would have come to fear him deeply.

The Queen gave a little delighted cry when she came to Margaret's chamber, just before the ceremony, to view Aleyne's handiwork.

'Oh, but you are quite beautiful,' she said, gently fingering Margaret's night-black hair which fell unrestrained past her waist to signify maidenhood. 'Guy will be overcome. I am glad you decided to put off your mourning, just for this day.'

She was wearing a gown in softest blue which highlighted the blue of her eyes and was kind to her pale cheeks. Aleyne wore a yellow gown trimmed with brown brocade, colours which suited admirably her vibrant personality. She had fashioned a flower garland of copper, gold and white roses to crown Margaret's dark mane and had handed her two copper roses to carry. The Queen made her a present of an exquisite book of hours, and this Margaret took with her to the altar, the two blooms affixed to the cover with white ribbon.

The King, with Dominick, Sir Francis Lovell and Sir Richard Ratcliffe, met her at the chapel door and reached out to take her hand.

'Guy will be very proud.'

Margaret curtsied low. 'Thank you, sire. Everyone has been so kind, especially Her Grace the Queen.'

He nodded, his grey eyes shining.

The ceremony was short and seemed dream-like. Margaret stole only one glance at Guy, who stood with Owen in attendance near the altar. His fair hair shone like an aureole in the candlelight and she saw that he wore a doublet of murrey velvet with blue hose, Yorkist colours, which became him well. The enamelled white roses gleamed against the glint of gold in his neck-chain and she thought she had never seen a man so handsome.

She murmured her responses and felt the coldness of gold upon her fingers as Guy finally put the wedding-ring in place upon the third finger of her left hand. She was his at last, and he bowed to the King as, after nuptial mass, he took her firmly by the hand and led her from the chapel.

The supper which followed was taken in one of the private chambers of the royal apartments in the presence of the King and Queen, their principal attendants and friends, which naturally included Sir Dominick and Aleyne. Margaret was grateful that she had not to face the bawdy ribaldry of a celebration in the great hall of the palace. Though there was some good-natured banter by Guy's former companions, the meal was pleasantly informal and more suitable to Margaret's mourning state. Guy was attentive and served her morsels from the golden dishes, which she ate sparingly. The King toasted the newly wed couple and was clearly in high spirits. This marriage suited him well. He had wanted his loyal captain to make a good match and all appeared to be going as he had planned. Margaret found Aleyne's smiling regard on her when she turned once, a little bewildered by some jovial remark from Sir Richard Ratcliffe. Aleyne inclined her chin slightly as if to reassure her nervous young friend.

When the Queen rose with Aleyne to accompany the bride to the nuptial chamber, the men rose too and once more lifted their drinking-cups high to wish her well.

After the King's chaplain had blessed the bridal bed the Queen kissed Margaret and withdrew. Aleyne stayed until Jonnet had turned back the silken coverlet, undressed her mistress and combed out her hair. She curtsied and left. Aleyne came close and took Margaret's hands.

'You are not ignorant?'

Margaret shook her head. 'I had a practical nurse and a sensible mother.'

Aleyne kissed her soundly on the forehead. 'I'm sure you have nothing to fear. I'll try to see to it that Guy does not linger too long over the wine.'

Margaret smiled and watched, a little wistfully, as

her friend left, closing the door very quietly behind her. She looked curiously round the chamber. It was small and, clearly, Guy had only moved in very recently. There were signs of hurried unpacking—gauntlets, points, a cambric shirt spilling from one saddle-bag. If he had been in his own manor, Margaret mused, there would have been a hawking stand, possibly the bird itself, hunting dogs to be chivvied out. Guy lived constantly on the move, from one armed camp to another, only temporarily in castles and palaces. He was unused to luxury. Would he want her to accompany him, or would she return to Cold Ashby to live a neglected, lonely life until he came occasionally to warm her bed in hopes of siring an heir? Here the walls were painted, adorned with two good tapestries to keep out draughts in winter, the wooden floors polished and strewn with sweet-smelling herbs. Idly Margaret moved to the half-opened saddle-bag and withdrew a book of etiquette printed at Caxton's shop of the Red Pale, newly installed by the late King in Westminster. So Guy found time occasionally to read, and wished for books of his own, or perhaps this was a present. She wondered vaguely if by its very subject it had been given by some noble lady of Guy's acquaintance.

Her reverie was cut short by his entrance. Aleyne had kept her promise, then, and chivvied him above stairs. Margaret found herself suddenly tongue-tied and stood with the book in her hands, like a naughty child who had been found prying into another's secrets.

He came to her side at once. 'I ordered that the last time I came south. It seems it might prove more useful than I had then thought. I had never expected to wait in attendance on kings.'

'I thought you had hoped to ride north soon.' She hoped her tone was level and betrayed no uneasiness.

He nodded. 'After the coronation, when the King leaves on royal progress. I promised you would go to Rushton for the burial of your father.'

She looked away to the bed. Custom demanded that she await him there but she had been too restless. He followed her gaze and laughed softly.

'You have nothing to fear. I am a considerate and experienced lover.'

Her face flamed and she moved back from him, but she was too late. He lifted her high into his arms and carried her to the bed, laying her gently back against the piled silk-covered cushions. One ringed hand reached out and took a tendril of her scented hair.

'How very, very lovely you are, and no longer a child.'

She made to speak but he touched her lips gently.

'This is no time for words. I have waited over five years.'

Tears were very near the surface now and she dashed one hand against her eyes as he quickly began to divest himself of his doublet and hose. He did everything with consummate grace, in swift, fluid movements, she thought. The candlelight gleamed on his slim, well-muscled form. There was not an ounce of surplus flesh on him, and she let out a little strangled gasp of appreciation of such manly beauty. How could she ever have thought him effeminate?

He came to the bed and reached out again, this time to undo the ribbons of her fine cambric night-shift, sliding it down over her shoulders to bare her lovely firm young breasts.

His touch was feather-light on her flesh, his lips warm

on hers, then sliding lower to her throat and breasts, gently teasing the nipples until she arched back with further little gasps of excited anticipation. Her own arms stole up round his shoulders, pressing him down over her, her tears wetting the satiny smooth flesh.

He was, as he had promised, so véry experienced, arousing her to a torment of longing until she was ready to receive him, and the pain of taking was so very small and so quickly forgotten in the delight of their union. She had not thought to experience such ecstasy: her body flamed and pulsed to his touch and it seemed that they fused and became one. She was outside herself, flying about the earth with the freedom and wild joy that a bird must feel when it flew free to the heavens.

When it was over she lay in his arms, her eyes closed, wanting only the comfort of his body close to hers, his strong arms holding her tight.

She had surrendered herself and she rejoiced with a savage exultation at the knowledge. At last she belonged to him as it had been destined since her childhood, and he was the lover of her dreams, handsome, strong, brave, competent to protect her and keep her safe forever. She gave a little purr of satisfaction and nestled even closer.

In the subdued gleam of the candlelight he looked down at her, her raven hair tumbling free over the silk of the cushions, her ivory flesh alive with the gloss of their lovemaking. He gave a little secret smile and bent to nuzzle her hair again.

She moved fretfully, as if at this moment she wanted to lie undisturbed, and he ran a light, tantalising finger down the length of her spine. She gave a little shudder of delight and turned on her back to smile up at him.

His lips bent to her ear so that she heard only a faint whisper of sound.

'I have not hurt you?'

'No, no,' she protested, and her cheeks and throat flushed rosily.

'I have given you pleasure?' He bent lower, his kisses soft on her closed eyelids.

'Yes,' she murmured dreamily, 'I had never thought—believed love could be so wonderful. . .'

'I'm glad.'

She gave a soft sigh.

'Then you would be happy to be loved by me—often?'

Her lips trembled, then broke into a smile. 'Of course. Am I too forward, my lord and master?'

'No.' His answering smile was enigmatic.

She was suddenly alarmed and pushed herself up in the bed, staring intently into those very blue eyes which flashed almost silver and green lights in the candle-flame.

'What—what is it. . .? Have I. . .?'

'You have proved yourself a dutiful and—responsive wife, my dear.'

She felt abruptly cold and reached for the silken sheet to pull round her breasts and shoulders. Something was very wrong. She had displeased him. How? She sought frantically for an answer. Should she have been more reluctant. Had he wanted her to resist so that he might have the pleasure of conquest? Her heart was beating very fast now and she was conscious of a deadly chill in the air, despite the earlier warmth of the day.

He said softly, 'You are my wife now, truly mine, wedded and bedded. There is no way of escape. But, my dear Margaret, the next time I come to your bed it will be at your invitation, *your* pleading. I wanted you to know the burning desire for love. When you want me, wife, send and beg me to come. I shall be waiting.'

He moved from the bed then, and she sat hunched, watching in horror as he gathered his discarded garments and left the chamber.

How long she sat frozen in one huddled position she could not afterwards have said. Humiliation burned in her. She had given herself totally and now he was rejecting her cruelly. She gave a little wounded cry like an animal in unbearable pain, then turned and buried her face in the cushion, sobbing, muffling all sound until, spent, she lay silent and tearless, waiting for the dawn.

CHAPTER TEN

MARGARET sat miserably huddled against the pillows when Jonnet arrived to pull back the bed-curtains. She chattered brightly, clearly not realising something was very wrong. Margaret had glanced briefly at the indented hollow where her husband's head had lain beside hers, but Jonnet appeared to think it in no way unusual that Sir Guy had taken an early departure from the nuptial chamber.

'It was getting late, mistress,' she said, waiting while Margaret climbed from the bed and donned her bed-gown. 'I waits for your bell, but, since I didn't hear it, thought it best, like, to come and wake you. It be the day before the coronation and I thought as 'ow the Queen might want you with her at the Tower. I suppose Sir Guy is already in attendance on His Grace?'

Margaret nodded, her heart hammering.

Jonnet gave her one bright, enquiring glance, and she forced a smile.

'Yes, it was necessary for him to leave early.'

Jonnet gathered up the crumpled, stained sheets, pushed them quickly into a wicker laundry basket and set about preparing her mistress for the day.

Margaret felt oddly numb. The horrifying humiliation Guy had dealt her the previous night had left her bereft of coherent thought. She found it hard to concentrate and answered Jonnet's queries about her choice of gowns and jewellery mechanically. She thanked the Virgin that Aleyne had not arrived. Unlike Jonnet,

Aleyne would quickly have sensed that her friend was deeply unhappy and would have pressed her for an explanation. Even if Jonnet suspected that Margaret's experience had been disastrous she would not have dared to ask any questions.

She found her voice to request that breakfast be served in the chamber, and Jonnet scampered off in search of a page who could be sent to the kitchens.

Margaret dreaded the summons from the Queen, who also might be mildly curious and anxious that Margaret had fared well on her marriage night, but she learned that the Queen had indeed left for the Tower and was quite willing to excuse Margaret from duties until the afternoon, when she was requested to join the other ladies in the royal apartments there.

She spent an unhappy morning speculating about the whereabouts of Guy. Fortunately everyone at Westminster was busy preparing for the momentous occasion on the morrow, and finally she was forced to send for one of her husband's troop to procure her a place in one of the barges which would carry her to the Tower. It was the ubiquitous Will Scroggins who finally arrived and Margaret, feeling his inquisitive eyes fixed on her, kept her face averted while he escorted her to the King's steps and settled her comfortably in the barge.

The Queen seemed pleased to see her when she presented herself, but was obviously flustered and made only perfunctory enquiries concerning her welfare, then sent her off to see to her own concerns.

'I shall be quite adequately attended, Margaret,' she said graciously. 'I'm sure you have other thoughts on your mind than these tiresome but necessary preparations. Go and find Guy, unless he is occupied with the King. If so, go and sit in the garden. It is pleasant there. You may take your place with Aleyne tonight to help me prepare for bed.'

Thus dismissed, Margaret wandered disconsolately into the small garden. Despite the heat she found the massive, white walls of the White Tower and the still grimmer grey ones of the outer fortifications chilling and, since the last thing she wished to do was to find Guy, she set about exploring the environs of the most ancient of the palaces of England. The sight of the caged animals in the royal menagerie did nothing to lighten her spirits and she left their apartments and fled, shuddering, into the garden again. Some little distance from her, on the Tower green, she saw a little group of men practising at the butts, but they were too far away to witness her despair and she allowed herself the solace of silent tears.

So sure was she that she was unobserved that she jumped, startled, when a gentle hand was placed upon her bowed shoulder as she sat on a wooden seat.

'I cannot imagine what should so upset one of my subjects on this day of all days,' a well-remembered voice said then, revealing surprise at seeing her thus. 'Mistress Margaret, whatever can be so terrible that you must give way to tears?'

The King's voice had lost its usual teasing note and Margaret looked up, shocked by her own foolish weakness, and began to dab ineffectually at her reddened eyes.

He sat himself down beside her after looking up once to wave away some importunate page who wished to attend him, though two of his gentlemen kept watchful guard some paces distance out of earshot. He was quietly and unobtrusively dressed in a grey velvet doublet today, far removed from the ostentatiously splendid garments he must assume in the morning. His grey-green eyes regarded her thoughtfully, then he looked away to give her an opportunity to compose herself.

'Like you I came out to get away from these hectic arrangements.' His voice was half amused again. 'You can have no idea how these bishops and archbishops can quarrel and bicker and prove tiresome in the extreme when it is a question of jockeying for position in the procession tomorrow. My gentlemen, Guy among them, are all concerned that I shall be coddled and guarded and I felt I could not breathe. The air is more pleasant here, for moments at least. Soon I must return to my duties again.'

She was calmer now and as he turned back to her she recognised his kindness in giving her time. She made to rise and curtsy but he pulled her gently back on to the seat.

'Do not tell me I was wrong in my assessment of Guy and that he used you ill last night. I find that hard to believe.'

His voice was low-pitched so that no one even near by could hear what was said, and unaccountably she was not embarrassed by the direct question.

She shook her head. 'No, Your Grace,' she said very softly. 'Sir Guy was—was very considerate.'

'Good.' He leaned back, crossing one leg over the other, outwardly at his ease, but she noted the mannerism habitual with him of fiddling with the ring on his left hand, twisting and turning it on his finger. 'You must believe me, Margaret, when I assure you that I chose Guy as a fitting mate for you, sure that he would guard your interests and treat you lovingly.' He stressed the final words, one brow raised, and she gave a little smothered sob which brought his brows together then in a frown of concern. 'I was convinced that Guy truly wanted you and that this was no simple marriage convenient to his financial needs. You probably think I have used you harshly, Mistress Margaret. Anne will tell you it is my custom to tease, but I would never willingly have given you pain. It was necessary, at Northampton, to secure your person and recently I had hoped to ensure that your father returned to his allegiance, so enabling me to overlook his past negligence in coming to my side. As it turned out, mercy was not possible.'

She glanced down bleakly at the plain grey gown she had again chosen to wear as sign of her continued mourning.

'I understand, Your Grace,' she said tonelessly. 'I know now that you have treated me well.'

'Is it that you so dislike Guy?' he asked bluntly.

'No——' Her cry was hurriedly choked off and again his brows rose interrogatively. 'No, Your Grace, I—I love Guy. . .'

'Then, child, why do I find you in tears on this lovely afternoon so soon after your wedding night?'

'I—I. . .' She could not tell him. She could not tell anyone and yet. . . 'He doesn't love me,' she breathed softly, and he leaned closer, his eyes warm with compassion.

'You quarrelled? Surely you do not still believe him responsible for your father's death?'

'No, no, sir. I know—it was someone else——' She broke off again, her eyes, brimming with tears, following the movements of the archery contestants. 'It was something he said. . .'

'Said, not did?'

There it was again, his instant understanding, and she gave another sob of despair.

'I know that there will be no one ever for me but Guy—but—but he said—he said—he will not come to my bed ever again unless—unless—I beg him to.'

There, it was out, her terrible secret that she had thought she could never divulge to anyone, let alone her sovereign—and there was a brief silence.

At last he gave a little sigh. 'You dealt a terrible blow to his pride when you rejected him all those years ago, Mistress Margaret. Oh, yes, I know it was your father who forced your compliance but you were there, witnessed it, and I know how deeply he was hurt, and so he hits back, even now, after all this time.'

She stared at him blankly and he smiled. 'But if that is all, you have the simple answer to your own problem. You do as he wishes.'

'Oh, no,' she murmured piteously. 'Oh, no, Your Grace, I couldn't.'

'Yes, you can, little Mistress Margaret, not, perhaps, today or tomorrow, but you will find the courage—that is, if you truly love him. You see, I too loved very deeply and found it necessary to swallow my pride when the time came for protestations and sacrifices. I had been responsible for the deaths of Anne's father and uncle, to say nothing of her husband—though we will say nothing more of that—albeit not directly, and in some respects opposed to my own will. But she suffered deeply and I had to convince her that I truly loved her. I would have done and said anything, Mistress Margaret, to ensure that she accepted me. I have never regretted my decision and I do not think she has.'

He fell silent, as if remembering, and Margaret said impulsively, 'I know she loves you with all her heart, sir, and—' She broke off, startled by her own temerity, and he laughed and took her hand within his own.

'Then heed my advice, Margaret. Do not let pride stand in the way of your achieving your heart's desire.'

He turned and remarked, 'Young Richard is doing very well at the butts, almost as well as his brother, and Edward has had the advantage of living in the Welsh Marches these past months and having an opportunity to observe the Welsh in action. There is nothing like the Welsh bowman for true skill with the longbow, Margaret.' He had shaded his eyes to watch the little group in the distance and Margaret followed his gaze. Of course, the two boys in the group were the princes, the sons of the late King. Something touched a latent chord in her memory and she gave a startled gasp which brought the King's attention back to her.

'Your Grace,' she murmured hoarsely, 'I had forgotten until now—the boys! My father spoke of the boys. He meant the princes. . . .'

Richard was leaning slightly towards her now, his brows drawn together in concentration.

'He spoke of the princes—before he died?'

'Yes, he begged me to come to you—to warn you—of danger to the princes.'

'What exactly did he say, Mistress Margaret?' the King asked quietly, but there was a new, steely note in his voice.

She hesitated, her eyes on the two youthful forms she could see drawing together, laughing at something which had amused them. She was struggling to recall those last dreadful moments of her father's life.

'He said, "Tell Gloucester the boys are in peril,",

then, "Tell him—watch Buckingham."' She turned to him, wide-eyed with doubt. She was warning him against his greatest ally and closest kinsman. His grey eyes were fixed on her intently and he inclined his head, indicating that she should go on with her story.

She swallowed hard and put a hand up to her aching brow to try to remember exactly. 'Then he said something about the Tudor planning to wed the Princess Elizabeth. He was very gravely hurt, sir, and I do not know if he was thinking coherently. There wasn't much more. I kept urging him to stay quiet. . . But wait—he said something about the Marquess of Dorset wishing to come back. I think he meant he wished to return to his allegiance and I understood him to mean Dorset was being kept a prisoner by—Henry Tudor?' She looked back at the King questioningly. 'I am so sorry, Your Grace, I should have reported all this to you the moment I was brought back to Crosby, but—I was so grief-stricken and the marriage came so soon and. . .'

'Of course,' he said softly. 'Do not disturb yourself, Margaret; you have risked no one by this delay. Some of this I had already considered. Not that I thought Buckingham. . .' His voice trailed off abruptly as his eyes narrowed. 'No, I had not considered that Harry Buckingham—yet it is possible your father was mistaken or deliberately misled. It is not an unusual ploy to attempt to divide friends by instilling a lack of confidence in the one for the fidelity of the other.'

Margaret's thoughts were racing now and she said between her teeth, 'That is why he was killed, wasn't it? He overheard what he should not and wanted to return and warn you. Bennet Hartwell silenced him—or thought he had. He botched the job. Perhaps he was interrupted by some other arrival. . . But, my lord, I do not understand. How can the Princess Elizabeth be wed except by your consent and, even so, how could that imperil the boys, her brothers?'

He was sitting bolt upright now on the bench, one hand tightening upon the arm-rest so hard that his knucklebones were whitening under the flesh.

'Because, my dear Margaret, Henry Tudor could only claim the throne through her if she were once more declared legitimate, and were she to be so her brothers would also be legitimate and have prior claims.'

It was said so clearly and deliberately yet so succinctly that Margaret could instantly see the danger to those boys only yards from her, playing so innocently and happily in full view of the King's attendants. A sudden chill went through her and she leaned against the seat-back for support.

'My father had allied himself with the Marquess of Dorset,' she said unhappily. 'Do you think the Marquess now knows the danger to his own half-brothers?'

The King gave a slight shrug, frowning. 'While, as I said, my thoughts have already run on these lines, it seems I would be wise to take stronger precautions. Mistress Margaret, I must insist that you say nothing of what has passed between us to anyone, not even to Guy.'

She nodded obediently. 'I will be silent, Your Grace. You have my sworn word.'

He looked down at her and the grey eyes were shining in the old, half-sardonic fashion. 'And what are your thoughts on this matter? Do you trust me to keep my nephews safe, as your father apparently did, or do you consider it would be to my advantage to have them underground?'

She gasped at the harshness of the statement and coloured hotly. 'I—I think, Your Grace, that, knowing you as I now do, the boys could not be in safer hands.'

The tight line of his mouth relaxed in a smile and she understood suddenly why Guy and Dominick and Aleyne and all his gentlemen were prepared to put their lives in peril for his sake, and knew herself one of their number.

'It is well. I will not speak to the boys tonight. Edward particularly, on this day of all days, is in no mood to accept my plans for his—security.'

She stammered, 'Surely y-you will take all pains to keep the Princess Elizabeth equally—secure?'

Again he gave that half-regretful little smile. 'I would never force the Lady Bess into a match hateful to her.' Then he laughed out loud. 'Forgive me, Mistress Margaret, that was a crass observation, likely to hit you hard.'

'No, sire,' she said, crimsoning again, 'I have said if things could be arranged between Guy and me I would be well—satisfied.'

He chuckled. 'Somehow we must make it so. You will be in the abbey tomorrow?'

'If the Queen has ordered it, sir, but the honour. . .'

'*I* shall so order it. Guy will be in attendance and I want my newest supporter present.'

He rose and she hastily did so too, curtsying low. He took her hand and raised it to his lips.

'Give your heart peace, Margaret. Both these matters we discussed are in my hands now. I shall do my best to see to it that both end satisfactorily, but I urge you to do your part also.'

She was flustered and embarrassed and he released her hand gently, bowed his head to her and turned away to summon his page. She stood uncertainly, one hand clutching the bench-arm, until he had passed through the door of the royal apartments and was gone from her sight.

She flinched violently as someone touched her shoulder and turned quickly to find Guy's blue gaze fixed on her intently.

'It would seem you are truly bemused,' he observed. 'May your husband know the name of your gallant admirer? I saw only his back.'

'It was His Grace the King who talked with me,' she snapped. 'Talked only, mind you.'

'Ah.' He grinned at her amiably. 'Then I would be unwise to take offence.'

She was about to retort that there was none to take, when she thought better of it. People on the green were looking this way and she was not about to give them cause for gossip. She allowed him to take her arm and lead her towards the Queen's apartments.

'I regret I was forced to leave you to your own concerns for so long on this first day of our new life together,' he said evenly, and she stared at him uncomprehendingly. How could he behave so normally after what had passed between them only a few short hours ago?

She was silent and he made no further comment as they entered the building. Throughout supper Guy remained at her side, attentive and protective, since some of the younger knights in the King's household were already celebrating the great occasion tomorrow and drinking unwisely. Margaret wondered if they would be clear-headed enough to carry out their important duties, but she noticed that Guy was abstemious. Once or twice she caught his eyes on her, watching for her reaction, but he made no reference to anything which disturbed him and she was glad when the Queen rose from her position on the dais and Margaret hastened with Aleyne to attend her.

Margaret walked with Aleyne in the great procession which made its way to Westminster Hall and, from there, the King and Queen walking barefoot, on to the Abbey. Like all the Queen's ladies she was dressed in a white and gold gown and carried white roses, the symbol of the House of York.

The principal nobles bore the regalia, Northumberland carrying the sword of mercy, Stanley the Lord High Constable's mace. The Earl of Kent and Viscount Lovell came next with the pointed swords of justice. The Duke of Suffolk, the King's brother-in-law, followed them, carrying the sceptre, then the Earl of Lincoln, his son, with the ball crowned with its cross. The Earl of Surrey, Norfolk's son, bore the sword of state, holding it upright, and the Duke of Norfolk himself, the Earl Marshal, bore the crown.

The King was dressed in purple velvet and escorted by two bishops under the cloth of estate. His long train was held by the Duke of Buckingham and Margaret could not forbear wondering just what the King's thoughts were at this moment about his cousin, considering what she and he had discussed yesterday afternoon in the gardens of the Tower. Buckingham's glittering garments threatened to outshine those of his sovereign, and Margaret pursed her lips in distaste for this vulgar show of wealth and ostentation at so holy a moment.

The Queen, clad in white samite and cloth of gold, was attended by Lady Stanley, who carried her train. Henry Tudor's mother, Margaret thought wryly. What thoughts were passing through the mind of that great dame now? The Duchess of Suffolk, the King's sister, came next and then the Duchess of Norfolk. Margaret followed within the train of the Queen's attendants, walking with Aleyne. Guy, she knew, was with the members of the King's household. All passed along the length of red cloth which would be fallen upon after the ceremony and divided up by the waiting multitude as custom decreed.

Margaret was placed too far behind the other, nobler ladies round King Edward's chair to see or hear much of the wonderful ceremony, but she saw the flash of gold and gems in King Edward's crown as the Archbishop held it aloft before placing it upon the new King's brow and the ancient abbey rang with the shouts of acclamation which followed. Guy and Dominick were still with the King's gentlemen and separated from them. Margaret could not tell whether she felt sorry or relieved that she had been forced to spend the night in the Queen's antechamber and that she would see little of her husband today.

The press of people was great on this hot day, July sixth, and she was glad when the organ sounded a paean of rejoicing and the royal party left the Abbey for the great banquet in Westminster Hall. Here she found that Guy and Dominick were freed from their duties to join their wives, but she found herself too exited to eat the rich delicacies Guy pressed on her. The King and Queen left the hall for an hour but Margaret was not summoned to attend, and she thought how pleased the Queen must be to have a temporary reprieve from the onerous task laid upon her today. Poor Anne, she must be longing for the informality of life at Middleham, a peace and quiet happiness she would never know again.

When Sir Robert Dymoke rode into the hall on the return of the royal pair to challenge any who opposed the King's right, he was cheered and handed the traditional cup from which he drank to the new sovereign's health, then retired.

Margaret watched as the nobles came one by one to make their obeisances to the music of trumpets and clarions. It was growing dark in the high-roofed hall and flaming torches were lit. At last the King led his Queen from the hall and Guy rose and held out his hand to Margaret.

'You must be totally exhausted. Let me lead you to your chamber.'

They went out into the warm velvet darkness. Margaret thought on the gorgeous ceremonial she had witnessed. Never again would she see such a magnificent sight, she who had hoped only to catch a glimpse of the young King in Northampton on the day when she had left her home only months ago. Now it seemed aeons of time away. She sighed. If Guy were to join her in their chamber as Dominick would Aleyne, for the two were laughing together companionably behind them, she would feel her cup of happiness filled to the brim.

At the door of her chamber, he stopped and faced her. She felt her pulse racing and hoped the agitated rising and falling of her breast would not be noticeable. Guy had behaved so normally—would he repent now of his harsh announcement and accompany her into the chamber as if nothing had happened to change their relationship? She knew her eyes were pleadingly fixed on his. The King had advised her to request that he enter, but how could she bring herself to do such a thing?

As if from a distance she could hear his cool, impersonal voice.

'I will instruct Owen to sleep across your threshold tonight. There will be considerable drunkenness. The celebrations will have gone to too many heads. I bid you goodnight, madam.'

There was no frostiness in the tone, simply politeness. She found herself rooted to the spot, unable to reach up to the door-latch or to find a satisfactory answer. His nearness was a torment. How handsome he appeared in his blue velvet doublet, his Yorkist collar with its enamelled roses glinting in the light from the flaring sconces along the palace corridor. She swallowed hard and managed to find her voice.

'Thank you, sir.'

'I will wait on you early. I shall shortly know how soon I can be excused from my duties so that we can make arrangements to ride north.'

Again she nodded, her teeth biting down hard on her nether lip.

He turned. 'Well, goodnight again.'

She watched him move down the corridor and made a little convulsive movement.

'Guy. . .'

He turned instantly. 'Madam? You have some need of me?'

She stared at him helplessly. Had need of him? Sweet Virgin, couldn't he understand her great need of him? What would he do now? Would he seek solace in the arms of some other noble lady? There had been many admiring glances fixed on him during the banquet.

'No, no,' she floundered. 'I wanted to thank you again for your—your care of me during the feast. . .'

His smile was coldly courteous.

'Sleep well, or try to. I imagine the palace will prove a rowdy place tonight. Should you need me you only have to send Owen. I will come immediately.'

As he disappeared round a bend of the corridor she wondered if the last remark had been a direct invitation to send him the message he demanded. If so, he must remain disappointed. At least Owen must be informed of his sleeping place tonight. Did that mean that he would sleep alone? The thought was comforting but no real answer to her problem. She sighed and entered her chamber where a yawning Jonnet was waiting to unhook her from her elaborate court gown.

The next morning she was summoned early to wait upon the Queen. Anne looked somewhat drawn after that long and exhausting ceremony but talked happily of the wonderful ceremonial that had culminated in the placing of St Edward's crown on her beloved's head. There can be no doubt, Margaret thought, that she adores Richard. Isn't she aware that there must be many about him who still have doubts concerning his right to the throne, and that some will soon be busy in plots to overset him? She thought again of her conversation in the Tower garden, and of the most puissant Duke Harry of Buckingham. Plans were being made for the great royal progress around the country to enable the people of England to see their new king in the flesh. The Queen was full of the arrangements to install her young son as Prince of Wales. He was to meet them in York and it seemed most appropriate that the ceremony would take place there. She had been parted from young Edward too long, she said wistfully. Margaret wondered about the other young man in the Tower, another Edward, who was now no longer Prince of Wales. The King had sworn that he would take steps to ensure the boy's safety and that of his brother, and she believed him implicitly.

She looked up, startled, as Aleyne pulled her sharply away from the circle of the Queen's attendants.

'I have been wanting to speak to you all morning. Whatever is wrong?'

Margaret was immediately on the defensive. 'I don't know what you mean. Nothing is wrong.'

'Margaret, I have known you long enough now to know when something is badly wrong. Have you quarrelled with Guy?'

'Why ever should you think that?'

'You looked very strained yesterday. I thought perhaps it was the bustle and confusion, then that you were thinking of your father, then, later, that Guy had—well, ill-used you in some way.'

'No, certainly not. Guy is the soul of honourable knighthood.'

'You are thinking, then, of your former betrothed?'

'Of Bennet Hartwell?' Margaret looked outraged. 'I detest the man—worse, have nothing but contempt for him.'

'I thought you had some—deep feeling for Guy.' Aleyne was gently searching, her eyes anxious, and Margaret flushed to the roots of her hair.

'I—Guy and I will come to some arrangement over our difficulties in due time.'

'Are you——' Aleyne searched for the right words to

put her question delicately. 'You are not afraid of him—afraid of what he expects of you?'

'No,' Margaret said unhappily. She looked away from Aleyne, her eyes brimming with tears. 'I—I want Guy to love me, but—but he has not been near me since—since our marriage was duly consummated.' Again she was relieved that it was out, but worried in case she was asked further difficult questions.

Aleyne made to speak then hesitated. 'You have said Guy is the epitome of honour. I am sure you are right. It is probably that he fears to burden you too quickly, especially since he knows this is a difficult time for you. I understand he has promised to take you home soon. Once there I'm sure matters will improve. There will be no pressure of court events and. . .' She shrugged. 'I could wish, with you, that Dominick were not so close in the King's counsels. I want to go home and soon, but Dominick is ordered to attend on progress.' Her eyes became warm. 'I shall be forced to remain here for a while. I haven't told him yet but——' She finished in a little rush, 'I am to have another child in the new year. Since the early months can be dangerous for the unborn child, it will be some time before we meet again.' She gave another little regretful upward movement of her shoulders.

Margaret hugged her friend warmly. 'I'm so very happy for you, Aleyne. Dominick will be delighted, I'm sure.'

Aleyne moved off to resume her duties and Margaret remained where she was, a little pensive. There had been that deep glow of happiness around Aleyne that she could not fail to envy. Would she ever be able to present Guy with an heir? Unless matters between them could be successfully resolved, he would most likely abandon her on the Northampton manor, and she would remain there over the years, a neglected and bitter wife.

Guy rose from his obeisance to face the King, his eyes a trifle wary. He had not been received with Richard's customary warmth of manner. Today the King seemed abstracted, a frown drawing his brows together. Something had clearly displeased him and Guy had been summoned to attend him in his private chamber with summary haste. The page who fetched him had urged no delay. Had Margaret complained to the Queen of her husband's treatment of her and was he to be taken to task for it? Guy's mouth hardened involuntarily. King or not, Richard must be made to understand that in his own household he, Guy, reigned supreme, and he would suffer no interference in his dealings with Margaret.

The King gestured to a stool near his chair. 'I'm sorry I had to fetch you from your preparations for departure, Guy, but my business is urgent.'

Guy sat a little stiffly, still fearing the worst.

'I had begged to be excused attendance on progress, Your Grace, and formerly you did indicate that you would grant my request. The business of my wife's father's burial will brook no delay and——'

'There will be no need for that, Guy. In fact I have sent for you to command that you leave for the north at first light tomorrow—on my business as well as your own.'

Guy's expression revealed astonishment.

Richard moodily turned the ring on his finger and Guy noted the hard line of tension about his mouth.

'I spoke to Margaret in the Tower gardens the day before yesterday. . .'

Guy's resolve stiffened and he opened his mouth to defend himself but the King cut him off.

'She revealed to me something which her father had apparently told her with his dying breath.'

Guy's blue eyes widened.

'I think he was murdered to prevent his coming to me with his tale. He warned me of the danger to the lives of my nephews, Edward's boys. I have my own spies, of course, and was not unaware of the state of affairs but there was something else—concerning a man whom I have most loved and trusted. . .' He paused wearily. 'I had intended to put off the need for action until I returned to London but now it seems I must separate the boys and quickly, both for their own good and mine. I want you to escort young Edward north.'

'To Sheriff Hutton?'

'I think not. Young Warwick is there, George's son, and Edward could foment disharmony. So far young Warwick is inclined to trust me and is happy there, but Edward, naturally, is resentful and distrustful of my intentions. He will not be an easy charge.'

Guy nodded. His earlier alarm concerning his private life had begun to dissipate in his understanding of the King's expressed need. The boy must be guarded well and he was aware that there would be more than one man ready and waiting to snatch the person of the displaced King from his charge. This errand looked to be even more demanding and difficult than guarding Margaret had been.

'I want you to convey him to Barnard. He will be far enough from the capital there to be out of public view for a time and the castle is remote and well-fortified. I need you, Guy, to remain with him until I send you further word.' He smiled a little bleakly. 'It will give you and Margaret opportunity to get to know one another without pressure of Court duties, and I know you prefer a life of action to one of dalliance here.' He gave a short, revealing sigh. 'In some respects I envy you the opportunity. God knows I was ever happier keeping the peace on the border, and it may be necessary for you to support Northumberland if any outbreak of reiving should occur soon. It is more than likely that it will. The Scots wait only some state activity on my part to divert me from the need to keep a careful watch there. Your first duty will be to guard the boy. While you are at it, see that he is trained in the arts of war. I want him to be well able to defend himself from an assassin's knife if it should come to that, as it very well might.'

Guy looked doubtful. 'Your Grace, would it not be better for your peace if he were to be placed within the walls of a monastery?'

Richard gave a small, crooked smile. 'Ah, I see you have my cause at heart. There he would not produce an heir. Yes, that might solve my problems, if the lad were of a mind to the tonsure, but I doubt he is. Nor is he likely to be. Once before it was suggested that someone in my family would solve a mound of problems by taking the veil. I was against such pressure then, and I am just as firmly against it now. Anne became my bride and has made me the happiest of men. The boy might be dispossessed of his hopes but I'll not have him denied a natural existence. He will not prove co-operative. I have spoken with him and I know the problems ahead. I would have preferred to wait, as I said, and allow time to heal the humiliating wounds, but Margaret has reminded me that, certainly while I am from the capital, the boy is in very real danger—from the Tudor.'

He paused for Guy to take in the inference and added, 'Henry Tudor has been consorting with Lady Stanley and the Dowager Queen in an offer for the hand of the Lady Bess. You can see, I am sure, that such a move would place her brothers in the way of any hopes the Tudor would have of profiting from such an alliance.'

Guy nodded again thoughtfully. 'But Your Grace could counter that move by insisting that she take the veil. . .' His voice trailed off as he saw the King's rueful smile and shake of the head.

'What have I just said, Guy? I'll have no unnecessary force of such a nature. Bess has had disappointments enough in her time.'

'While the lady is in sanctuary she is safe enough, I grant you, sire, but you ask me to train the prince in martial skills. Surely. . .'

'You will have to wait a while until the resentment dies down somewhat, but he will need to watch his own back. You are the man I trust to teach him. Fetch Jehan Treves from Sheriff Hutton if you need him.'

The old man, Treves, had trained the young knights at Middleham, Guy among their number, and he had an admiration for the old soldier's ability.

A knock sounded on the door and the King rang the hand-bell on a table near him as a signal to admit the waiting page.

'I have sent for your lady. It is necessary that she hear my further orders.'

Margaret was ushered in by the page and the King gestured to the boy to withdraw. Margaret curtsied low, then, rising, her eyes went doubtfully first to Guy and then to the King.

'You sent for me, sir?'

'Yes, Mistress Margaret. Please be seated.' He indicated a high-backed chair facing his own.

She obeyed him, though nervously, and her trembling fingers toyed with the folds of her silken gown.

'Guy is to leave with you first thing tomorrow for Northampton.'

'So soon?' She betrayed her astonishment as Guy had done earlier.

'I have been telling Guy about our conversation within the Tower gardens.' The King's grey-green eyes danced somewhat mischievously as Margaret stared at him aghast. 'About the danger to my nephews,' he explained, and saw her visible relief. 'I have decided to act on your warning. Prince Richard is to be sent abroad. I have already made arrangements and I think it wiser that none but myself and those concerned should know where. Edward is to go north with you both. I want him to travel as your page, Mistress Margaret. Once away from the capital he will not be recognised and, though I think he may be somewhat difficult to manage, I trust to your womanly skills to handle him. It will not seem unusual for a boy of his age to wait upon his mistress, nor for a husband to keep a watchful eye on both—a protective eye.'

Margaret and Guy exchanged glances.

'Your Grace, if the prince refuses to obey me. . .'

'You have my permission to castigate him as you find necessary. I mean it, Guy. Do what you must.'

Margaret said hesitantly, 'He will miss his brother, sir.'

'I think not, Mistress Margaret. He has had his own

household away from young Dickon, so they will not be deeply affected by the parting. As for their mother——' his lip curled a trifle bitterly '—she will profess to miss her sons, but she will survive the unhappiness, I'm sure.'

There was a brief silence. 'Guy will explain why I need you both to reside at Barnard Castle for some months at least.' The King held her eyes with his own. 'I am sure you will find there the happiness you desire.'

She swallowed and nodded mutely.

It was clear now that they were being dismissed.

'Attend me at the Tower at seven of the clock tomorrow, Guy, where you will meet your charge. He will have received my personal orders by then.' There was a steely note to Richard's voice as he added, 'You may find him sulky but he will not dare flout my wishes.'

At the door Margaret turned, her face troubled.

'Sire, the disappearance of the princes will cause you some—difficulties.' The last word was breathed so softly that he had to come closer to catch her meaning.

'True,' he said quietly, 'but what are my difficulties compared with the possible consequences of leaving the boys in public view and together?'

She bowed her head in acknowledgement. The King was a proud man who would not stoop to offer explanation of his conduct to detractors, but she understood what his silence concerning the wherebouts of his charges would cost him. He bent to kiss her fingers.

'Go with God, Mistress Margaret. Pray to him for guidance and he will grant you your heart's love.'

She looked back at him once and curtsied again, and her eyes were brimming with tears as Guy led her out of the presence chamber.

* * *

Margaret looked back towards the open door of Rushton church as the funeral party emerged after the requiem mass. Guy paused with one hand on her arm and she smiled back at him tremulously through the dark veiling she wore forward, over the frontal of her hennin. He had been a constant source of strength and comfort to her throughout this sad day. Behind came Owen Lewis and the young page, Ned Weston, who had travelled with them from London. For once his fair features bore no trace of the sullen expression they had all come to recognise and expect during the journey. Margaret had discovered that, once the prince had understood her father's allegiance, he had been only too anxious to attend the ceremony and appeared suitably chastened by the experience. Sir John Rushton had been a gentleman in Dorset's household and had given his life for the cause of his young sovereign, and Edward had expressed his sincere condolences to Margaret in private. His change of heart towards her had not suited Owen, who had been frankly jealous of the boy's constant presence at her side. Owen had a special admiration for Margaret, who had helped to save his life at St Albans, and he could have wished that he had been granted the particular tasks of ensuring the comfort of his young mistress during the journey.

Guy had remarked once to Margaret that he had thought it possible that Owen would recognise their charge and, since he had been forbidden to reveal to anyone in the party his identity, save Will Scroggins who had accompanied them, albeit unwillingly, he was relieved that Owen had failed to do so. The squire had seen the prince only once in Northampton, but perhaps his eyes had been blinded by his apparent resentment of the new page's position in the household. Clearly Guy had needed the services of Scroggins, the most experienced captain in the company, in case they should be attacked on the road, and had been forced to explain the necessity for him to desert his place by Aleyne and his wife, Kate, who had steadfastly refused to leave her mistress in her delicate condition.

The King had been right in his assumption that the prince would accept his changed circumstances and see the need to appear to serve Margaret in his pose of Guy's new page. Edward of York was used to subservience from all members of his household, but he had formerly been trained in the duties of a page, serving at table, carving meat, waiting on his lady, running errands, as a matter of chivalric practice, so the tasks had not come hard to him. Though he'd obeyed with scant good grace, Guy had had no reason to threaten reprisals and the journey had gone as he'd hoped. Scroggins had seen to it that a good watch was kept on the prince, and Guy had insisted on his new page sleeping near his own person whenever they stopped for the night. Margaret had told herself that such a need gave Guy further excuse to remain clear of her bedchamber, but she too had been glad to admit, even to herself, the unpleasant fact of the very real need.

The King had enjoined on them silence regarding the prince's danger. He was not to be told, and the boy's continued resentment of the close guard served further to irritate the company. How long Guy could accept this flouting of his authority without an explosion of anger she could not bear to think.

Edward looked younger than he actually was, tall, slender, fair and with the flamboyant good looks of the Nevilles he had inherited from his grandmother, Proud

Cis. He'd appeared to Margaret to shout to the world in general that he bore royal blood and to wonder who, in the various inn households they'd slept in, could be unaware of the fact. However no one had passed any undue comment upon the behaviour of the overbearing young man and she had breathed a sigh of relief with Guy. Once at Barnard the reason for the prince's banishment from the capital would be revealed and she hoped that Guy's task would then become easier.

Her father had been laid to rest within the table tomb near the chancel where her mother was already buried. Few villagers had attended, many not knowing yet of her father's untimely death, but most of the manor servants had been present and Margaret had been satisfied with the quiet dignity and beauty of the simple service. Her father would have been honoured indeed if he could have known that his young sovereign attended his burial, and was being kept safe due to the warning for which he had lost his life in his effort to inform Gloucester.

Perhaps it was because she alone of the party was shaded from the strong sunlight by her mourning veil that she was able to see the man in the tree clearly. As they emerged from the church she looked up and froze in horror as she saw him lying full out along the branch of the oak tree near the church door, crossbow already loaded and levelled at the doorway. She gave a strangled gasp and acted instinctively, stepping back straight into the path of the young Edward who was following close on her heels. The crossbow bolt hissed through the air and buried itself in the partially opened oaken church door. One of the manor serving wenches screamed shrilly and Guy went immediately into action.

He pushed forward and threw Margaret down on to

the ground, crying to Owen to do the same service for Edward.

'Get the prince down on the ground and stand back, the rest of you.'

Margaret was already scrambling back half crouched towards the shelter of the church door. Men-at-arms came instantly on the alert, appearing seemingly from nowhere at their commander's call. Margaret could hear Scroggins issuing further orders and men were being deployed to search the churchyard. She moved to help Owen draw the startled prince to his feet and get him inside the sanctuary of the church interior. Manor servants had jostled and pushed to get clear of danger and the prince was now surrounded, no longer a possible target. She turned frantically for sight of Guy.

The prince was pale and wan with shock. Even in the dim light within the shaded church she could see that, but he quickly recovered his courage and allowed himself to be escorted back towards the chancel by two of Guy's men. Now, at last, he realised the need for their earlier precautions.

There was no sign of Guy. Margaret panicked as she realised he had gone in search of the assassin. How had the prince been discovered? They had been so careful. She thrust back her veil impatiently. Perhaps they had been followed, or, more likely, someone within the King's closest circle had known of the plan to remove the boy to the north and had betrayed them. Had Buckingham known? She doubted it. After her father's implied accusation, the King would have been at some pains to keep him ignorant of his plans.

Owen put out a hand to detain her as she gathered her skirts and made to run from the church. The shape in the tree had been indistinct but she could not rid herself of the deadly fear that the hidden killer had been Bennet Hartwell. If he had murdered in cold blood the man who had believed himself a trusted comrade, he would prove a formidable opponent to Guy. That her husband had immediately gone for the man in the tree she could not doubt for a moment. She shook off Owen's grasp and nodded sharply towards the prince.

'Stay with him. Do not let him out of your sight for a moment. He will argue and the guards will be inclined to allow him to do what he wishes, but he must be kept safe.'

She did not turn to see if she was being obeyed but emerged from the church, pushing past the ashen-faced priest who stood with his hand on the door-latch staring at the path from the lych-gate where two men fought in hand-to-hand combat.

Understanding that she must not draw attention to herself and give any advantage to Guy's antagonist, Margaret stood beside the priest, her frightened eyes following his to every move in the deadly battle. Round the combatants Scroggins had drawn a half-circle of men-at-arms between them and the lych-gate, fencing off any attempt at escape, and Margaret could see that already they had taken two prisoners. So Hartwell had not travelled alone! Now she saw clearly that Guy's enemy was the man to whom she had almost been betrothed. She kept very still but her heart was beating wildly and her breath coming in harsh rasps.

From this distance she could hear no sound save the heavy breathing of the fighters. Both looked to be expert with the heavy broadsword and dagger. Neither wore armour. Obviously Hartwell had not wished to draw attention to himself by the glimmer of sunlight on his breastplate, as he'd lain in ambush, and Guy had not deemed it necessary to come armoured to the burial service, though he had taken no risks for the prince's safety and had surrounded the quiet little churchyard with his own men once he had realised that the prince was to attend the mass.

Why, oh, why, Margaret thought desperately, had he not allowed Scroggins to take Hartwell prisoner? The wily old captain caught her eye and made a helpless gesture of two spread hands, so she knew he had been forbidden to come to Guy's assistance.

Both men had come fresh to the combat but surely Hartwell had stiffened during his long wait within the tree. It occurred to her to wonder why he had not trusted the murderous task to one of his menials but knew instantly that he had dared take no risk of failure. He had been issued with orders from those malcontents in France, likely enough from Henry Tudor himself: Kill Edward of York while he is within your grasp. The fate of the second prince can be tackled later.

Equally she knew why Guy had not relinquished the work of punishing the assassin to another. Hartwell had betrayed his allegiance, he had stooped to the contemptible attempted murder of a boy, too young yet to be able to defend himself, and—most tellingly—he had been Margaret's suitor, so doubly incurred Guy Jarvis's hatred.

She could not withdraw her gaze even when the end came. Slowly, relentlessly, Guy was forcing the man back towards the lych-gate and his men fell back before the onslaught. Hartwell was sobbing now in desperation and looking huntedly from side to side of the path as if he was in hope of some miraculous reprieve, but he was doomed and soon knew it. He fell to his knees as Guy's sword tore the neck of his padded jerkin and the point pierced the skin near his palpitating Adam's apple, and he gave a shrill animal cry, throwing up his hands in surrender. His dagger and sword fell to the ground with a metallic clash. Margaret watched petrified, waiting like Hartwell for the *coup de grâce*, and then, with a muttered oath, Guy drew back his weapon and Scroggins and one of the men came at a run and dragged the prisoner to his feet and back towards the lych-gate.

Slowly Guy began to return to the church. Margaret gave a startled cry as she saw the ominous stains on his mourning doublet. Wearily he pointed his stained sword to the ground and then stood, waiting. It seemed to her that he stumbled awkwardly and almost fell, but he righted himself with an effort. She ran into his arms, her fingers searching expertly for the seat of the wound or wounds, then, half muffled by the velvet folds of his garments, she forced herself to say quietly and deliberately, 'We must get you back to the manor, sir, so that I can dress your wounds and check the bleeding. If there is need we must summon a physician.'

Guy waved away testily all efforts to help him and walked beside her steadily enough until they reached the house. She was only dimly aware that Scroggins had organised the rest of the party and taken responsibility for his royal charge. Guy made no objection when she tersely ordered him to his chamber and sent startled maids scurrying for hot water and bandaging. Jonnet hastened off to the still-room for the medicaments she knew her mistress would require. Silently Margaret blessed the changes time had wrought in her maid, and knew she could rely on her now to do what was needed. A white-faced Owen presented himself and Margaret nodded to him to help remove his master's doublet and shirt.

She turned her attention to the things she needed when they were brought and quietly dismissed the maids. Jonnet looked stolidly back at her and Margaret nodded.

'I shall be glad if you will stay to hold the basin for me and hand me my salves and bandaging when needed.'

'Of course, mistress.'

'Is your Will back with the other men?'

'Yes, mistress, and the young—page.' It was clear from the hesitancy in her maid's tone that there was some doubt now about the newcomer's true identity.

Guy was snapping at his squire. 'Hold steady, lad. You've seen blood before. There's nothing here to cause anxiety.'

Margaret went to examine for herself the truth of this statement and was relieved to have the diagnosis confirmed. There was a long, jagged wound running down the length of his right arm from just below the shoulder to the elbow, which appeared to be the source of much of the blood-staining, and another deep scratch on the shoulder itself, but as her fingers probed gently she could find no evidence of broken bones nor even torn tendons or muscles. The wounds looked worse than they were and she gave a half-suppressed sigh of relief. There would be no permanent disablement of Guy's sword arm, of that she was sure, but despite that she found her legs trembling beneath her. Whether he could determine that by her stance so close to him she did not know, but his blue eyes looked steadily into hers reassuringly.

She staunched the blood with gentle pressure, cleansed the wound, pouring in wine then drawing the jagged edges close so that they would heal true. Finally she applied tansy salve and bandaged the arm and shoulder. Guy leaned against the back of his chair with a little sigh.

'Thank you, mistress,' he said tiredly. 'I am sorry that you were forced to watch that, especially after so distressing a day.'

Margaret's eyes filled with sudden tears. 'As long as you are safe—and—and our youthful guest, all is well. Now you must take wine with water and a light meal and rest. You have lost quite a deal of blood.'

There was a ghost of a smile around his lips as he nodded obediently and took her hand, raising it to his lips.

At the door she said, 'What of the prisoners? You know the would-be assassin was Bennet Hartwell?'

'Yes. That disturbs you?'

'Somewhat.' She hesitated. 'I cannot bear to think of any man doomed to a terrible death.'

He sighed again. 'I shall dispatch all three to Leicester Castle. The King will eventually reach there on progress and I'm sure he will wish to have his prisoners closely questioned.'

She gave a shudder of revulsion.

'I know you think it would have been better if I had dispatched him. I did consider that, but the King must have as much information as he can about his enemies. In no other way can he ensure the peace of the realm and the particular safety of the two princes.'

'I know.' Her words were barely whispered.

'You still have some feeling for this man?'

Again she shuddered. 'No, I have nothing but contempt for a man who lies in ambush to kill a boy and—and I am almost sure he killed my father.'

'We shall know the truth of that in good time.'

She shook her head sadly and left the chamber.

Guy took her advice and did not come to hall for supper. Margaret saw Owen preparing to take up a meal and checked to see that it was light and nourishing as she had ordered. The young prince insisted on attending her at table though she felt acutely embarrassed. Afterwards she retired to the solar with Jonnet and he followed and prepared to take down her lute which hung on the wall.

'Please, sir,' she said quietly, 'will you come and sit down? I do not think either of us is in the mood for music.'

He smiled a little tremulously and Margaret made a hurried signal to Jonnet to leave them.

'You will wish to know that Sir Guy has made arrangements for your attackers to be escorted to Leicester.'

'So I understand.' He was sitting in the window embrasure, idly swinging one leg. 'The whole business was very revealing. Please inform Sir Guy that he will get no more sulks from me. He is not badly hurt?'

'Fortunately not.'

He frowned slightly. 'One of the men—not the one with the crossbow, the taller one—I seem to recall was close to me on the ride from Northampton, in His Grace of Buckingham's train, I feel sure.'

Her expression revealed her sense of shock despite her previous suspicion. Even now she could not believe that any man who had been so favoured by the King could be so arrantly false. The prince raised one brow in faint amusement. In this sardonic mood he somewhat resembled his uncle, King Richard, she thought.

'Do not be too shocked or amazed, Lady Jarvis,' he said as he stood up, stretching lazily. 'My brother and I have come to expect changes of circumstances and allegiances every moment these days. At least I can be grateful that my uncle appears to have made provision for my safekeeping. I had begun to have fears and suspicions even about that.' He bowed low and her eyes followed him doubtfully as he took his leave.

She sat on until the long summer day faded to twilight and at last rang for Jonnet and retired to her own chamber. Owen had already reported that Sir Guy had eaten well of his solitary supper and seemed relatively free of pain, though his arm had stiffened. Jonnet chattered happily about Will Grimshaw and Margaret only half listened. She dismissed her maid finally with a smile and her gratitude for the girl's competent assistance at her treatment of Guy.

Unwilling to get into bed, she stood for a while at the open window. The shutters stood wide to the cool night air and she had forbidden Jonnet to close them. Her father had always planned to get these upper windows glazed but now she was glad that the scents of roses and lavender drifted in from the nearby pleasance. A hunting owl hooted somewhere close by in the meadowland. The day had been so strange. She had dreaded the final parting with her father and yet she knew he would have been glad to be returned here and lie in peace on his own land. Guy had been truly supportive. He had organised everything, from the bringing of the body to the manor church to the order of the final requiem, to save her pain—and then there had been that terrible scene in the churchyard.

Her whole body was trembling now at the thought of how close to death her husband had been—and would be many times in the future while he served the King in the northern castle so close to the warring Scots border.

He would go from her time after time into danger—and she could not bring herself to say truly the words which would tell him how much his loss would mean to her. Despite the pleasant warmth of the night she drew her brocaded bed-gown more closely round her.

Owen had said Guy was well, that there were no undue ill effects. She must see for herself.

Since their arrival Guy had continued to sleep in the guest chamber he had occupied when she had considered him her gaoler. She hastened to the door and knocked before her courage failed.

'Come in, Owen. What is it, boy? I told you to ensure that——' His voice broke off as he saw Margaret framed in the doorway. 'My lady, please come in.'

He was still clothed in shirt and hose and had not yet retired. Her eyes went to the bulge of the bandaging beneath the fine linen and slowly she moved closer.

'Owen told me you were well but—but I thought it best to see for myself.' Her voice was very low, hesitant, apologetic.

'I am honoured.' He bowed slightly and she looked up sharply. Was she being deliberately mocked?

He held up his arm. 'See, there is no more bleeding. You did your work well.'

'Good.' Her breath was coming unevenly. 'Is there undue pain? If so I can provide a mild——'

'No pain, or so little as to cause me no inconvenience.'

'Yes.' There was a silence and then she said with a rush, 'I was so terribly afraid. . .'

'That he would kill me?'

'Yes.'

'I see.' She saw him swallow hard and the pulse in his throat move rapidly. 'I'm sorry you were——'

'Please,' she said a trifle harshly, 'let us not continue this game. You must know I was frantic.'

In the dim purple light she saw the brightness of his hair outlined against the window opening. She could not see his features clearly enough, and tears were now perilously close to revealing her distress.

'Guy,' she said piteously, 'you said you wanted me. . .'

'Oh, yes, I wanted you—desperately.'

'Then please—please come back with me to—to my chamber.'

He had her within his arms before she could move even a fraction. Her body was crushed close to his and she heard him utter the faintest gasp of pain as his wounded arm caught her tight round her waist. Instantly she was alert to his suffering.

'No, no, I had forgotten that you——Please, you must rest and recover. . ..'

He laughed as he nuzzled her disordered dark hair which was cascading in glory over her bed-gown.

'Margaret, Margaret, do you think me such a weakling that I would let so trifling a wound come between us now?'

He lifted her high into his arms despite her protest and carried her along the corridor to her chamber, one push of his good shoulder closing the heavy studded door and leaving them enclosed in the scented half-darkness.

As he removed her bed-gown and laid her back against the pillows she looked up pleadingly. 'I was afraid you might reject me—and perhaps I deserved it. . .'

'No, no, sweetheart, I was the one who allowed foolish pride to cut to the quick. I wanted you the moment I saw you. I had that triumphant rush of joy that you were promised to me, mine, and then your father was objecting and you were—'

'Please,' she whispered. 'I was a stupid child and it was so long ago.'

'You were a child indeed, and I should have understood that you were acting only on your father's order, but do you know how much it hurt to be so humiliated by a child, a beautiful, wilful child?' He put a hand gently over her mouth as she was about to protest. 'The child is a woman now and all mine. That she should come and tell me that she is proves how deeply I am blessed. Never regret those words, my love, nor think they denigrate you in my eyes. They are the proof that our love will last. I should not have asked them of you, yet how can I make you understand how uncertain I was, even when the King's chaplain had bound us together and I had made you mine in the marriage bed?'

He was undressing hurriedly and she heard him give a muffled curse as his unwary fingers caught at his wounds.

'Guy?' She was concerned for him instantly.

He was beside her at once, leaning above her, tracing a gentle finger across her brow and down her straight, well-shaped nose, then he was bending even closer to kiss her eyes.

'Hush, my love, I told you all is well.'

She lay back in rapturous delight as his hands now explored her body, bringing her even greater joy than they had the first time on her marriage night. She was less afraid now, eager for him, and the moment of taking was without pain and filled with ecstasy.

As she lay back, nestling against his broad shoulder,

she gave a little sigh of satisfaction. She was lying so close now that she was again afraid that she was hurting him, but he laughed triumphantly when she expressed her anxiety.

'Not in the least, and if you were I would bear it willingly.'

After a few moments she said hesitantly, 'Guy, you do not think that—that men who are promised to me are all cursed?'

His answer was tinged with laughter as he twined a lock of her curling hair around one possessive finger. 'What? My darling, what is this foolish notion you have?'

'After—after I repudiated you, the man to whom I was to be betrothed died—and then—then there was Bennet Hartwell and—' she gave a little sob of panic '—he will die—horribly. And now—and now—Guy, I could not bear it if you. . .'

He did not ridicule her dread as she had feared he might but drew her up into his arms again. 'Oh, my darling wife, there is nothing to fear. Believe me, I have no intention of going recklessly into danger, not now I have you to come back to each time.'

'But there was danger this afternoon. As I watched I realised that we are going north where there will be constant campaigns and perhaps more attempts on the prince's life. How did they know, Guy, where to find him?'

He considered. 'I don't know, but there are always men around kings who will betray through lust for power.'

'My father warned the King about Buckingham, and the prince said he was sure one of those men we took prisoner was formerly in the Duke of Buckingham's train. He had seen him at Northampton.'

In the half-light from the unshuttered window she saw Guy's eyes gleam. 'Then we must be doubly on our guard.'

'Why should Buckingham wish to harm the princes? They are no threat to him.'

She felt the slow rise and fall of Guy's chest pressed close to her own breast as he considered again. 'Perhaps it would be to his advantage to have Richard's reputation harmed. He himself is very close to the throne.'

'But the King has rewarded him with great offices and lands.'

'Indeed, but for some men rewards are never great enough.'

'I still fear for you in this guise of special guard to the prince.'

He was nuzzling her hair and one of her hands reached up to touch, wonderingly, the damp golden curls at the nape of his neck. 'You will be very cautious, Guy. Swear to me.'

'Margaret, my heart, can you not see that you were meant for me from the beginning? Because of that I shall live a charmed life, but——' he stared down into her anxious eyes '—if you are still fearful we must make very sure.'

'How?' she mouthed fearfully.

He laughed joyously. 'Why, by performing the ritual demanded by the god and goddess of love.'

Before she could fully understand him, he had covered her mouth with his own and when, at last, she was able to breathe again she was willing enough to take part in the necessary rites.

Join the festivities as Mills & Boon celebrates Temptation's tenth anniversary in February 1995.

There's a whole host of in-book competitions and special offers with some great prizes to be won–watch this space for more details!

In March, we have a sizzling new mini-series Lost Loves about love lost...love found. And, of course, the Temptation range continues to offer you fun, sensual exciting stories all year round.

After ten tempting years, nobody can resist

Temptation 10th anniversary

LEGACY *of* LOVE

Coming next month

A REMEMBERED LOVE

Laura Cassidy

English Civil War 1643-46

Christopher Rokesby, Henry Carrington and Alice Ashley were long-time friends, becoming adults as the black clouds of civil war began to appear. Henry was determined to marry Alice, as much to gain his inheritance to put towards Parliament's cause as because he wanted her. But Alice didn't know where her heart lay, and would only agree to an engagement—until war broke out, and Christopher was hurt fighting for the King. Flying to his aid, Alice knew that their childhood trio had broken asunder—would that remembered love keep them all from harm?

SERAFINA

Sylvia Andrew

Regency

'Lady Aldworth is looking for someone who will give her grandson an heir, is meek, content to let others do her thinking for her, and is ready to allow Lord Aldworth to continue in his present mode of life—'

If acting like a brainless ninny would net Serafina a wealthy husband, and so get her family out of difficulty, she would do it—until Charles caught the *real* Serafina in action. The only recourse was to pretend to be her 'sister' Sally…

LEGACY of LOVE

Coming next month

THE NAKED HUNTRESS

Shirley Parenteau

Seattle, USA 1889

Lyris Lowell's foray into investigative journalism turned into disaster when she found *herself* exposed—stark naked!—in a painting of Diana the Huntress. Seattle society would be shocked and her parents humiliated unless the canvas was destroyed. But the buyer, saloon bar owner Nicholas Drake, had other plans for his purchase.

Nick's life was a rags-to-riches story; marrying Lyris would cap his social achievement, and now that he had that chance—surely that meant more than love?

CASTAWAY

Laurel Ames

Bristol 1818

Nathan Gaites was not inclined to respond to belated overtures from his father's family, until told that his grandfather did not have long to live. It was clear that the family had the wrong impression of Nathan, and their misconceptions amused him—until he realised that his cousin, Margaret Weston, was under pressure to marry him!

The more he learned of her, and of the growing passion between them, the more Nathan wanted to free her to make her own choices...but how to manage it?